THE HELLION AND THE HERO

"Sullivan expertly exposes her characters' emotional depths and keeps the pages turning with a steady undercurrent of mystery. Series fans are sure to be pleased."

—*Publishers Weekly*

"The latest in Emily Sullivan's League of Scoundrels series will satisfy those who yearn for a second-chance romance."

—*Paste* magazine

THE REBEL AND THE RAKE

"*The Rebel and the Rake* will steal readers' hearts before they even realize it's gone, entangling them in the storytelling with much the same stealth as Rafe's investigations."

—*Entertainment Weekly*

"After wowing readers with her superb debut, rising historical romance star Sullivan returns with another entrancing addition to her League of Scoundrels series that brilliantly showcases her mastery of deep characterization as well as her gift for crafting a wit-infused plot that effectively threads the needle between desire and danger without dropping a single stitch."

—*Booklist*, Starred Review

"The subterfuge provides an intense backdrop that only enhances the complex romance between Sullivan's intelligent, progressive protagonists. Readers will be taken by independent Sylvia's quest for love and companionship."

—*Publishers Weekly*

A ROGUE TO REMEMBER

"The literary charms of Sullivan's superbly written debut are many, including a full cast of deftly nuanced characters, an exquisitely evoked Italian setting that would impress E. M. Forster, love scenes that deliver both emotional intensity and lush sensuality, and vivacious writing enhanced by ample measures of wit."

—*Booklist*, Starred Review

"[A] winning debut... This satisfying love story will especially appeal to historical romance fans looking for a break from the typical English setting."

—*Publishers Weekly*

Duchess Material

ALSO BY EMILY SULLIVAN

A Rogue to Remember
The Rebel and the Rake
The Hellion and the Hero

Duchess Material

EMILY SULLIVAN

FOREVER

New York   Boston

Forever
Hachette Book Group
1290 Avenue of the Americas, New York, NY 10104
read-forever.com
@readforeverpub

First edition: November 2024

Forever is an imprint of Grand Central Publishing. The Forever name and logo are registered trademarks of Hachette Book Group, Inc.

The publisher is not responsible for websites (or their content) that are not owned by the publisher.

The Hachette Speakers Bureau provides a wide range of authors for speaking events. To find out more, go to hachettespeakersbureau.com or email HachetteSpeakers@hbgusa.com.

Forever books may be purchased in bulk for business, educational, or promotional use. For information, please contact your local bookseller or the Hachette Book Group Special Markets Department at special.markets@hbgusa.com.

Print book interior design by Taylor Navis

Library of Congress Cataloging-in-Publication Data

Names: Sullivan, Emily, author.
Title: Duchess material / Emily Sullivan.
Description: First edition. | New York : Forever, 2024.
Identifiers: LCCN 2024022645 | ISBN 9781538742341 (trade paperback) |
    ISBN 9781538742365 (ebook)
Subjects: LCGFT: Romance fiction. | Novels.
Classification: LCC PS3619.U4237 D83 2024 | DDC 813/.6—dc23/eng/20240521
LC record available at https://lccn.loc.gov/2024022645

ISBNs: 9781538742341 (trade paperback), 9781538742365 (ebook)

Printed in the United States of America

LSC-C

Printing 1, 2024

For the sisters of my heart

Duchess Material

One

May 1896
London, England

Will Margrave stared up at the imposing brick building and narrowed his eyes. Yet unlike with dogs, people, and even the occasional horse, his legendary glare made no impression whatsoever on the weathered edifice. It remained indifferent to his mood, which currently hovered somewhere between extreme irritation and reluctant curiosity. Around him, the pavement teamed with passersby, but everyone instinctively gave him a wide berth. They may not have known he was the Duke of Ellis, but Will always made sure his bearing radiated a certain amount of importance, wealth, and power. Such gravitas either provided an advantage or acted as a deterrent, depending on what the situation called for.

Given that he was currently standing in front of a police station, he needed all the outrageous privilege an aristocrat such as himself was bred to expect. He pulled the note that had upended his day from his pocket and read it again, though he had already memorized every word:

A Miss P. Atkinson has requested your assistance. She is currently in my custody at the Bow Street Police Station. Please come at your earliest convenience.

Regards,
Detective Inspector Holland

Phoebe Atkinson was the younger sister of his old friend Alex, who was away on a business trip in New York with their father until the end of the month. Given that, it was understandable why Phoebe had reached out to him. What remained to be seen was what kind of trouble a *schoolteacher* could have gotten into. Phoebe had always been rather impetuous as a girl, but that had been mere childhood mischief: stolen puddings and soiled shoes. Nothing that required the intervention of the police.

She's a menace, Alex had once seethed after Phoebe snuck into her room. She had been looking for a book Alex insisted she didn't have and accidentally knocked over an open bottle of ink in the process, ruining a treatise on whatever arcane subject Alex had been engrossed in that week and ensuring that Phoebe's stained fingers marked her as the culprit.

A faint smile tugged at Will's lips as he recalled the absolute melee that followed. Apparently age and wisdom had not dampened Phoebe's riotous spirit. He then rolled his shoulders back and ascended the steps. Time for the duke to get to work.

When he gave his name to the gangly young officer manning the front desk, the lad's jaw went slack for a moment.

"We were sure she was mad, asking for a duke."

Will paused for a moment and raised an eyebrow. "No. Not mad."

The lad then sprung from his seat and gave a quick bow. "Right this way, sir. I mean, my lord."

"Actually, it's Your Grace," Will drawled.

"Of course," the lad said with a blush. "Your Grace."

Will would always be grateful for the many ways his title made it easier to pass through the world, but that didn't make the gross unfairness of it all easier to swallow. However, he had learned long ago it was best to keep such complaints to himself, as those who weren't at the top of the social ladder were often the most invested in it. Instead, he followed the young officer at a leisurely pace, as dukes did not rush for anyone—save the queen. Though the station was bustling with activity, he could still feel every eye in the room fix upon him as he passed by. They continued down a dingy hallway that smelled of damp and stopped in front of a closed door.

"The jail's nearly full and Inspector Holland said it didn't feel right, putting her in with the rest of the rabble. He's familiar with the school she works at, you know. Does a lot of good for the neighborhood girls, so she's in his office," the young man explained as he unlocked the door. "I'll go and fetch him for you."

"My thanks."

The lad gave another awkward bow and scurried off.

Now thankfully alone, Will glowered at the closed door. He was hesitating, though he couldn't account for *why*. It was only Phoebe Atkinson on the other side, not some man-eating lion. And yet, Will couldn't ignore the distinct sense of unease buzzing under his skin. He had worked very hard over the years to remove the element of surprise from his life and thus rarely found himself in unfamiliar situations he couldn't completely control. This, however, was the closest he had come to facing the unknown in quite some time. Will did not much care for it.

He let out a huff of irritation and had just reached for the doorknob when the memory suddenly came to him, unbidden and unwelcome. It had been an afternoon in late June and the air was thick with the heady scent of Mrs. Atkinson's prized roses. Alex and Phoebe had been busy making paper fans for a picnic they had organized for later in the week. A picnic Will could no longer attend. Alex had gone inside to fetch some lemonade, leaving the two of them in the back garden of her parents' country estate, which bordered his own family's property. Will spent so much time at their house as a boy that it felt like a second home, and the three Atkinson girls almost like sisters. But Phoebe had grown up while he completed his first year at Oxford, and Will had spent the last month or so trying to navigate this bewildering new development.

Even Alex had reluctantly acknowledged that her sister had become *interesting*. Whereas Phoebe used to beg to be included in whatever they were doing, now Alex invited her to join. Phoebe was quick-witted and full of energy and, as Will was finding it increasingly difficult *not* to notice, quite pretty. Cal, his younger brother, had also proved to be interesting and they became a quartet of sorts that summer. If Alex was holed up in the library or Cal was busy with his painting, Will and Phoebe would often take walks by the river together to pass the time. But as those hazy days crawled by, he found himself seeking out her company more and more. Or idly wondering what would happen when he returned to Oxford. Would she allow him to write to her? And, perhaps not quite so idly, would she write him back?

Until all that wondering came to a grinding halt.

Will had come that afternoon to break the news of his unexpected elevation from young country gentleman to duke's heir after his father's cousin, a man he had never even met, lost his only surviving son from injuries sustained in a bar brawl with a Sicilian sailor on the Continent—or so the story went. From what Will gathered, the recently deceased had been a roguish sort of fellow who never took his duties seriously after the death of his elder brother some years before. *That* brother had died of typhoid. It was hard not to think the title was cursed. Will certainly felt that way. He wanted to be a barrister like his late father—not a damned bloody duke.

But Will's opinions on primogeniture were irrelevant. Thanks to an above average number of girl children in his generation as well as a tendency for his more promiscuous relatives to only have boys out of wedlock, not mention plain old bad luck, it appeared that Will was to have a dukedom, whether he wanted it or not. Now instead of whiling away the rest of summer in this very spot like he had planned—had been looking *forward* to—Will had to go to Derbyshire and meet with some crusty old man.

Phoebe had been awfully quiet since he arrived and her sole focus was on twisting the paper fan in her hands. That made Will feel even more out of sorts than he already did, so to fill this unnatural silence, he began to speak—ramble, really—about all the various properties he would one day inherit, which included an obscene chunk of Derbyshire. It was a bit daunting to list them all aloud but he hardly wanted to sound out of his depth in front of her. Bad enough to be taken by surprise by a blasted dukedom. So instead Will spoke with his usual irreverent tone. As if this were just another one of his silly larks.

I mean, really. Him a *duke?*

It was laughable—if it had happened to anyone else.

"I suppose that makes me rather like your Mr. Darcy now," he said, unable to resist the chance to tease her. "Perhaps I should start attending country dances and stand in the corner looking down my nose at the rabble." Ever since Phoebe finished the Austen novel earlier in the month she had been endlessly sighing over the hero's quiet transformation after being delivered a set-down by the sharp-tongued heroine. Though Will had not read the book himself, he was quite tired of hearing about the handsome and so very noble Mr. Darcy who changed just for the mere *hope* of winning the heroine's esteem.

The whole plot sounded like utter rubbish to him.

But Phoebe only grunted in response while keeping her gaze fixed firmly on the fan. Her face was partially obscured by the thick waves of light brown hair that hung well past her shoulders. And while it was considered unseemly for a girl of sixteen to still wear her hair down even at home, to Will she almost resembled some kind of veiled medieval maiden. This combination of indecency and modesty was strangely titillating and perhaps that was why Will couldn't stop staring at her even as he rambled on.

What if he wrapped one of those soft tendrils around his finger? What if he then gave it a tug? He flexed his hand and pressed it against his thigh, resisting the sudden, bone-deep urge to reach for her and find out. He was so distracted by this procession of thoughts that he left a pause in his little recitation and that was when Phoebe's head snapped up. Sprays of sunlight gleamed off the crown of her head, making her hair shine like a halo made of burnished gold. But her expression was not anything close to the innocent adoration he had been imaging. Instead, the unfamiliar contempt in her hazel gaze was like a swift blow to the chin. For a moment he wondered if he had somehow spoken one of his indecent thoughts aloud instead of the acreage of his Oxfordshire estate, but she quickly set him to rights.

"I would imagine given that you're such a well-endowed member of the ruling class now," Phoebe said crisply. "You'll be far too busy doing your important *dukely* things to come around here very much anymore, let alone a country dance."

Her barely veiled sarcasm at this tumultuous turn of events had quite effectively doused his fledgling desire. "You think I would so easily forget where I came from," he said, hot with indignation. "And everyone here."

Including you?

Phoebe matched his glare. "Why not? You can't even be bothered to stay for our little picnic."

"No, Phoebe," he said through his tight jaw. "I *can't*."

Something that could have been regret flickered in her eyes, but then she threw the fan down on the table and ran inside. It could just as likely have been disgust. Will reached out and picked up the crumped paper, trying to smooth it back into shape. Then his heart sank. She had written his name on the side. Will placed the fan back on the table and pinched the bridge of his nose. He had needed her to understand. To see what he was up against. But she was too caught up in girlish nonsense.

Because she is *still a girl.*

Well, Will could hardly fault her for that. A day ago he had been caught up in the very same nonsense. But now…

Let her go, cautioned the voice in his head. *It will be easier this way.*

But for whom?

Eventually, Alex returned with the lemonade.

She gave him a quizzical look. "Did Phoebe leave?"

"It would appear so." Will then shrugged in an attempt to affect unconcern. "I believe she has heard enough from me."

The feeling was *extremely* mutual.

Alex remained skeptical, but Will changed the subject. And that was the last they ever spoke of her.

Will rarely saw Phoebe after that beyond the occasional stilted hello at a ball during her one and only season or a passing nod at an exhibition. His social circle changed significantly once he was named as the duke's heir and given the courtesy title of Viscount Middlefield. Nearly every day he received piles of invitations to all sorts of balls, soirees, and clubs. Schoolmates who had never given him a second glance now sought him out, while women treated him like a god among men. If Will were being *very* honest, he...got a little caught up in it all for the first few years.

Only his friendship with Alex remained unaffected, mostly because she didn't give a damn about his title one way or the other. Yet whenever he crossed paths with Phoebe, however briefly, an undercurrent of irritation leftover from that long-ago afternoon hummed between them, usually accompanied by that hint of contempt in her eyes. But Will never did make it back to the Atkinsons' Surrey house. Not since the summer when everything changed.

It irked him now to realize Phoebe had been right.

He *had* been too busy with dukely things.

Will opened the door to the inspector's office with more force than necessary and as it hit the wall with a satisfying thud, someone let out a startled yelp. It was Phoebe, standing in the center of the room dressed in a dark blue skirt and matching jacket with a striped shirtwaist. Her straw boater hat was a little askew and obscured most of her hair, which, he thought with a pang of regret, was tied back.

And he hated that he noticed.

Her mouth dropped open and her hazel eyes went wide with astonishment rather than the usual contempt. "You actually came."

She still thought so little of him, then.

"Of course I came," he said, unable to control the sharpness in his tone.

Phoebe looked chastened. "It's just that Alex is away, you know. And it all happened so fast. But I really didn't expect you to—"

"Well I'm here now," he cut in. No need for her to elaborate any further on her utter lack of confidence in him.

"I hope I didn't interrupt anything important," she said. "I know how busy you are."

Doing dukely things.

Will pointedly looked away and adjusted his cuffs. "You did, actually."

He decided not to mention that it had been a carriage ride through Hyde Park with Lady Gwendolyn Fairbanks, the most celebrated debutante of the season and the ideal candidate for his future duchess. This whole courting business was deuced irritating, but as his mother had become so fond of reminding him, he was nearly thirty and it was long past time to find a wife.

If it had been up to Will, they would already be betrothed, but apparently ladies liked to be wooed a little—and Lady Gwendolyn had no shortage of admirers. That meant far too much of Will's time lately had been spent coordinating the most insipid activities around the young lady's packed schedule. No doubt Lord Fairbanks would be furious that Will had canceled on his daughter with so little notice, but he couldn't in good conscience ignore Miss Atkinson's message, however much he regretted it now.

"I'm sorry."

The apology sounded genuine enough to faintly tug at a spot in his chest.

That's your heart, you idiot.

Will cleared his throat as he met her gaze, but he found no trace of the expected contempt.

Yes. Definitely his heart.

"No apologies necessary," he said curtly. "Just doing what Alex would want."

Her eyes dimmed. "Right."

"Now then. Would you mind telling me exactly *why* you are in police custody?"

But just as Phoebe began to speak, the door opened again. A dark-haired man with a thick mustache and a strong jaw entered. He looked around Will's age but had several inches and a good thirty pounds on him—all of which appeared to be muscle.

"Afternoon, Your Grace," the man said with a brief nod while his expression remained stern. "I'm Detective Inspector Holland."

"A pleasure," Will replied, shaking his hand. "Miss Atkinson was just about to tell me what grave offense has landed her in your care. Surely there has been some kind of misunderstanding," he added with an apologetic smile that the inspector did not return.

"I'm afraid not, Your Grace. She was trespassing on private property. The constable who arrested her witnessed it himself."

Phoebe scoffed, "As I already told you, I was simply trying to locate my student."

"According to the property's maintenance man you were causing a disturbance," the inspector countered. "And refused to leave."

"I didn't have the chance to before the constable came! And

I would think the fact that a fifteen-year-old girl has completely vanished would be of far more importance to the police."

The inspector's impressive jaw hardened. "There are proper channels for reporting missing persons. You can't just go around accosting people in their own homes."

"I did no such thing," Phoebe said hotly. "I was merely asking the other residents of the building when they had last seen her. And everyone I encountered was happy to share any information they had. Which, I believe, is *your* job."

Will shifted on his feet. Alex was right. She *was* a menace.

Detective Inspector Holland sighed and pinched the bridge of his nose. "I understand your concerns, Miss Atkinson. Truly, I do. But you were still trespassing and it is my *job* to enforce the law."

Before Phoebe could further antagonize the man, Will intervened.

"Inspector, with all due respect, has Miss Atkinson been charged with a crime?"

The inspector reluctantly shook his head. "It's up to the building's owner to press further charges."

"But until then she is free to go, correct?"

Detective Inspector Holland had a glare to rival Will's. "As long as her fine is paid."

"Consider it done."

After an awkward silence, the inspector shot Phoebe a dark look before addressing Will. "Just make sure she doesn't go near the property again."

"Of course."

As the inspector turned to leave, Will held out his hand, a folded banknote in his palm. "And thank you for your assistance."

Detective Inspector Holland stared at the money before he met

Will's eyes, not even trying to hide his disgust. "As I said before, Your Grace, it is my *job*. Good day."

Will stared at the inspector's departing back and the door closed with a slam. "An honest policeman," he murmured. "Haven't met many of those."

"Excuse me," Phoebe said crisply. "But you certainly do not get to dictate where I go."

Will turned to her. "Naturally. But I thought it would move things along if I kept up the pretense." At her look of confusion, he arched a brow. "You do realize he probably assumed you're my mistress."

Phoebe's mouth fell open. "*What?*"

"Well, you can hardly blame him." He held out his arm. "Why else would you have called for me?"

She stared at the appendage as if Will had offered her a writhing snake. "But what if he *says* something?"

Will couldn't help bristling at her reaction to the mere thought of being his mistress. "So you were fine with being arrested, but that is a bridge too far?"

Her jaw tightened, which drew his attention to her perfectly pointed chin. "I'm not *fine* with any of this. But yes, I find the idea that I would be any man's mistress appalling—let alone a duke's," she added under her breath.

It was an entirely reasonable sentiment for a proper young lady, and yet Will couldn't control the resentment thundering through him. "Then try to remember that next time you get brought in," he snapped as the hot flush of humiliation worked its way up his neck. "And I'll make sure to ignore any future summons from the police."

Her cheeks turned a becoming shade of pink as she glanced down. "I'm sorry. I wasn't trying to insult you. I really am grateful."

Will cleared his throat. Her apology made him even more uncomfortable than her rejection. "Yes. Well then," he grumbled and held out his arm again.

This time Phoebe took it without resistance. She still smelled the same, he realized. Like clean cotton. Will stared at their joined arms for a moment before meeting her gaze. The corner of her mouth lifted in a small smile. "I'd forgotten how eloquent you are."

Will frowned as her eyes twinkled with devious delight entirely at his expense. And to his utter horror, he liked it. Quite a lot.

Two

*A*s the carriage pulled into traffic and headed toward her flat near Bloomsbury, Phoebe stared at Will Margrave's commanding profile through the veil of her lashes.

No.

He could not simply be "Will" to her anymore, but the Duke of Ellis.

Your Grace.

When he first burst into the inspector's office it had taken Phoebe a moment before she recognized him—though perhaps that wasn't terribly surprising given how little she had seen of him these last eight years. And even when they had happened upon one another, he was usually too preoccupied with the pompous gentlemen and fawning ladies surrounding him to spare her more than a passing nod—and sometimes not even that.

His posture had been stiff and his manner imposing, like every other man who thought himself terribly important. Though she supposed it was warranted in his case, if one felt anything other than contempt for the English aristocracy. Nevertheless, the old and illustrious title he had inherited eight years ago seemed to have seeped into his very bones, snuffing out any trace of the cavalier young man with the lopsided grin who had once invaded her thoughts far more than she would ever admit—to say nothing of her heart. But then his narrow-eyed gaze had fixed upon her, setting off an irritating flare of heat as her mind caught up to what her body already knew.

He actually came.

The incident in the tenement house had unfolded rather quickly once that awful maintenance man Mr. Felton appeared. Phoebe explained that she was simply looking for her missing student Alice Clarke, but he accused her of trespassing and immediately found a constable passing by. Phoebe had only invoked the duke's name in a last, desperate attempt to put the constable off. After all, he was the most powerful person she knew—never mind that they were barely on speaking terms. Still, Phoebe issued the command with all the outraged self-importance she could muster. She was fairly certain she even said *Unhand me*, like a silly maiden in a penny dreadful. But her protest had done nothing. The constable just shot her an irritated look and hauled her off to Bow Street, muttering something like *Damn modern girls never know their place.*

"How long has your student been missing?"

She turned at the question and met her reluctant rescuer's eyes. They were darker inside the carriage, closer to black than brown. Or maybe it was just the way he was looking at her. A mediocre novelist might describe them as *piercing*, but that was the only word that came to mind. Phoebe ignored the answering shiver of interest. "A week, Your Grace."

"Don't call me that," he said with a sudden scowl.

She let out a short, surprised laugh. "Why? That's how one addresses a duke, is it not?"

He rolled his eyes. "Your sister doesn't."

"That's because Alex doesn't have any respect for the peerage."

A very undignified snort erupted from him. "And you do?"

Phoebe had spent enough time among people who thought that because their great-great-great-grandfather had been Groom of the Stool to Charles II or some other such nonsense that they were entitled to act however they wanted whenever they wanted to whomever they wished. She and Will had once mocked such people, until he became one of them.

"Touché." She lifted a shoulder. "Very well. I will call you Ellis. Is that better?"

"No," he said sullenly.

She couldn't help smiling at the trace of petulance in his tone. He didn't really expect her to call him Will anymore, did he? That was a relic from a far different era she would rather not revisit. When nobody knew he would become a duke and Phoebe could still delude herself into desperately hoping these feelings weren't hers alone.

"But Ellis is your title."

He gave an unduke-like shrug and turned back to the window. "I'd prefer Margrave."

Then he fell into a short brooding silence and Phoebe was grateful she could look freely upon him for a moment. As the carriage took a turn, a beam of late afternoon sunshine illuminated his face to devastating effect and drew attention to his sharp cheekbones. Really, it was *outrageous* that a man would possess such cheekbones. One could allow the chiseled jaw and the full lips, but the cheekbones were simply too much. A lock of his thick, dark hair fell across his forehead and as Will absently pushed it back, Phoebe's heart twinged at the familiarity of the movement. She wasn't sure what angered her more, that he still retained the mannerisms of his former self or that she still remembered so very much.

"Doesn't this girl have parents?"

She startled at the question and met Will's eyes. He raised a brow, waiting for a response. Had he noticed her staring at him? And if so, for how long? Phoebe cleared her throat to hide her embarrassment.

"Ah, no. She is an orphan. Her mother had been sick for some time and passed on earlier this year, while her father died when she was very young. No other family to speak of."

"Do you know such intimate details of *all* your students?"

Phoebe lifted her chin at the disapproval in his tone. "Unfortunately Miss Clarke is hardly an outlier. There are many girls in similar situations. The school tries to provide as much assistance as possible, but funds always fall short of the need." She then gave a pointed look around the grand carriage.

Will shifted in his velvet-clothed seat. "Not that I need to explain myself to *anyone*, but I inherited this conveyance."

"And I suppose you inherited your cashmere coat and silver-handled walking stick as well?" Phoebe smiled widely as she said this. She may not have much respect for the peerage, but she usually saved this level of sarcasm for only her sisters.

Will gave her another narrow-eyed look. "All right. You've made your point, Atkinson."

"Is that how you'll address me?" She was far too pleased by the idea, not that she could ever admit it.

"Seems fitting given your sister refuses to be called Alexandra."

"Yes, but as you know only a select few are permitted to call her Alex."

His mouth curved in the faintest hint of that lopsided smile at the mention of his dear friend, and Phoebe felt a distressingly familiar pang of jealousy. As a girl, she had often felt like the odd man out in their company, though Will had always tried to make her feel welcome even when Alex did not. Yet another old memory she did not wish to revisit. "Have you heard from her lately?"

"I received a letter last week."

Phoebe hesitated for a moment. "Is she enjoying New York?"

He cocked his head at the question. "Don't you know?"

"We had a disagreement before she left," she admitted. "I...I don't suppose she said anything to you about it?"

Will turned thoughtful. "Even if she had, I wouldn't break her confidence."

Phoebe let out a breath and nodded. "Good. I'm glad she has you," she added quietly.

Alex didn't have many friends. Not that she seemed to notice. Or care. She preferred financial portfolios to people. It was her single-minded dedication to profitability at any cost that had led to their argument in the first place. Still, Phoebe didn't like fighting with her. She could always send a letter rather than wait another month until Alex returned to London, but it was nearly impossible to gauge her sister's mood over correspondence. One felt as though they were conversing with a letter-writing machine rather than an actual person. No, definitely better to wait.

Will was giving her that piercing look again. The one she could feel in her chest. "And how is Cal?" she asked a tad too brightly. "I haven't been back to Surrey since Christmas."

He returned his gaze to the window yet again. "Fine. Not much changes with him."

Will's younger brother had been a promising art student when he was injured in a terrible carriage accident that claimed the life of his best friend and left him with a debilitating shoulder injury. As far as Phoebe knew, he hadn't picked up a paintbrush in years.

"I don't see you around town much," Will continued, deftly steering the subject away from his younger brother. "Though Winifred is everywhere I go. I'm not sure that girl even sleeps."

Phoebe had wondered the very same about her vivacious younger sister.

"Yes, well, that is because Freddie is the only Atkinson sister who actually *enjoys* society. And thank God for that. She keeps Mother occupied so Alex and I can do as we please." Will smiled at that and Phoebe ignored the answering shiver of interest again. "I mostly keep to my corner of London. There is little to tempt me to venture towards Belgravia and beyond."

"Aside from your family, you mean."

She offered a half-hearted shrug in response. That was a thorny topic these days. Her mother was the granddaughter of an earl, but had committed a grave faux pas when she married Phoebe's father, the brilliant, dashing son of a successful accountant-turned-banker—and *new* money. Then, instead of being ashamed of their poor match, her parents had the audacity to be happily married, even when they had only three daughters and no sons. Some of the more conservative members of society still snubbed them to this day, but they didn't much care. Thus the family was considered, well, a bit eccentric. Their reputation had helped create a close-knit, nurturing atmosphere at home that, as Phoebe found, could quickly become suffocating.

Will gave her a searching look but didn't press further. "What will you do about Miss Clarke now?"

"I'm not sure," Phoebe said with a sigh. "If I wait for the police, nothing will ever happen."

"That detective seemed like a competent fellow."

"Perhaps, but I doubt Miss Clarke will be much of a priority to him."

Will frowned. "You've become quite cynical, Atkinson."

Phoebe held her tongue as anger flared inside her, hot and quick. That was rich, coming from him. Men like the duke were the very reason it was so blasted hard *not* to be cynical these days. "I'm merely a realist." She glanced out the window and noticed they were close to her flat. "Drop me off here, please." This unexpected reunion had grown tedious.

Will followed her gaze. "But we haven't reached your street yet." Even still, he tapped the handle of his walking stick against the ceiling and the carriage slowed to a stop.

She mustered a coy smile. "You can't possibly think I can be seen by my neighbors alighting from a duke's carriage. I'm simply trying to preserve my reputation. And yours."

His frown deepened as he moved to open the door for her, but she was faster.

"Nice to see you again, Margrave," Phoebe called over her shoulder as she practically leaped onto the pavement. She almost meant it too. "And thank you again for your help."

He called after her, but she didn't turn back. The words faded into the street noise as she lifted her chin and made her way home, alone once again.

As Will watched Phoebe march down the street like a woman who had not just spent the better part of the day in police custody, his mother's long-ago warning echoed through his mind: *That Atkinson girl is not for you anymore.*

She had been referring to Alex—for Will could *never* convince his mother that they were only friends—but the words had been an unsettling reminder of all that had changed thanks to a fearsome Sicilian's dagger and his degenerate cousin's habit for cheating at cards.

His father had never once spoken of the possibility that the dukedom might fall to him before his own early death, and his mother was just as shocked as Will by the news. She had been estranged from her late husband's family upon their marriage, as Will's grandfather expected his only son to marry the daughter of an important business associate, not an impoverished country squire in London for the season. But they had happily settled in Surrey and Will's father had become a successful country barrister in spite of the estrangement.

On occasion when his father had too much brandy at Christmas he spoke of his grandfather's distant cousin descended from a more illustrious branch of the Margrave tree, but it was treated like just another fairy tale: "Hansel and Gretel," "Briar Rose," and the Duke of Ellis with a dozen estates. What boy could imagine all that? What man? Will's imagination hadn't been big enough.

So although the Atkinsons may have been a perfectly acceptable family to unite with when he had been Mr. William Margrave, gentleman's son, they were not the right sort for a future duke. They had money and connections, but their blood simply wasn't blue enough. Only Mrs. Atkinson, the granddaughter of an earl, could claim a direct line to the aristocracy. Will knew nothing of Mr. Atkinson's ancestry, which said enough. He was meant for more now. The daughter of an earl or better would be ideal. Someone to help him adjust to his new station. Someone who had been born and bred to understand what it took to be a duchess. Someone like Lady Gwen.

Will snapped the curtain shut and sat back in his seat. He didn't need any reminders of how limited his choices were. That knowledge had followed him for years. He let out a sigh and checked his pocket watch. There was still time to pay Lady Gwen a short call, though he would have to come up with some reason to excuse his absence. Will winced. They weren't even engaged yet and he was already lying to her. That wasn't exactly an auspicious beginning, but he could hardly tell her where he had been all afternoon, could he.

Because you don't trust her.

The wince turned into a grimace. Damn that Phoebe Atkinson. Will didn't need more complications in his life, especially now. He needed to focus on his future and all the great things that lay ahead, not waste time wading through past memories—and Phoebe was *firmly* a part of his past.

Will instructed his driver to take him to the Fairbanks' home and reached for the satchel on the seat beside him. Now seemed as good a time as any to go over Parliament business. He didn't agree with many of the positions of the Conservative party, but the old duke had been an important fixture and a confidant of Lord Salisbury, the current prime minister. Upon his death, it was just assumed that Will would take his place and he had been too overwhelmed at the time to give it much thought. Besides, he wasn't a young idealist anymore, but a man with responsibilities. With dozens, nay, hundreds of people who depended on him for their livelihoods. And Will couldn't leave anything to chance, which meant following the guidance of the old duke's friends like Lord Fairbanks.

However, as the years passed and Will slowly found his footing, he began to bump up against the barriers constructed by powerful men who wanted the world to remain as it was. So Will chose his battles carefully, strategically, so as not to arouse any suspicion. If he was labeled a radical, those doors that had opened for him with such reluctance would slam shut and he could lose what little power he had amassed. This way he could advocate for gradual change from the inside. He was being pragmatic.

I'd say a coward.

Will gritted his teeth as Phoebe's contemptuous gaze flashed through his mind. This was insupportable. He flicked the curtain aside to glance out the window. They were still a good mile away from Mayfair, but Will banged on the roof. He couldn't sit here any longer. And certainly not while Phoebe's scent still hung in the air. Somehow it was more cloying than any perfume. As soon as the carriage came to a stop, he threw open the door and stepped down onto the pavement to the bewilderment of his coachman.

"Your Grace?"

"Thank you, John. I'll walk the rest of the way. I could use some fresh air."

His coachmen didn't even try to hide his confusion. This was Central London. There was no fresh air to speak of. But Will didn't need to explain himself. He was a duke, and dukes did whatever they pleased. So he turned swiftly on his heel toward his destination, grateful for every step that brought him farther away from Phoebe Atkinson.

Three

*P*hoebe had never been so happy to spend the night in her own little bed. She had done her best to appear blasé about the whole situation in front of the duke, as if she were hauled into police stations every day, but in truth she had been terrified. Then she came dangerously close to oversleeping the next morning. Luckily Marion Hartwell, her flatmate and fellow teacher, woke her with a cup of tea and a biscuit.

"Here. Drink this," she commanded. Marion was the school's mathematics teacher and had a fearsome reputation that was well earned. She was also an incredibly loyal friend.

Phoebe took the cup. "Ah, bless you, Mare."

As a young man, Marion's father had been a midshipman in the Royal Navy and met her mother while in Bombay. After a brief courtship, they married and returned to England, but the rest of the Hartwell family refused to accept his new bride on account of her Indian heritage. The estrangement was never mended and after her father's death five years ago, Marion embarked on her teaching career in part to support her mother and younger brother. Marion didn't waste a second dwelling on her father's family, but on more than one occasion she had implored Phoebe to make amends with her own.

"I did knock first, but you sleep like the dead." Then she narrowed her eyes. "Are you unwell? Did you catch something in that ghastly place?"

Phoebe took a restorative sip and shook her head. "No, I was just tired. Overwrought, I suppose." She had briefly related her ordeal to Marion yesterday before turning in early.

"Well, you best get ready. The headmistress sent a note last night while you were asleep calling for a meeting before the first bell."

Phoebe sat up a little straighter. "You don't think she's heard anything about Alice?"

Marion gave her an exasperated look. "If she had, she certainly wouldn't call a meeting over it."

Girls leaving the school was hardly an uncommon experience.

"I know Alice was your pet and I am sorry she's gone, but you'll run yourself ragged trying to save every one of them."

Phoebe ran her thumb along the rim of the chipped teacup. "It just doesn't make any sense. She was doing so well. And we had plans. She was very interested in the typist program"

"And where was she to get the money for that?" Marion said impatiently. They had had this conversation several times before. "Alice needed to *work*, especially after her mother died. We're lucky she stayed on as long as she did. This school provides a basic education for working-class girls, which is a miracle in itself. And heaven knows that isn't enough, but you can't be everyone's fairy godmother."

"I'm not *trying* to be. Only I…I hate seeing such potential wasted."

Marion's eyes softened. "I know. And I love you for your soft heart. But please, you need to do a better job looking out for yourself. What if Detective Inspector Holland hadn't been on duty when you were brought in?"

Phoebe hadn't mentioned Will's role in her release. "Do you think he'll say anything to the headmistress?"

"No, he's a good sort. Actually cares about doing the job."

Phoebe recalled the look of disgust on his face when Will tried to give him money. "Yes, I can see that."

"Now get dressed. If we're late, Mrs. Richardson will have us cleaning chalkboards after last bell," she said with a wink.

Once Phoebe washed and dressed, they took the omnibus to Langham Place School, which Mrs. Richardson had founded five years ago. It mostly served the daughters of the shopworkers in and around Oxford Circus, many of whom were the descendants of migrants from every corner of the empire. The diversity of the student body was also reflected in the teaching staff, as Mrs. Richardson believed it was important for the girls to see something of themselves in the women teaching them. The headmistress had grown up in the neighborhood herself, the exceptionally bright daughter of a milliner who had scrimped and saved to see her properly educated. She had been sent to board at the North London Collegiate School for Ladies on a scholarship, as the local schools didn't educate girls after age twelve.

It then became her mission to open an affordable neighborhood school for girls that offered the same educational opportunities as boys. One only needed to spend a few minutes in Mrs. Richardson's company to understand how she had managed such an accomplishment. An imposing figure who generally adhered to the usual stereotypes about headmistresses, she was sharp, direct, and suffered no fools. Phoebe admired her immensely.

Though she was called *Mrs.* Richardson, the headmistress was only married to her work, and there was an unspoken assumption that she expected the same single-minded focus from her teachers. That meant no other jobs, no other interests, and, most importantly, no men. If a teacher was courting, it was expected she would marry and *that* meant leaving the school. Of course, Mrs. Richardson's tacit disapproval didn't really stop anyone. It only meant they had to be quiet about it. But none of that was a concern for Phoebe, as she truly couldn't imagine a man worth the sacrifice of her hard-won career.

They made their way to the teacher's common room, which was already filled with their colleagues, and found seats next to Miss Cecily Sanderson, the unfortunately named music teacher.

"Any word yet on what this meeting is about?" Marion asked.

Cecily shook her head gravely. "No one knows a thing."

Marion exchanged a worried look with Phoebe. That didn't bode well. But before they could speculate further, Mrs. Richardson entered the room. Phoebe's stomach clenched as she took in the headmistress's expression, which was even more dour than usual.

Mrs. Richardson came to a stop at the front of the room and scanned the group. "Good morning, ladies. Thank you all for being here," she said, then paused for a tense moment. "I'm afraid I have some difficult news to share with you. Lady Montgomery has passed away—" Miss Blakenship, the drama teacher, let out a comically loud gasp, and the headmistress shot her a quelling look. "Given her advanced age and recent decline in health, that in itself is not a surprise, though it is sad. She was a great champion of female education, and as you are all aware, she held a charity auction during her annual garden party that greatly benefited our school. Those funds were crucial to our operations, and though she did leave a small bequest in her will, it does not make up for the loss of her patronage, especially given the ever-rising cost of rent and supplies. You all make a great many sacrifices to work here, so I am committed to keeping your wages intact, but that means we need to find another source of funding to keep our doors open. And quickly. I welcome your suggestions." She then folded her hands in front of her and looked expectantly at the audience.

The room fell silent for several long moments as people exchanged bewildered looks and hopeless shrugs until Phoebe slowly raised a hand. "What if we held a charity auction of our own?"

Cecily shot her a nervous glance. "But we couldn't possibly put on an event that compares to Lady Montgomery's garden party. She was *so* elegant."

Phoebe resisted the urge to roll her eyes. It was quite easy to be elegant when one possessed a great deal of money and a houseful of servants. "Then we'll do something different," she said, as her mind began to spin with ideas. "Perhaps we could put on a fair of sorts with the students. They could show what they've learned and how valuable the school is to them. We can open it up to the entire neighborhood and solicit donations from local businesses, so more people will attend."

Lady Montgomery's garden party was usually the purview of society women who attended rather less out of a sense of civic-mindedness and more so they could show off their newest afternoon gowns.

The headmistress's expression offered only the barest hint of interest. "What you're suggesting would be an enormous undertaking, Miss Atkinson."

Marion immediately raised her hand. "I'll help." Phoebe shot her a grateful look and a few other teachers raised their hands as well.

"We can form a committee," Phoebe said. "Organize it ourselves."

Mrs. Richardson seemed pleased. "And are you offering to lead this committee, Miss Atkinson?"

It wasn't really a question.

"Of course."

"Excellent," Mrs. Richardson said as one corner of her mouth slightly lifted. It was the closest she ever came to smiling. "Please come see me this afternoon so that we may discuss this further."

The headmistress then made a few other general announcements before they were dismissed. The rest of the morning passed quickly, as Phoebe was consumed by the gargantuan task of keeping a room full of girls ages twelve to fifteen interested in the works of Homer. As Phoebe explained the historical background that had inspired *The Odyssey*, her gaze wandered to Alice Clarke's empty desk by the window.

Each morning when Phoebe admitted she still hadn't heard from Alice, the girls' collective disappointment was palpable. It hung over the classroom like a fog, thick and impenetrable. They were a close-knit group with a genuine sense of camaraderie, which had made Alice's absence particularly distressing for them. Marion could think whatever she wanted, but Phoebe knew that Alice wouldn't have simply disappeared without a word to anyone.

When the bell finally rang for luncheon, Phoebe headed straight for the headmistress's office, as one was *never* late for an appointment with Mrs. Richardson.

Three years ago Phoebe had watched the headmistress give a lecture on the importance of public education for girls at her mother's social club, and working-class girls in particular. Phoebe had recently graduated from Bedford College and taken a position at a finishing school. She liked her students well enough, but they were mostly preparing for a life of upper-class luxury, and Phoebe often found herself bored. She approached the headmistress after her lecture and asked if there were any open positions. Mrs. Richardson had, rightly, been skeptical of Phoebe. She knew how she appeared, like the starry-eyed rich girl she was. But Mrs. Richardson had invited her to visit Langham Place School the following day and Phoebe never left.

The work was often challenging and many of her students had experienced the kind of profound loss and extreme hardship she had never experienced. But Phoebe loved her students and she believed in the school's mission. She saw firsthand how the girls grew more confident the longer they stayed there, and how they marveled at the skills they developed. They began to see more possibilities for themselves, and many went on to shape their own futures. Every girl should have a right to an education and learn as much as they wished. And Phoebe would do whatever she could to keep this school open.

She rapped on the open door, and the headmistress glanced up from her seat behind a massive desk piled with papers, books, and assorted bric-a-brac. Mrs. Richardson was surprisingly messy in her private quarters, but Phoebe knew she could locate anything she needed, and quickly.

"Miss Atkinson. Please take a seat," she said, gesturing to the chair across from her.

As Phoebe obeyed, Mrs. Richardson set aside the papers she had been reading and folded her hands.

"I liked your suggestions this morning very much. But to be frank, we need your family's connections to make this a real success."

Phoebe shifted in her seat. She kept the more grandiose details of her upbringing to herself, as she didn't want the other teachers to dismiss her as some kind of interloper. Only Marion and Mrs. Richardson knew just how patrician her background truly was.

"I don't see why we need to involve anyone outside of the neighborhood, ma'am."

The headmistress narrowed her eyes. "Unfortunately, we aren't in a position to be selective, Miss Atkinson. Though I'm sure your committee will come up with something unique, profitability is our primary concern. We must cast a wide net, and see what we can bring in."

Phoebe glanced out the window where the youngest students were playing with a weather-beaten ball in the tiny yard. She let out a sigh. Of course she would do it.

"I'll visit my mother after school lets out. I'm sure she will be happy to provide any assistance we need."

Even if it made Phoebe feel like a hypocrite.

The headmistress cracked another half smile. "Splendid."

Phoebe moved to rise, but Mrs. Richardson raised a hand. "One more thing before you go: I know you have been looking into Alice Clarke's whereabouts, but I can't have one of my most dedicated teachers ending up in *jail*."

"Ma'am?" Phoebe attempted a look of confusion that was undermined by the blush flooding her cheeks.

Mrs. Richardson was unimpressed. "Detective Inspector Holland is my neighbor. He told me what happened yesterday, and that he was able to let you go with only a warning. But you may not be so fortunate in the future."

Phoebe bowed her head in what must have appeared to be remorse but was actually relief. Mrs. Richardson didn't know about the duke then. Phoebe supposed she should thank the inspector for that little bit of discretion.

"I know you are concerned about Miss Clarke," she continued, her tone gentling. "But the inspector assured me he is looking into it."

A scoff escaped Phoebe's lips and her eyes widened. "I'm sorry, ma'am. You know the inspector far better than I do. I'm sure he is doing everything he can."

Mrs. Richardson gave her an arch look. "He is. Now you must leave him to his work so you can focus on your own. Make sure you aren't seen in that tenement house again." She then dismissed Phoebe with a wave of her hand.

Phoebe left before she could get into any more trouble. She found Marion in her empty classroom eating the remainder of her luncheon and correcting what looked like ghastly algebra homework.

"Mrs. Richardson knows," Phoebe said without preamble as she entered the room.

Marion glanced up and furrowed her brow. "Knows what?" As understanding dawned, she took on a look of horror that would have been funny under different circumstances. "She *knows?*"

Phoebe nodded and began to pace in front of Marion's desk. They only had a few minutes before her class returned. Marion sat back in her chair. "Goodness, you're lucky she didn't sack you on the spot!"

Teachers were supposed to conduct themselves according to the school's strict moral code at all times—or at least have the good sense not to get caught. They weren't supposed to be carted off to Bow Street in the middle of a Sunday, and they most *certainly* weren't supposed to be rescued by a bachelor duke.

"For now," Phoebe added ominously. At Marion's confused look, she winced. "There's a tiny, *tiny* detail I neglected to mention yesterday."

"Oh God," her friend muttered.

"When the constable arrived I panicked a bit and mentioned the name of an old family friend..."

Marion eyed her with suspicion. "And?"

"And he came down to the station—"

"He?" Marion nearly fell out of her chair.

"Yes. He. More specifically, the Duke of Ellis," she said in a rush.

"You know a *duke?*" Marion squeaked, and Marion had *never* squeaked before.

This was exactly the kind of reaction Phoebe had wished to avoid. Marion was now staring at her as if she had sprouted a pair of angel's wings.

"He wasn't always a duke," she said, only just a little defensively. "He was our neighbor growing up. And back then he was just a man. Well, not a *man* man. He was mostly a boy when I knew him best," Phoebe corrected, but she was blathering on and Marion only looked more and more confused. "The point is, he came to the station and asked the inspector to release me into his care."

"Don't tell me you *left* with him."

Phoebe hadn't known it was possible for a person's eyes to grow so large. "He insisted on taking me home, but I made him drop me off a block away."

"Well, at least you were discreet," Marion said dryly.

"I know how it looks, but the inspector didn't mention him to the headmistress."

Yet.

Marion mulled this over. "You aren't...involved with him, are you?"

Phoebe blinked. "Who? The duke?"

Marion rolled her eyes. "No, the postman, you goose."

"Of course not," Phoebe said far too sharply. "What would *I* want with a duke?"

As if it were even an option.

She instantly recalled the look of annoyance that had barely left Will's face the moment he entered the inspector's office. Lord knew what kind of elegant women he *actually* associated with. They certainly didn't spend most of the day in skirts smeared with chalk dust.

"Oh, I don't know," Marian said sarcastically. "Wealth, a title, power?" Then she paused. "Wait, he isn't one of those very old dukes, is he?"

If only.

"No, he's just a little older than my sister Alex."

Marion gave her a sly smile. "Is he handsome?"

Phoebe crossed her arms. "Who cares?"

"*Definitely* handsome, then."

"Don't look so smug."

"Excuse me, but a young, handsome duke rescued you from jail and you said nothing about it! Have I done anything to give you the impression that I would not be interested in such information? Because I *am*."

Phoebe shook her head. "You're making this into far more than it is. It's not as if I'll be seeing him again."

"Why not?"

Now it was her turn to roll her eyes. "Funnily enough, our paths don't cross very much given our respective positions in society."

"You could change that," Marion argued. "Easily."

You could probably see him this evening, if you wished.

Lord knew Freddie was invited everywhere.

"But I won't." She said it more for herself than Marion.

The bell then sounded, signaling both the end of luncheon and her interrogation. "We are far from done here," Marion said as she pointed her finger at Phoebe. "I want every little detail when we get home."

"Sorry to disappoint, but your inquisition will have to wait," Phoebe replied as she headed toward the door, suddenly grateful for the excuse. "I'm visiting my mother after school to discuss the charity bazaar."

"Perhaps you should invite the duke then," Marion teased.

Phoebe let out a burst of genuine laughter at the idea and headed back to her own classroom. As if someone like Will would *ever* lower himself to bother with her little school. How absurd.

Four

*P*hoebe stared out the window of the hackney as modest brick buildings gave way to tidy town houses and finally the grand classical-style mansions of Belgravia. At this hour the streets were mostly populated by pairs of finely dressed ladies no doubt heading to pay afternoon calls to other finely dressed ladies to trade thinly veiled insults mixed with bits of gossip. Phoebe suppressed a shudder and sat back in her seat. She already missed the vibrancy of her neighborhood.

As the carriage pulled up in front of a property that took up the top portion of a crescent of terrace houses, dread bubbled low in her belly. Her parents had caused a minor scandal when they bought two adjoining mansions years ago and combined them to create Park House, named for the impressive back garden. Her father had been inspired to commit this architectural offense while on a business trip to New York by the enormous Fifth Avenue mansions populated by robber barons and the nouveau riche. He liked to say that he had brought a little bit of that *splendid American gauche to the West End*. And while a number of neighbors whispered their disapproval, even more followed suit as soon as they could. Phoebe had once admired her father's unwavering commitment to riling London society at every opportunity, but the older she got, the more it felt like a gigantic waste of energy—to say nothing of the expense.

The carriage had long since rocked to a stop, but Phoebe took another moment to collect herself. She pasted a bright smile on her face before she stepped onto the pavement and had nearly made it to the front door before it swung open. "Good afternoon, Munson!"

The family's stodgy old butler gave a short bow as he stepped aside. "Miss Atkinson."

Munson was a relic inherited from her maternal grandmother's much more formal household, which made him a horrible snob who disapproved of Phoebe's living arrangements—not that he would *ever* be vulgar enough to show it. However, the housemaids liked to talk and they all claimed he was the biggest gossip in the neighborhood.

"Is my mother in?" She pulled off her gloves and cast a subtle look around the grand entryway.

"Madam is in the pink room. Follow me."

"Goodness, Munson. It hasn't been *that* long since my last visit," Phoebe joked, but the butler remained stone-faced. "I can find the way myself," she added quietly.

"As you wish." He then gave another short bow before shuffling off to grace another part of the house with his sparkling presence.

Phoebe let out a soft sigh and headed down the hall. According to family legend, when her newlywed parents were planning out Park House, her mother balked at her father's overtly masculine designs for the study and insisted on a separate space of her own. Her father jokingly replied, "I suppose you'll decorate it all in *pink* as well!" And she did just that.

While the composition of Park House may be considered

gauche by some, few could find fault with the elegant interior thanks to her mother's impeccable taste and eye for detail. Walls were either painted in soft shades of blue and cream, or papered in one of William Morris's exquisite floral prints, while the floors were accented with carefully matched rugs or intricate tilework.

Phoebe knew Marion didn't really understand why she lived in their little flat with the leaky roof that was too cold in winter and too hot in summer when she could stay here. Or why she bothered to work at all when she could spend her time going to balls and marry a perfectly nice man and have perfectly nice children. But Phoebe wanted no part of a society marriage's gilded cage, nor the largely unspoken rules expected of a wife.

Even her parents, who had most certainly married for love, could not entirely escape these expectations. Phoebe had watched her mother, an intelligent, curious woman, take up and discard a dozen different hobbies over the course of her childhood: painting, sculpture, astronomy, landscape design, flower arranging, and, for a brief, torturous period, the harp.

Unlike most husbands of their class, Phoebe's father doted on his wife and was indulgent of her many disparate pursuits, but they never veered from what was considered appropriate for a lady. A wife. A *mother.* And yet, Mrs. Atkinson was still considered an eccentric. Luckily she didn't seem to care. "You must try to do what makes you *happy,* my dear," she had told Phoebe once. "And as often as you can. No one else is as concerned with your personal happiness as yourself."

But at home Alex was their father's golden child, while Winifred was content reveling in the superficial delights of the ton with their mother, which often left Phoebe feeling like the odd one out.

So even though the little flat with the leaky roof was too cold in winter and too hot in summer, Phoebe could come and go as she pleased without interacting with at least half a dozen other people and their expectations of her, both silent and spoken. She could wear what she wanted and eat what she wanted *when* she wanted. Phoebe could, in short, just be. If the cost of that freedom was having to wear extra stockings in February or change her chemise twice a day for a week in August, that seemed like a fair bargain.

Phoebe paused outside the door to the pink room and took a steadying breath before knocking. At her mother's muffled response, she entered. Just like the rest of the house, this room was the picture of muted elegance. Phoebe didn't even particularly *like* pink, but her mother had dressed the space in warm, welcoming shades, silky textures, and sumptuous pieces of furniture that practically begged visitors to sit. Phoebe always felt immediately calmer as soon as she stepped across the threshold. Even her father couldn't resist the siren's call of the pink room—though he would *never* admit it. But on more than one afternoon he had been found dead asleep on the plush chaise.

Mrs. Atkinson, dressed in a fetching pale green silk afternoon gown, was looking at her reflection in a large gilt-framed mirror and adjusting her matching hat, but her hands stilled when she noticed Phoebe.

"Oh, hello Bee. I was just on my way out to see Lady Kirby. Is Freddie expecting you? She's having a lesson with Monsieur Laurent."

"No, Mother. Actually, I . . . I came here to speak to you. I need something."

Mrs. Atkinson let out a surprised laugh and whirled around to face her daughter. "I don't think you've needed anything from me since you were twelve years old."

Phoebe glanced away from her mother's deceptively sharp gaze. "It won't take more than a moment."

"Very well." Mrs. Atkinson sat down on the sofa and patted the space beside her. "Come here."

Once Phoebe had dutifully taken her seat, Mrs. Atkinson began inspecting her. "You're looking a bit tired. Perhaps you need a break from that school."

Her mother was always suggesting she take a break. Though Phoebe knew her concern was well meant, it was incredibly irritating.

"I'm fine," Phoebe grumbled.

"Is this about a suitor?"

She ignored the hope in her mother's voice. "It's about the school, actually." Before her mother could make any more guesses, she explained the situation while Mrs. Atkinson listened patiently.

"And since the headmistress has put me in charge of forming a committee, I thought I'd ask you for advice," she added.

Mrs. Atkinson gave her a conspiratorial smile. "I'm sure you don't only want my *advice*, darling."

"No," Phoebe admitted. "Obviously the headmistress would like it if we could attract the same people who attended the garden party, but we won't have anywhere near the same funds to spend."

Her mother didn't look concerned. "We will come up with something. Lady Montgomery's event was always lovely, but she was mostly concerned with keeping up appearances. If you're looking to compel people to open their purses, I have a few ideas." She paused to tap her chin. "Lady Graham and Mrs. Abernathy also have a fierce philanthropic rivalry we could exploit."

But Phoebe was too distracted to comment on her mother's scheming. "You...you attended the garden party?"

"Of course I did," she said, offended. "Every year, in fact. Did you think I wouldn't support the school my *own* child worked at?"

"No," Phoebe replied hastily. "I didn't mean it that way. I just...you never said anything."

"Well, you haven't been around very much. And when I do see you, we have far more important things to discuss than what society functions I've attended."

Phoebe looked down. It was true that her visits home had grown more and more infrequent since she started working at the school three years ago. Lately they were mostly relegated to holidays or family birthdays, as that was all Phoebe could take.

Though Mr. Atkinson had dutifully paid for Phoebe's education at Bedford College, a local women's institution, after she refused to endure another London season, he hadn't understood her desire to teach.

If you insist on working, come down to the office. I'm sure your sister can find something productive for you to do.

But Phoebe immediately rejected the suggestion and her father had gone on to treat her job as little more than a lark.

Let me know when you grow tired of reading nursery rhymes to street urchins and are ready to join your sister and do some real *work.*

Phoebe chose to avoid him instead. Besides, even if she *had* wanted to work for their father, it only would have caused more strife as she could never measure up to Alex, who had started working for him while still in the schoolroom.

At first it was something to occupy her busy mind when she grew bored with their governess's admittedly limited knowledge and Father found her in the library halfway through *The Wealth of Nations*. But not only was Alex brilliant, she had an uncanny knack for spotting incredibly lucrative business ideas. It was largely thanks to her that Atkinson Enterprises had grown into one of the top financial firms in the country.

But Phoebe didn't have a head for numbers like her sister, and she certainly didn't care about enriching their father's already wealthy clients. Alex viewed it as a kind of game, but to Phoebe it felt like the worst sort of excess. And recently, in a moment of frustration, she had told her sister just that.

Well that excess, *as you call it, helped pay for your education.*

The immediate rejoinder, delivered in Alex's famously cold, crisp voice, had been haunting her for weeks now. Phoebe's tendency to reverse numbers ensured that she would never follow her sister to Lady Margaret Hall at Oxford, but Bedford College had been all too happy to have her—and her family's money.

"I'll help you, Bee." Her mother's warm words cut through the ugly memory. "Only let me give it a think. I'll speak with Lady Kirby as well. She has far too much money as it is. She may as well spend some of it on a school instead of that racehorse she keeps going on about."

"Thank you, Mother."

Mrs. Atkinson held up a hand. "Before you agree, there's something I'd like from you in return." Phoebe braced herself. She knew what was coming. "When your father and Alex come back home, I want all of us to have dinner together on Fridays. Like we used to. And *no* arguments."

Phoebe's cheeks flushed. "Then tell Father to respect my job and stop acting like I'm a glorified nanny."

"I will speak to him about that," she promised. "But you must admit that calling him morally bankrupt didn't exactly help."

Phoebe winced. God, Christmas had been awful. Cook had made the punch stronger than usual and it had loosened all their tongues.

"I only said that because he called my students street urchins. And even if they are, what of it? Don't they deserve to learn to read?"

"They do," her mother agreed. "And your father did apologize for saying that. You don't have to like everything he does, but all of you need to be more respectful of each other. Your father and Alex both work hard, and though you might not see it, they try to do good in their own way."

Phoebe sensed she wasn't going to win this argument and simply nodded in reply. Her mother looked relieved.

"Oh, I'm *so* glad. I'll start planning the menu tonight. We'll have everyone's favorite dishes. You do still like lobster patties, don't you?"

Phoebe couldn't help but smile at her mother's enthusiasm. "Yes, that sounds nice."

"Wonderful! Even Cook will be excited." Mrs. Atkinson then glanced at the clock on the mantel. "I'm sorry, darling, but I really must be going. Lady Kirby will have likely fallen asleep in her chair waiting for me." Phoebe rose with her mother and accepted her cheek kiss. "Now make sure to see Freddie before you leave. She'll be terribly put out if you don't say hello."

"I'll go right now."

Mrs. Atkinson patted her cheek. "That's my dear girl. Be well! And come again soon!" she called over her shoulder as she glided down the hall with an enviable combination of purpose and grace.

As Phoebe made her way to the ballroom, she could hear Freddie arguing with Monsieur Laurent from down the hall—but that was nothing unusual.

"You dropped your arm."

"I did not!"

"You did," he calmly insisted in his delightful Parisian accent.

Then the sound of foils clinking commenced. Phoebe paused in the doorway and watched as her sister smoothly dropped to the floor to avoid Monsieur Laurent's lunge and thrust her foil against his chest. She let out a triumphant cry as she rose.

"That was *perfect*!" Freddie tore off her mask.

"It was better," the monsieur allowed as he much more gracefully removed his own mask and ran a hand through his dark hair. Then he noticed Phoebe and bowed. "Mademoiselle Atkinson."

Freddie turned and gave her a wide smile. "Did you see? We've been practicing that move all afternoon."

"Very impressive," Phoebe answered honestly.

Freddie immediately turned back to her instructor and gave him an arch look. Even the formidable Frenchman couldn't completely suppress a smile. "It was better," he repeated.

"I'll take it," Freddie said with a grin.

"I will see you next week then," he said as they shook hands. Then he gave Phoebe a wink as he strolled past her and inclined his head. "Mademoiselle Atkinson, always a pleasure to see you."

"And you, Monsieur Laurent."

Freddie rolled her eyes and sat down on a bench. "You're blushing."

Phoebe turned back to catch one last glimpse of the man in his tight fencing whites as he headed down the hall. "Can you blame me?" Then she faced her sister. "He really is so charming."

"It's the accent," Freddie said as she unbuttoned the collar of her fencing jacket. "He's an absolute monster."

Phoebe laughed and joined her on the bench. "You're getting awfully good though."

"Oh, he's a splendid teacher. I can't fault him there. His kissing, however, was quite lackluster."

"Freddie!"

"It was nothing," she said with a dismissive wave. "We both agreed it was a mistake that will not be repeated."

Phoebe frowned at her impertinence, though it wasn't exactly a surprise. Freddie didn't place much importance on kisses. Or men in general. She had barely entered her first season when she became engaged to a young marquess—and the most eligible bachelor in London at the time. But then she just as quickly called it off, and blamed her initial acceptance on the novelty of being proposed to which had dimmed considerably once she considered the reality of being a wife.

It had been a shocking turn of events and their mother had taken her abroad the following year rather than risk another scandal. But unfortunately Freddie was even more popular on the Continent and collected proposals from an Italian prince, an aging Texan oilman, and a chap claiming to be one of Napoleon's descendants before Mother hauled her back to England. Since then Freddie had behaved. Mostly. Or at least learned to keep her indiscretions well under wraps.

She pulled the jacket off and dropped it on the floor. "Much better," she said as she fanned herself with her hand. "Now then, what are you doing here?"

"I can't visit my favorite youngest sister?"

Freddie huffed. "You never want to come to the house anymore. I always have to meet you somewhere."

Phoebe bit her lip. She may be at odds with Alex, but she had always gotten along with Freddie. *Everyone* got along with Freddie. She made it impossible not to. "I needed to speak to Mother, actually."

Freddie raised one dark brow. "Oh?" While Phoebe's lighter coloring favored their father, both her sisters shared their mother's raven hair and brown eyes. But whereas Alex was tall and willowy, Freddie was shorter with enviable curves. "Do tell."

Phoebe explained the situation with the school and her intention to hold a charity bazaar. Freddie's eyes lit with interest.

"That's a splendid idea! I'll donate a fencing lesson."

"Really? That would be wonderful."

"You don't need to sound so surprised. I'd love to help."

Phoebe lowered her head. "I didn't mean it like that. It's just… you know how disapproving Father has been about the school."

"He's been an *ass*."

Phoebe chuckled. "Yes, well, I suppose I've also liked having something all to myself. And it's nice to go somewhere where people don't know that I'm the great Philip Atkinson's daughter, or the extraordinary Alex Atkinson's sister. You know?"

"I do," Freddie said softly. "Seeing as how you're the unconventional Phoebe Atkinson."

"I thought it was the *unnatural* Phoebe Atkinson." She tried to say it lightly, but the bitterness bled through. She had heard all manner of jeers both whispered and not during her London season. It was why she now avoided society as much as possible.

"To some, perhaps," Freddie said with a shrug. "But you're trying to do good in this world. There are plenty of people who find you admirable, besides me of course."

"Oh," Phoebe said dumbly.

Freddie gave her a pointed look. "Not *everyone* I socialize with is a spoiled ninny, you know."

"Sorry, Freddie," Phoebe mumbled.

"It's all right," she said with a wave of her hand. "Have you heard anything about your student? You were so worried last time I saw you."

Phoebe shook her head. "I went to her flat yesterday, but no one has seen her. It's like she simply vanished."

Freddie's brow furrowed with worry and she clasped Phoebe's hand. "That's awful."

"Something else happened while I was there," Phoebe added. "But you can't tell anyone."

She gave a solemn nod. "I swear."

As Phoebe relayed the events of yesterday, Freddie's eyes grew wider and wider. But when she got to the part about the duke showing up, Freddie's mouth actually dropped open.

"Will Margrave went down to Bow Street to *rescue* you?"

Phoebe shook her head at her sister's incredulous tone. "I didn't really give him much choice. And you know how loyal he is to Alex."

Freddie didn't look convinced. "He could have sent someone, Phoebe. I mean, the man *is* a duke."

She ignored her sister's pointed look. Time to change the subject away from Will. "I wish I knew who owned the building. Something just doesn't feel right. The maintenance man was so outraged that I was even *asking* about Alice. But why would he care?"

"Well, why don't you ask Will? He owns all sorts of properties around London. If anyone can find out I'm sure he can." Then her sister's eyes took on a gleam that usually signaled trouble. "Come with me to the Wrenhew ball tonight! You can ask him there."

Phoebe's heart beat noticeably faster at the thought of seeing Will again, and so soon, but she would rather return to Bow Street than a London ballroom.

"I have school in the morning."

"Then don't stay long," Freddie tossed off, as if an early wake time was the only thing preventing Phoebe from attending the kind of event most people spent weeks preparing for.

But rather than admit to feeling woefully out of place, Phoebe simply crossed her arms. "I thought the fashionable set don't show their faces until past midnight anyway."

"Yes, but Will is only going because he's courting Lady Gwendolyn Fairbanks. He'll get his two dances in and then leave as soon as he can," Freddie added.

Phoebe's mouth had gone strangely dry. "I...I don't think I know her," she said, managing to sound bored.

"She's Lord Fairbanks's eldest daughter. A little too fond of herself I think, but she is very popular. Not that Will has any real competition, being a duke and all. Lord Fairbanks would probably cart Gwen over to St. George's this second if Will proposed."

Of course. The daughter of an earl was perfect for him. "Naturally."

Freddie didn't seem to notice Phoebe's dry tone and suddenly grasped her sister's hand again. "Oh *do* come with me tonight. I promise we won't stay very late. Just long enough for you to talk to Will."

Phoebe couldn't deny that Freddie had a point. And a part of her was awfully curious to see the future Duchess of Ellis, though she quickly buried the pang in her chest that followed the thought. It felt distressingly close to envy and *that* was absurd.

"I have a gown you can wear," Freddie continued. "It's never quite fit me right, anyway. And Lucy can do your hair. She'll probably find it easy after battling with mine every day." Freddie gestured to the absolute mass of curls neatly pinned at the nape of her neck. As usual, a few strands had sprung loose around her temples, but they only made her look more fetching.

Though she had already made up her mind, Phoebe had a reputation to uphold so she let out a heavy sigh. "Very well. If you think the duke can help, I can't really say no."

Freddie grinned as she looped her arm through Phoebe's. "My thoughts exactly."

Five

*I*t was barely past nine, but the Wrenhews' ballroom was already a crush. Will stood at the edge of the dance floor and scanned the sea of too familiar faces chattering away about nothing of consequence and discreetly checked his pocket watch yet again. He had already danced once with Lady Gwendolyn Fairbanks. Now he needed to stand here for three more turns until he could claim his second and get the hell out of here, where a mountain of paperwork and a glass of single malt awaited him at home. Will shoved the watch back into his breast pocket. Best not to ruminate on *why* he was more interested in spending the evening locked in his study with inanimate objects rather than his soon-to-be-betrothed. Luckily, a distraction approached.

"Fairbanks, good evening."

The earl came beside him. "You and my daughter make a handsome pair."

"Any man is improved in her presence."

The earl chuckled and absently ran a hand down his short salt-and-pepper beard. Though he must be well into his fifties, he still garnered his share of flirtatious looks from matrons and maids alike. Every now and then there was a whisper about his days as one of London's most dissolute young gentlemen, but Will wasn't the kind to listen to rumors. Besides, former libertine or not, Lord Fairbanks had gone on to marry the beautiful daughter of a duke and was a well-respected member of society.

"You don't need to flatter me, Duke. I already approve, of course."

Will's brow furrowed. Then why was he wasting his time wooing her?

"Let the girl have her fun for a few more weeks," the earl continued, as if he were able to read Will's thoughts. "Before she takes on the role of a wife. I am given to understand it can be quite taxing," he added with a smirk.

"Of course," Will replied softly.

Lord Fairbanks had been a close friend of the old duke and mentored Will when he first took his seat in Parliament more than half a decade ago. He had been barely a man, fresh out of Oxford and still finding his feet in a world he had been thrust into just two years before. Will always enjoyed healthy political debate in school, or at the dinner table, but once he was in a position to actually *do* something, he was overwhelmed. The earl was a powerful member of the Conservatives and though they didn't always see eye to eye, Will owed him a debt of gratitude for his guidance for so many years.

It was only natural now that Will was of an age to marry that he would consider Lady Gwen. She was beautiful, refined, and had been raised from the cradle to be a duchess. The earl had also made no secret of his desire to see Will hold the highest office in the land, and promised she would be a valuable asset and support his political ambitions.

Will wasn't entirely sure he even *wanted* to be prime minister—being a duke was more than enough work on its own–but he had learned it was always better to be prepared for both the expected and the accidental. Though some might argue that was impossible, Will had arranged his life in such a way that he would never again be at the mercy of something as erratic as fate.

"Just a few more weeks of this nonsense and you can announce your engagement," Fairbanks continued. "My wife is hoping for an early June wedding. Something about the peonies being in season."

Will cleared his throat. That was rather soon.

The earl raised an eyebrow at his noticeable silence. "I thought you *wanted* a short engagement."

"I did. I do," Will amended. But that was before. When it had merely been a strategy, rather than an actual life decision.

"Glad to hear it." Fairbanks punctuated his words with a clap on Will's back. "Though a great many ladies will be very disappointed," he added with a nod toward a passel of mamas nearby who all had daughters out and were utterly failing to hide their interest in him.

Will's shoulders tightened as two women cast him very obvious looks before whispering to one another behind a fan. No doubt they intended to cajole him into dancing with one of the wallflowers lining the room, but Will was not in the mood to be charitable this evening. He was the only unmarried duke under sixty in all of England and every time he entered a ballroom, he had the distinct sensation of being stalked by a bloodthirsty predator. But they would not make a meal of him tonight.

"Fly, good Fleance," the earl said, quoting *Macbeth* with a devious little grin. "Fly, fly!"

Will shot him an exasperated glance and wove his way through the crowd, while the earl's cackle nipped at his heels. Once he made it out of the ballroom, Will swiftly rounded a corner right into the path of a young lady coming in the opposite direction.

"My apologies," he burst out as he steadied her shoulders before she could tumble over. But as the girl lifted her face to him, Will was dumbstruck. He blinked a few times before he found his voice.

"Phoebe?"

She wriggled out of his grasp and stepped back to smooth her skirts. "You needn't sound so shocked."

Will begged to differ, given the sight before him. Phoebe Atkinson was trussed up in a pale blue ball gown that showed off her lithe figure, while her hair, now fully on display, was plaited in an intricate knot at the back of her head.

She looked lovely, to be sure, but quite different from the last time they met. Only her hazel eyes, sparkling with that familiar edge of defiance in the hallway's low gaslight, remained unchanged.

"Can you blame me? You never come to these things."

Phoebe looked away. "Yes, well, tonight I have a reason."

Something skittered in Will's chest. Had she come here for a man? The thought unsettled him far more than he cared to admit. But before he could press her further, Freddie Atkinson called to them as she hurried over.

"There you are!" Then she shot Phoebe a knowing look. "And you've already found Will."

He immediately perked up. Phoebe was looking for him? That shouldn't be so pleasing to hear.

But Freddie wasn't done interrogating her sister. "Why didn't you wait for me?"

"You were having quite an engrossing discussion with Lord

Danvers," Phoebe said with a shrug. "I didn't think you would notice."

Freddie dismissed the idea with a flick of her wrist. "Oh please. I was only making small talk. It's generally expected at social events," she added pointedly.

Phoebe responded with a huff and crossed her arms.

Will's curiosity finally got the better of him. "You were looking for me?"

Both sisters turned toward him then. A weaker man who hadn't grown up with these girls might have cowered in the face of their uncommonly direct gaze.

The Atkinson sisters were not known for being shy and retiring. Most gentlemen avoided Alex whenever possible and very few could match wits with Freddie, while Phoebe had simply taken herself out of the equation for reasons Will still didn't understand.

"I dragged Phoebe here with me tonight because she needs your help, even if she is reluctant to admit it," Freddie explained.

Will cast a glance at Phoebe, who did indeed look like she would rather be fed to wild dogs than stand there.

"How intriguing," he said. "I'm all ears."

"I want to know who owns the tenement building where my missing student lives," she said in a rush. "Freddie seems to think you can find out." Though Phoebe herself looked skeptical. And that didn't sit right with him.

Will turned to Freddie, who simply shrugged her shoulders, before addressing Phoebe. "I should be able to, yes. But why do you want to know?"

"The more I think about what happened yesterday, the stranger it becomes." Phoebe shook her head in thought. "That maintenance man was so determined to stop me from finding out about Alice. But why? He must know something or is trying to protect someone."

Will exchanged another look with Freddie. "Or you may be reading far too much into your brief interaction with him."

"It might not mean anything," she acknowledged, "but it's the only lead I have on Alice. I need to see it through."

"And then what? You'll confront this person? You've already been arrested for trespassing on their property. You heard the inspector. They could still press charges."

"I can be careful."

"You should *always* be careful," Will insisted, well aware that he sounded like a fretful nursemaid.

Phoebe appeared undaunted by his little outburst. "Something is amiss here. Something bigger than Alice's disappearance. I'm sure of it."

As she continued to stare at him with her solemn gaze, Will could actually *feel* his resolve weaken. Later, he would wonder if that was the precise moment he lost all good sense.

"All right," he groused. "I'll look into it. But I make no promises."

Phoebe suddenly broke into a dazzling smile. "Oh, thank you. Truly. Anything you find would be helpful, I'm sure."

A full peal of bells clattered in his head. Good lord. The things he was prepared to do to have her smile like that again went *far* beyond a little fact-finding. Will needed to leave. Immediately. But before he could make his excuses they were approached by Lord Danvers, who was gazing at Freddie with the kind of anxious hopefulness normally reserved for small children asking for a second dish of pudding.

"Miss Atkinson? I believe our dance is coming up."

"Oh! I nearly forgot," she said airily, as if she had left behind her hat and not one of the most eligible bachelors in London. As Freddie took Lord Danvers's arm she glanced back at Will. "Dance with her, will you?"

The alarm bells were now deafening, but it would be the height of rudeness to say no.

Phoebe shot her sister a murderous glare just as Will offered his hand. "My pleasure."

Her eyes widened in surprise but she took it without comment. Will led her back into the ballroom and onto the dance floor. As the music started, he swept her into his arms. Though he had waltzed with dozens of women over the years, holding Phoebe felt decidedly different. They were attuned to each other in a way he hadn't experienced. Though he must have whirled her around the Atkinson's parlor a time or two growing up, Will struggled to recall any particular memory now. Still, dancing with her was easy. Familiar. After a few moments Will lost himself in the movements and had completed two full turns before he realized people were staring at them. Or, more precisely, at *her*.

Phoebe seemed to read his thoughts. "Did it not occur to you that we would draw attention?"

"I'm used to it." Will had not enjoyed any kind of anonymity for many years. Not since he became the heir to a dukedom.

He felt the sigh that escaped her. "I don't know how you stand it. I couldn't."

Will had the sudden urge to point out that he hadn't much choice in the matter, actually, but he swallowed the bitter reply. No one liked a bellyacher, especially when he was a duke.

"The end justifies the means," he grumbled instead.

She arched a brow. "Still doesn't seem worth it to me. But then,

I don't expect to ever marry," she added as she cast a dull gaze around the room.

"I'm sure there are any number of gentlemen who would be happy to have you as a wife," he said gently.

Her eyes snapped back to his face and Phoebe let out a laugh. "Oh, heavens, look at you! Good lord, I don't *want* to."

Will couldn't hide his shock. "Why not?"

"I already earn enough to support myself," she said. "What use would I have for a husband?"

Will suddenly felt very stodgy. "Love? Companionship? Protection?"

Phoebe laughed again, but this time with a dismissive edge that rankled him for some reason. "Surely you know one doesn't have to be *married* to experience such things. And that would not necessitate me giving up my autonomy or becoming nothing more than chattel."

He hadn't really considered that. "Nearly every woman I know talks of nothing but marriage."

"Well, can you blame them?" Phoebe challenged. "Society tells us that a single woman is at best an inconvenience and at worst an aberration. I can understand why so many choose the safety of marriage—even if it isn't always in their best interest," she added.

Will cleared his throat. "What about children?"

Phoebe's chin lifted. "What about them?"

"Do you . . . do you not want any?"

This conversation had become highly inappropriate for a ballroom. Though he couldn't think of anywhere it *would* be appropriate. And yet, he couldn't stop himself from asking such a personal question. He wanted to know her answer. Wanted to know what kind of future she envisioned for herself.

Phoebe looked past him. "I haven't given it much thought," she said. "And I'd rather be available to help my students."

It was a perfectly reasonable response, and yet Will felt a strange pang of disappointment. "Your dedication is admirable," he said stiffly.

But Phoebe shrugged off the compliment. "I'm no different from the other women I teach with."

"Tell me about the missing girl," he said after a moment. It was well past time to move away from matrimony and babies. "What was her name again?"

Phoebe perked up at that. "Alice Clarke. She's a bright girl and a hard worker. She wants to go to secretarial school."

"And you don't think it's possible that she ran off? Maybe she found work outside the city." Though as he said the words, Will realized how silly that sounded. People were pouring into London every day looking for work.

Phoebe shook her head. "Not without telling anyone. And she was so determined. She wouldn't just disappear. Not unless—" Phoebe swallowed hard and cleared her throat. "I need to know that she is safe. She has no other family. There is no one else looking for her. She'll become yet another girl swallowed up by this city." Then her jaw hardened as she met Will's eyes. "Which is why I'm going back to that tenement house."

"But Inspector Holland—"

"Has far more important things to do than look into another missing girl," she cut in. "You *know* this, Margrave. I can't waste any more time waiting for him."

In the space of a moment, her entire bearing had changed. She seemed more confident. Determined. Unapologetic. It was the exact opposite of the modest serenity a young unmarried lady was expected to embody, especially at a ball. But it seemed safe to assume that Phoebe didn't give a damn about any of that.

"Then let me accompany you."

"There's no need—"

"I promised the inspector that I would be responsible for you," he reminded her before leaning in a little closer. "And I take my responsibilities very seriously."

Her hazel eyes darkened and Will found he could not look away.

"Give me two days," he urged. "I'll see what I can find about the owner of the tenement house as well."

"All right," Phoebe said after a breath. Then she arched a brow. "But I won't wait longer than that."

The corner of Will's mouth curved up. It had been a long, long time since anyone other than his mother demonstrated such utter disregard for his opinion. "Understood."

It was another moment before he realized the music had stopped and they were the only couple still holding each other. He immediately let her go and escorted her off the floor, but there was no chance their faux paus had gone unnoticed. As they rejoined Freddie, she didn't even try to hide her smirk while he could nearly feel Lady Gwen's sharp-eyed gaze raking his back from across the room. Will stiffened. He had let Phoebe distract him long enough.

"Thank you for the company, Miss Atkinson," he said with a short bow. "Good evening, ladies." Then he walked away before either could reply. By the time he reached Lady Gwen, she had managed to resume her bored expression—aside from the slight crease between her brows.

"Who is that with Winifred Atkinson?"

"Her sister."

Lady Gwen wrinkled her nose. "The one that supposedly works for their father?"

Will's lips pursed at her skeptical tone, but it was hardly the first time someone questioned the nature of Alex's role in the company. "That is Alexandra," he replied. "Phoebe is a schoolteacher. She doesn't move much in society."

"Oh." Lady Gwen's shoulders relaxed. "I suppose that's why she's wearing a gown from last season. For a moment I thought it might be someone important," she drawled.

Will ignored the impulse to reprove her, as that would only arouse her suspicions once again. "No," he said, making sure to match her careless tone while he watched the Atkinson sisters retreat out of the corner of his eye. "Not at all."

Six

*P*hoebe gazed idly around her classroom. It was a balmy afternoon and her students were growing antsy. They were separated into groups and supposed to be debating the themes present in *The Odyssey*, but more than one had strayed from their task in favor of school gossip. Class would be dismissed for the day in just a few minutes, so Phoebe decided not to scold them. There would be plenty of time to discuss the intricacies of Homer tomorrow.

There were many who thought teaching these girls the classics was beyond useless, but every boy that attended Eton read this text. And Phoebe strongly believed that literature shouldn't be reserved for only the upper classes. Odysseus's treacherous journey back to Ithaca had survived for thousands of years because it relayed something universal about the human experience. Something that spoke to people across eons and captured their imagination. Perhaps Phoebe could have devoted the hour to more tedious grammar exercises or penmanship practice, but these girls deserved a little adventure too.

She intended to have one of her own soon. Once school ended, she would head directly to Alice Clarke's flat. Phoebe had not so patiently waited two days at Will's request, but he was likely too busy with whatever it was dukes did to come all the way over here now.

I take my responsibilities very seriously.

Her neck warmed at the memory of those words spoken in his low, deep voice so close to her ear. If he ever learned how many times she had thought of that over the past two days, she would perish on the spot. Especially considering the elegant young woman he had left them for.

That's Lady Gwen, Freddie had whispered. *People say they'll be married before Ascot.*

As Will moved to stand beside her, even Phoebe couldn't deny they made a striking pair.

So it did not matter what he whispered as they moved around the ballroom, nor the feeling of comfort that had washed over her while in his strong arms. And she must have imagined the spark in his dark eyes at the very end, just before he pulled away. After all, she had mistaken his attention for a deeper interest once before and had no wish to repeat the experience.

Phoebe gave her head a sharp shake, forcing the enticing memory to scatter.

"Who is *that?*" Mabel Taylor suddenly rose from her chair and pointed to the window that looked out onto the street. "He looks like the king!"

"We don't have a king, you idiot," Florence O'Conner said, joining her. "He must be a lord."

Next was Lizzie Abrams. "What's a lord doing *here?*"

"Girls, stop gawking," Phoebe called out, but it was no use. The entire class was now crowded around the window. Girls were standing on their tiptoes and craning their necks for a glimpse. Phoebe glanced at the clock. The bell would ring any moment.

"Oh, he's handsome," Lizzie cooed. "I think he's waiting for someone."

"From *this* place?" Florence sneered. "Don't be daft."

"Well, why else would he be standing right there?" Lizzie countered.

Phoebe rose, prepared to intervene in case they continued to quarrel but then the bell rang. "All right girls, class dismissed."

A chorus of groans rose up but Phoebe knew they were only sorry to lose their vantage point. "We'll continue with *The Odyssey* tomorrow, when Odysseus encounters a cyclops."

That managed to catch their attention, especially after she promised there would be blood. Then they gathered their things and dutifully filed out. Phoebe said her goodbyes and answered a few last-minute questions mostly regarding *just how much blood* until the room was finally empty.

Then she headed toward the window to see this supposed lord creating such a fuss. It was probably a clerk waiting for his sweetheart who worked in one of the nearby shops, she reasoned as an irritating flicker of hope began to kindle in her chest. The girls thought *any* well-dressed man was an aristo. It wasn't him. He was too busy. Too important. Too—

But the rest of her well-reasoned points vanished as she caught sight of the man standing on the pavement across the street. The girls were right. This was no mere office worker. Even from this distance Phoebe could tell he wore an expertly tailored suit only the very wealthy could afford. And was indeed handsome. Exceedingly so.

Just then Will glanced up and caught her staring at him. He gave a little wave and pointed at the school's front door with a questioning look. Phoebe immediately shook her head. If he came in here she would have to explain who he was and then she would *never* hear the end of it. Will seemed to understand and raised his hands in supplication. She held up a finger and he nodded.

Phoebe gathered her things as quickly as possible and rushed down the stairs just as Marion was coming up them, likely to see her.

"I'm late for an appointment," Phoebe explained before she could ask. "But I'll see you at home!"

Marion called out something but Phoebe just raised a hand in goodbye. She would answer for her abruptness later. As Phoebe exited the school, she looked over her shoulder to make sure no one was watching. Then and *only* then did she cross the street.

"Come this way," she said to Will without stopping and headed away from the school.

"Is this how you always greet people?" he replied drolly as he followed her.

Once she rounded the corner and was safely out of sight, Phoebe came to a stop. She then discreetly looked back but no one seemed to have noticed them. She let out a breath and faced Will, who stared at her curiously.

"Worried about being seen with me?" He was clearly joking but Phoebe nodded.

"It would cause talk," she explained. "My students all saw you from the window."

"And you'd rather skulk about than just tell them the truth?"

"That I know a *duke*?"

Will narrowed his eyes. "I meant that I'm a friend—" The scoff erupted from her without warning. "Of the family," he continued.

Phoebe's cheeks flushed. "Sorry," she mumbled. "I didn't mean—"

"It's fine," he said as he looked away to adjust his cuffs. "And you're probably right to be so cautious. I don't wish to make things difficult for you."

Before she could reply, he continued on. Phoebe watched for a moment as he strode down the pavement, his smooth movements suddenly *achingly* familiar. But even if he had been a stranger, it would have been quite impossible for her not to notice such a dashing figure.

Will paused and looked back, his gaze now steady. "Aren't you coming?"

A sense of familiarity washed over her. Back in Surrey he had always waited for her, even when she had been nothing more than the annoying little sister clambering after him and Alex, desperate to be included in their adventures. Phoebe's heart clenched for one wrenching beat, then she trotted after him, suddenly feeling ten years old again. Once she was by his side, Will continued on. He fixed his gaze straight ahead as he addressed her:

"My secretary retrieved the location of the tenement house from Inspector Holland and from there was able to uncover the building's owner."

Phoebe brightened. "Oh? Who is it?"

Will glanced at her and shook his head. "It's owned by a company. We're trying to find out who is behind it, but that will be difficult. Usually people set up these companies to ensure their privacy. Whoever owns this flat also owns a few other properties in the area, including a music hall of ill repute."

"Then perhaps it is someone with a reputation to protect."

"Quite possible. But that doesn't exactly narrow the suspects."

Phoebe sighed. This was going to be even harder than she expected. She gestured up ahead. "There it is."

They came to a stop across the street and took in the three-story structure. Like most of the buildings in this neighborhood it was verging on derelict. The front steps were in need of repair and the windows were clouded over from years of grime.

"Whoever *does* own this place is doing a shoddy job keeping it up," Will said, his words dripping with aristocratic disapproval.

"Most of my students live in places like this. The landlords don't care as long as they have paying tenants, and no one holds them to any kind of standards."

"Well, someone should."

Phoebe let out a snort at his priggish tone.

The duke turned to her. "What's so funny?"

"Nothing," she amended. "Only that of *course* someone should do something. The deplorable living conditions of the poor isn't exactly a new problem. There was talk of erecting something like the Katharine Buildings in this neighborhood," Phoebe explained, referencing the East End apartments built for the working class by a philanthropic society a decade ago. "But whoever owns this block refuses to sell. Meanwhile, the people with the power to enact real, lasting change don't care."

Phoebe kept her eyes on the building, but she could feel his gaze on her.

"You mean people like me."

"I suppose." Phoebe shrugged. "But even you are only one man. This is a problem that will take more than a single duke to solve."

"There's that cynical streak again," he said after a moment.

"Hardly. If I were a true cynic, I don't think I'd be working at my school. Or standing here." She turned to him then. "I still have hope that my students' lives can be improved. But I know that for so many their days are filled with unnecessary pain, loss, and endless drudgery. That won't ever change. At least, not in the ways that would make the most difference in their lives. Perhaps you call that cynical, but I'd be a fool to think otherwise."

Just as his eyes began to soften with pity, Phoebe looked back to the building and straightened her spine. She wasn't interested in any cloying remarks from him. She had enough of those from her mother. "Now come along, Margrave. We don't have time to waste."

Seven

*W*ill froze in place as Phoebe marched across the street with the kind of determination decorated generals spent a lifetime honing.

Who was *this woman?*

In so many ways, she was little more than a stranger to him, yet she remained hauntingly, relentlessly familiar. Though he knew next to nothing about how she spent her days or the path that had led her to this broken-down corner of London, there were still flashes of the impetuous girl she had been—not to mention the beguiling young woman he had been a bit of a fool for that fateful summer. Will had known her once, and he couldn't ignore the growing need to know her now. To understand the person she had become during their time apart.

She had nearly reached those derelict front steps before he remembered to move. He hurried over with a speed he usually reserved for the ring of his boxing club. There was no need for a duke to hurry when everything was brought to him. But just as Phoebe lifted her skirts to take that first step, Will was beside her, offering his hand.

"Allow me," he said as he braced one foot on the step. As she turned to him, he saw the hesitation in her gaze until her gloved hand slid against his waiting palm. Will's fingers closed over hers and something like an electric shock jolted down his arm. If Phoebe felt it, she gave no indication.

She had not wanted his help, but Will would do his best to convince her he could be of some use. Together they gingerly ascended the steps and entered the building, where they were greeted by the choking scent of mildew and decay. The only source of light in the cramped entryway was whatever could filter in from a cracked window above the front door. Will squinted at the staircase before them. It looked even more hazardous than the one outside. There were broken planks and holes in nearly every step.

Will turned to Phoebe. "You came here *alone?*" He couldn't help his scandalized tone. It *was* scandalous.

She didn't bother to respond and instead moved toward the stairs. "Her flat is on the third floor."

Will followed closely behind, prepared to catch her the minute she took a wrong step, but Phoebe moved with a careful confidence that could only come with experience.

"Sunday wasn't your first visit to this place."

"Especially after Alice's mother took ill," Phoebe replied without looking back at him.

"That's how the maintenance man knew you," Will added. "And what you were doing here."

To this she merely nodded. They continued on in silence, though they were surrounded by noise. The walls must be paper thin, as the din of conversations, the rattle of cookware, and the cries of a child filled the dank air. Will scrunched his nose against a particularly pungent aroma he couldn't begin to place as they passed the second floor.

"Do you know where he is now?"

Since the man clearly wasn't busy doing his job.

"His room is in the basement, but he drinks," Phoebe explained. "I'm hoping he's in a stupor. I . . . I wasn't so lucky last time."

Will was shocked that she spoke of such degeneracy so casually, and then annoyed with himself for being naive.

"Go on, then." She glanced back to give him a wry smile. "Tell me how much you disapprove."

Will rolled his shoulders. Like hell he would. "You're a grown woman," he said. "You can do as you like."

"Yes." Her smile turned into a grin as she turned away. "My thoughts exactly."

Just as they reached the third-floor landing, an old man entered the hallway. Phoebe leaned closer to Will and the softest hint of her fresh scent kissed his nose.

"That's Alice's neighbor," she whispered. "He wasn't home on Sunday."

Phoebe shifted away to approach the man, but Will caught her shoulder.

"Let me. He may be more willing to talk to a man."

Phoebe looked primed to argue, then relented. "You're probably right."

Will's mouth curved. "Can I get that engraved? Preferably on something small like a pen, so I can carry it around."

She let out a dramatic sigh and tried not to smile. "Just hurry up."

He nodded. "Pardon me," Will called out as he stepped forward and the older man slowly lifted his head. His narrow shoulders were heavily stooped and his stiff movements betrayed the frailty of age, but he met Will's gaze with a fierce directness that took him by surprise. "What'd you want?"

"I'm looking for your neighbor, Miss Alice Clarke." Will smiled broadly but the man's scowl only deepened.

"Why?"

Phoebe ducked around him and held out her hand. "I'm her teacher, Miss Atkinson."

The older man eyed her hand for a moment before taking it. "Cartwright," he replied.

"Mr. Cartwright," Phoebe said with a smile. "A pleasure."

The man seemed far more charmed by her than Will and his scowl nearly disappeared. "You work at that school for the young chits?"

Phoebe nodded graciously at the coarse description and Will felt a pang of jealousy. She had shown this man more cordiality in the last minute than she had toward him, well, ever. "Alice has been missing these last two weeks and I'm worried about her."

Cartwright grunted in reply. "Just as well. Girls like her don't need to be taught reading and the like. Gives them too many ideas."

"On that I'm afraid we must disagree," she said tactfully. "But I'd be so grateful if you could share the last time you saw her."

The man grunted again. "Hard to say. She mostly kept to herself. Her and her ma. A good woman. God rest her soul."

"Anything would be helpful," Phoebe stressed.

Will was certain he would give them the brush-off but then Cartwright tilted his head in thought. "I haven't seen Alice in a long while. But I did see another chit leaving her flat not long ago."

Will glanced at Phoebe, who shot him a puzzled frown.

"Could you describe her?"

The scowl returned as Cartwright addressed Will. "She looked *fast.* The sort that has no business coming up here. This is a respectable place, and she's naught but trouble."

"Then you know her."

Cartwright hesitated. "She hangs about at the music hall round the corner. Goes by Maude, I think. Only a certain type is seen there. Not ladies," he added with a nod to Phoebe.

Will gave him a skeptical look. Cartwright seemed to know a fair amount about a woman he claimed to disapprove of, but Will resisted the urge to challenge his assertion.

Phoebe still managed that congenial smile even in the face of the man's hypocrisy. "Can you tell me when you last saw her, then?"

"More than a week gone now," he said with a shrug.

She met Will's eyes. That was around the time Alice disappeared. It couldn't be a coincidence.

"Thank you for your time, Mr. Cartwright," Phoebe said. "I appreciate it."

"And we would appreciate it even more if you didn't mention this conversation to anyone." Will pulled out a banknote.

Cartwright took the money while grumbling something about "useless toffs" before he shuffled down the hall.

Once he was out of earshot, Will turned to Phoebe. "Charming man. Shall we explore the flat?"

She balked. "You mean to break in?"

"I mean to try. No promises though. I haven't needed to pick a lock in nearly two decades. I had a penchant for roly-poly pudding as a boy and our poor cook couldn't keep up with my stomach," he said, smiling at the welcome memory. "She had to start locking the larder so I wouldn't go looking for a jar of her raspberry preserves. Desperate times and all that."

Phoebe let out a laugh and gestured to the door. "Well, let's see if you've retained the skill."

But when Will reached out to inspect the doorknob, he found it unlocked. They exchanged a glance. Will pressed his ear to the door, but no sounds came from the other side.

"It's empty." He turned the knob and the door opened easily. Phoebe grabbed his arm just as he was about to enter.

"Careful," she whispered, her hazel eyes wide with apprehension.

"It's all right." He patted her hand, then simply rested his palm on top for as long as he dared. It felt remarkably good. Together they entered the tiny room, which was just as dank and dim as the rest of the building. Phoebe immediately headed for the lone window and pulled back the threadbare curtain. The neighboring building blocked most of the direct sunlight, but they could now see a space that, while small, was quite clean. A cot took up one wall, while a table with two mismatched chairs took up the other. Phoebe moved around the cramped space, pulling back the patched bedspread and looking under the sparse furniture. Her worried frown deepened the more she took in.

"There's nothing here," she finally said. "Her clothes, her things, it's all gone."

"She must have left." It was the only reasonable explanation.

Phoebe sat down hard on the cot. She looked defeated. "Then I failed her."

His chest tightened. It wasn't right seeing her without that confounding sense of determination. Like a crow that couldn't fly or a lion tamer without a whip. Will shook his head. Those were terrible analogies, but the point remained: Phoebe couldn't blame herself.

"Come," he prompted. "We're going to find that blasted maintenance man."

Phoebe looked up. "What for?"

"I've a few questions to ask him."

"He won't cooperate."

"Perhaps not, but we're going to ask anyway."

Phoebe stared at his offered hand for a moment before taking it. "So sayeth the duke," she replied as he pulled her to her feet. A faint spark had returned to those hazel eyes and Will relaxed. All was right with the world again. At least for now.

Eight

$\mathcal{A}$s they made their way down into the decrepit building's equally deplorable basement, Phoebe practically clung to Will's sleeve.

"I can barely see a thing," she explained unprompted. Their path was illuminated only by the faint daylight that came in from a small window. "It will be a miracle if we don't break our necks."

"Not to worry," he said with a smile as they reached the door to Mr. Felton's quarters. "I have excellent reflexes."

Before she could respond to that remark, he knocked so hard that Phoebe jumped and grasped his arm even harder.

"Sorry," Will said as he patted her hand. "If he is dead drunk, I want to make sure he can hear me."

But there was no answer.

"Excuse me," he called out. "Is anyone in there?"

Then he knocked again even harder, while the worn door creaked in protest.

"Careful or you'll break it down!" Phoebe hissed.

He shot her a wry look. "That would be helpful in this situation." After a moment of taut silence, Will rattled the knob and let out a dry laugh. "Does no one lock their doors in this place?"

Phoebe's shoulders tensed and the sinking sensation that had begun upstairs only grew. Nothing about this was right. Not Alice's empty flat, not the mysterious visitor, and certainly not another unlocked door. People here knew better.

Will pushed the door open and entered. Phoebe followed a few steps behind him. She had faced Mr. Felton's wrath once before and had no desire to repeat the experience.

It was larger than she expected, as it appeared to double as the man's living space, but it was in a sorry state. Like the room preceding it, this one had a small window that let in enough natural light to make out their surroundings. A tattered sofa was littered with old newspapers and bits of soiled clothing, while used cutlery and the remnants of several meals covered a battered table. Phoebe's nose wrinkled at the stench of rotting food. How could anyone live in such a place?

She was just about to make the comment to Will when he came to an abrupt halt. Phoebe walked right into him.

"So sorry," she gasped, trying not to focus on his surprisingly firm backside.

Will didn't respond, or even seem to notice. He was too busy staring at something.

She peered around him. A battered wooden desk took up the back half of the room and a pair of trouser-clad legs were sticking out from under it. Phoebe's stomach turned.

Will slowly approached the body, then turned to her. "Well," he said as he let out a breath. "Now we know why he didn't answer."

Phoebe braced herself and moved beside him. Behind the desk was Mr. Felton, faceup in a pool of dark blood that had begun to dry around the edges. His lips were parted and his pale blue eyes,

so unsettling in life, were wide open, staring up into nothing—
and taking whatever secrets he had to the other side.

"Bollocks," she muttered. Will raised an eyebrow. "Sorry."
Then she made a quick sign of the cross in supplication.

"You did that backwards," he said and turned back to the body.

"I don't make it to church very often," she admitted.

But he just shrugged. "Only weddings and funerals for me."

Phoebe stared at the body. "Could this have been an accident?"

"I suppose it's possible, given his drinking. He could have fallen
back and hit his head. But that unlocked door..."

If he had settled in for the night to drink himself into a stupor,
it would have been locked. She was certain of it.

Phoebe nodded in agreement. "Then if that's the case, and this
is a murder scene—"

"We need to get out of here. *Now.*" Will backed away and
grabbed Phoebe's arm. "Don't touch anything," he said as he
hauled her out of the room. He didn't stop until they were outside
and around the corner.

"We can't just leave him like that," she protested as they caught
their breath by the side of a building.

Mr. Felton might have been an awful man, but he could be lying
there for days until someone else came across him. The thought
sent a shiver down her spine.

Will closed his eyes and leaned his head against the brick wall.
"I've an idea," he said after a moment. Then he cracked one eye
open and leveled her with a look. "But you must do *exactly* as I
say."

As Phoebe began to balk, he opened both eyes. She crossed her
arms and huffed. "Fine. Lead the way, Duke."

Detective Inspector Holland took a long sip of his pint then set the glass down and folded his hands on the table. Will shifted in his seat. They were in a back room of a quiet pub in Holborn and the wooden chairs in this place were damned uncomfortable. But that was nothing compared to the glare the inspector was leveling at him.

After discovering the body of Mr. Felton, Will made Phoebe wait in his carriage while he went to fetch the inspector, who unsurprisingly had not been pleased to see him. Since Phoebe couldn't risk returning to the station again without drawing attention, the inspector suggested they meet here.

Now the man continued to stare at Will in cold silence, mulling over the story they had just shared. He was beginning to feel like an unruly schoolboy in the headmaster's office, which was absurd. He was a blasted *duke*.

"Please allow me to explain—"

But the man held up a hand. "No need, Your Grace. I believe I understand perfectly. After I explicitly told both of you to stay away from the property," he said, looking between Will and Phoebe. "You disobeyed me, broke into the building—"

"The door was unlocked," Phoebe corrected.

Detective Inspector Holland narrowed his eyes. "Interrogated a tenant—"

"We merely asked him a few questions," Will clarified.

"Then broke into Alice Clarke's flat—"

"Again, it was unlocked," Phoebe said.

"And interfered with a possible *murder* scene."

"That was an accident," Phoebe pointed out. "We didn't know

Mr. Felton was dead. But who knows how long he would have been down there. *And* we told you immediately. Surely that must count for something."

Detective Inspector Holland rubbed a hand over his face. "That was the only thing you did right. I was able to say I got an anonymous tip about a body, but I can't protect you if you keep inserting yourself into dangerous situations."

Phoebe bowed her head. "Understood."

The inspector didn't look the least bit convinced.

Smart man.

"I assure you that it won't happen again," Will said but the man gave him an equally skeptical look.

"Beg your pardon, Your Grace, but that didn't work out so well last time. I shouldn't need to tell you that it is Miss Atkinson who is incurring the greatest risk here."

The back of Will's neck heated. It was true. Phoebe could be ruined by all of this.

"Never mind that," she said briskly, as if her reputation was a trivial detail. "We need to find this Maude woman Mr. Cartwright saw. If she truly was at Alice's flat, then she has to know something. We can go to that music hall she frequents."

"There is no 'we' here, Miss Atkinson," Detective Inspector Holland said with exasperation. "You are not to have any more involvement into Alice Clarke's disappearance."

"But—"

"I will look into it," he insisted. "I promise you. But you must give me some time. I will write to you within the week. Is that satisfactory?" he added mockingly.

Phoebe sat back in her seat. "I suppose," she said with a pout. "But do you at least know Maude?"

The inspector's pause was telling. "Possibly."

Phoebe narrowed her eyes. "Is she a prostitute?"

He let out an awkward cough and turned to Will. "Is she always like this?"

"It appears so," Will said with a helpless shrug.

The inspector looked scandalized. He finished his pint in one long swallow and rose. "As I said, *I* will look into it." Then he addressed Phoebe as he pulled on his overcoat. "And for God's sake, don't go to that music hall." Then he pointed to Will. "He won't last five minutes there."

Will began to bristle but the inspector shot him a pleading look, so he kept his mouth shut. Phoebe gave a meek nod, but the inspector still didn't look convinced.

"Your Grace," he said and touched the brim of his bowler hat.

Will nodded in return and the inspector then exited the room, leaving them alone.

Phoebe stared at her untouched glass of cider. She had removed her gloves when they first sat down and now Will couldn't tear his gaze away as her pale, slender fingers idly tapped the table. It was easy to imagine her writing on a chalkboard with smooth, confident strokes.

"I should have done more to help Alice," she said softly. "I knew she was struggling after her mother died. Maybe then she wouldn't have been so vulnerable."

Will leaned an arm on the table, though what he really wanted to do was take her hand in his own. Her skin would be cool to the touch, and so soft—except a working woman like her might have a callus on her finger. The thought was unexpectedly exciting.

"I'm sure you did all you could," he began. "And remember, she is not the first girl to fall prey to the empty promises of a scheming madam."

Phoebe's head rose sharply, but not with the look of appreciation Will expected. "You're making an awful lot of assumptions about the both of them, Margrave."

Will's cheeks flushed at her unexpected admonishment. "They're hardly outlandish though," he pointed out, suddenly feeling defensive. "The peddling of flesh is a scourge in this city."

Her eyes narrowed slightly. "It is," she agreed.

Will relaxed a little, glad they had found some common ground. "Thankfully Lord Fairbanks is drafting a bill aimed at punishing the culprits, like this mysterious woman."

Phoebe let out a harsh laugh. "You can't seriously be suggesting that the *prostitutes* are to blame."

"Well, no. Not entirely," he amended.

"Ah, so then their clients will face penalties?"

"I—"

"And, pray, what provisions will be in this bill to help these women when they've lost their livelihoods?" Phoebe snapped. Her cheeks had taken on a becoming rosy color he would have enjoyed had her eyes not been bright with anger and fixed solely on him. "Or do you plan to lock up everyone who's ever *dared* to sell their body? Out of sight, out of mind, is that it?"

"No," Will insisted as his mind spun wildly. "But something must be done—"

"There are a great many things that need to be done to improve the lives of the people who live in this city," she interrupted. "But it appears we disagree on what exactly needs changing. People turn to prostitution for all sorts of reasons. If you really *are* interested in ending this scourge, rather than punishing those that do, you should explore what is driving them down that path in the first place. Men like you are all too happy to indulge in vice in private while condemning it in public," she added.

Whatever guilt Will had begun to feel at his thickheadedness immediately vanished and his jaw tightened. How dare she so casually accuse him of such hypocrisy.

"I agree that you've made some salient points, Miss Atkinson, and I will take them up with the earl directly." Then Will took a breath and leaned over the table until her damned enticing scent filled his nostrils. "But do not presume to know what kind of man I am," he growled.

For her part, Phoebe remained undaunted and simply held his gaze for a heart-shattering moment. "Then tell me what kind you are," she finally murmured.

Will blinked. He must have imagined the suggestive note in her voice. *Had* to. Even still, his gaze dropped to her mouth and Phoebe's breath caught. The air grew hot and thick around them. Then, after what felt like eons but had only been a matter of seconds, he pulled back. "The kind I've always been."

Phoebe stared at him in silence but while her chest rose and fell in quick breaths, her expression was more shuttered than ever. "I should go," she said abruptly as she pushed her chair back. "It's getting late. My flatmate will worry."

"Take my carriage," Will said.

"Absolutely n—"

"My driver can return here after he drops you off. I'd like to be alone," he added.

Phoebe stood there gaping until Will raised an eyebrow. "Is there something else you'd like to accuse me of," he drawled, "or have you had your fill this evening?"

Her mouth snapped shut at his sarcastic reply and she left without another word. Will slid down in his chair until his knees nearly touched the underside of the table, but neither his vulgar posture nor having the last word made him feel any better.

Men like you are all too happy to indulge in vice in private...

Will had never once engaged in the kind of vice she meant, as the exchange of money for bed partners had never sat right with him. As silly as it sounded, he wanted to be with someone who chose him out of desire, not obligation. Will preferred experienced widows, like his most recent paramour, Mrs. Hunt. After the death of her much older and mostly indifferent husband, she had been eager to make up for lost time and they embarked on a passionate affair. But their liaison ended nearly a year ago, after she received an offer of marriage from a very respectable doctor and Will didn't counter it. Though he enjoyed spending time with her, Will had to be strategic in his choice of wife. Mrs. Hunt was a pretty woman with a pleasant demeanor and a healthy appetite in bed, but that didn't make her duchess material.

His refusal to offer for her himself had caused her great pain.

I suppose I came to think of you as my fairy prince—or duke as it were.

Her tearful admission still made him blush all these months later. It was the first time one of his paramours had admitted to harboring hopes of marriage and the incident had weighed heavily on his conscience afterward. He may not have been in love with Mrs. Hunt, but he did care for her and didn't like thinking that he may have inadvertently given her false hope.

All in all, it was frustrating to realize that he was still uncovering new depths of power related to his title. He hadn't pursued any more romantic entanglements afterward. And once he decided to marry, it seemed best to remain celibate until his wedding night.

Perhaps that was why he found Phoebe Atkinson so damned distracting. It had nothing to do with *her* in particular. He was simply…overwrought. Will finished the rest of his pint in one gulp and rose to procure something stronger while he waited for his carriage to return. Yes, that was definitely it. Phoebe wasn't the most attractive woman of his acquaintance. Certainly not more than Lady Gwen. And though she was intelligent, intelligence was overrated—especially when it was accompanied by a tongue as sharp as hers

Once Will reached the empty bar, he ordered a double whiskey. As the barman poured it out, Will decided that Phoebe could think whatever rubbish she wanted about him. It didn't matter, as her opinion was of absolutely no consequence in his world.

Then he raised the glass, made a silent toast, and downed the contents.

To hell with Phoebe Atkinson.

Phoebe collapsed against the cushions of Will's carriage and cast a dark look around the sumptuous interior. That old familiar anger rose inside her once more, pushing away the guilt that had begun to claw up her throat in the pub. He had a lot of nerve, freely judging what far less fortunate people did to survive while an eye-watering fortune had fallen into his lap. Phoebe let out a sigh and closed her eyes, but all she saw was his darkly forbidding gaze as he leaned in close to her.

Do not presume to know what kind of man I am.

He had been undoubtably angry as he said the words. Yet the deep command had skated across her skin and left a distressing neediness that was only exacerbated by his painfully familiar scent of cedar, spice, and warm skin. Together they created the kind of fierce, carnal urge that could only be born from a thousand girlhood idles—and one she would absolutely take to the grave.

Then tell me what kind you are.

The brazen question had slipped past her lips and for one dazzling moment she indulged in this practically biblical personal fantasy, pretending he was the dashing country upstart once more without his towering rank standing between them. He was simply Will Margrave. The same boy who had argued with her father over the benefits of profit-sharing, asked her mother about the time she met Eleanor Marx, and helped her rescue a wounded bird they found in the forest before giving her a sympathetic forehead kiss. Then he had to go and ruin it.

The kind I've always been.

Phoebe let out a snort in the quiet carriage. Will could say whatever he liked, however he liked, but he was *not* that person anymore. Not since the day he strolled into the back garden and ruined the little fantasy she had been carefully constructing in her heart by rattling off the list of extravagant homes he would inherit as if it were all a terrible inconvenience and not the stuff of fairy tales. And what had he gone and done with that twist of fate? Nothing of importance. When the time came, he simply took his seat in the House of Lords and blithely supported an agenda he once would have declared immoral.

He was just another man in a bespoke suit with too much power and not a clue what to do with it.

"Here we are, miss."

Phoebe blinked in a daze and turned to the speaker. It was his coachman. She must have dozed off. Not surprising, given that this carriage seat was softer than her own bed. She quickly sat up and let the man hand her down. They were right in front of her building and the curtain fluttered in the window of her second-floor flat. Blast. Marion must have seen her. And there was no hiding who she had been with. Phoebe cast a frown as the Ellis crest glinted in the moonlight. How on earth could a piece of *wood* manage to look so superior?

She thanked the coachman and swiftly headed up the front steps, until the thought of Will still sitting alone at the table back in the pub brought her to a halt. Phoebe knew something about lonesomeness. Of how one could feel alone even while surrounded by people. And title or no, there was no mistaking the expression on his face.

"See that His Grace makes it home safely," she said over her shoulder, and turned away just as a look of surprise flashed on the coachman's face.

Phoebe tried to enter the flat as quietly as possible, but her effort was for naught. Marion stood in the entryway with her arms crossed and a thunderous expression on her face. No wonder her students called her Mad Marion behind her back.

"You were with that duke again, weren't you," she said without preamble. "Don't deny it. Your students were gossiping about him before they even made it out of the building. Unless some *other* well-dressed toff just happened to be hanging about the school."

Phoebe winced. "It isn't what you think."

Marion raised a mocking eyebrow. "And what, pray, would I be thinking? You only disappeared for *hours* before getting out of the finest carriage I've ever seen. I suppose you were inside playing checkers?"

It had been a very long day and Phoebe lacked the patience to deal with Marion's usual sarcasm.

"I'm not involved with him." Phoebe pushed past her into the flat and took off her coat. "Not that it would be any of your business if I was," she added, unable to control the defensive note in her voice.

"You're acting like a child," Marion scolded.

"And you're acting like my mother!" Phoebe shot back. "I told you before, the duke is a family friend. He had some information for me that could help with finding Alice."

Marion remained unconvinced. "That he needed to relay in person until nine at night?" She then let out a sigh. "Sorry. I—that wasn't fair. I was thinking of myself. Of what happened."

Phoebe's irritation faded. Marion had an ill-fated love affair last year with a promising law clerk who was all but engaged to his boss's daughter—and had no intention of throwing the girl over for her. Marion had immediately ended things and insisted she was better off, but there were still moments when she couldn't hide her broken heart.

"I know," Phoebe said softly. "But this isn't like that at all. Truly. He just wants to help."

As she said the words, her cheeks flushed with embarrassment. Perhaps she had judged him a little too harshly back in the pub.

"All right then." Marion gave her a thoughtful look. "What does he know about Alice?"

Phoebe relayed everything that had happened up until they found Mr. Felton's body, as the inspector insisted they keep it between them. But Marion was still shocked.

"I can't *believe* you went back to the building."

"We found a lead."

"What, some woman who sounds like nothing but trouble?" Marion clucked her tongue. "If Alice *is* involved with her, then she really is as good as gone."

Phoebe's mouth dropped open. "You would cast her aside so easily?"

"That is the way of things," Marion said with distressing finality. "She will have ruined what little reputation a girl like her has by now anyway. And there is no returning from that. Not around here."

Phoebe crossed her arms. "I refuse to believe that."

Marion gave her an enraging look of pity. "You have always been an idealist. And I admire that so much. But you need to be realistic."

Phoebe could only laugh to herself, given that Will had called her a cynic only a few hours ago. Perhaps she was a mixture of the two. A cynical idealist.

"And there are other girls you can still help," Marion continued. "Girls who wouldn't dream of *looking* at a fallen woman, let alone inviting one into her home."

"But we don't even know if that is what has happened," Phoebe countered. "If I could just go down to that music hall and talk to her, I'm sure—"

"No," Marion said firmly. "That place is frequented by the lowest sort. The inspector was right to warn you off. If anyone even saw you there—"

"Then *I* would be ruined?" Phoebe scoffed.

Marion sat back in her chair. "You say that like it's nothing. Though I suppose for someone like you, it is," she added.

"What's that supposed to mean?"

"That you have a loving family and a mansion you can always return to if things go wrong. No one will ever have to know about your little dalliance with the lower classes."

"That's not fair, Marion."

"No, it isn't," she said as she rose. "And it's well past time you learned that's the way things usually are for the rest of us. Good night."

Phoebe remained in place for many minutes afterward, mulling over Marion's sharp words. It was not lost on her that she had lobbed a similar accusation at Will. Much like there had been truth in her accusation of Will, there was truth in Marion's. Now she understood his desire to remain alone in the pub. It seemed a perfectly reasonable reaction to having one's faults pointed out so candidly.

"I'm an idiot," Phoebe murmured as she pressed a hand to her face. She'd have to apologize to Will as well, then. And there was a decent chance he wouldn't accept it.

Nine

Will gave a slow blink. Once again he stood in a crowded ballroom watching Lady Gwen dance with another man while he was supposed to patiently await his turn. He let out a sigh and shifted on his feet while his rebellious mind wandered toward thoughts of Phoebe, as it had far too often over the last several days.

Her words still stung, and if he lingered on them for too long he would feel the urge to crawl out of his own skin. But that would fade in time. Realizing just how bored he had become with his own life would take a bit longer to get over, however. Though Phoebe could irritate the hell out of him, she was undeniably fascinating. He felt a sense of excitement around her. Of unpredictability. If he wasn't careful, he might start to want more.

And there wouldn't be a damned thing he could do about it.

Just as a heaviness began to settle in his chest, the earl approached.

"Don't look so morose, Duke," he said with a devilish smile. "You know Lord Whitby doesn't stand a chance with my daughter."

The young baron had inherited a crumbling estate in Northumberland and a mountain of debt. He would need one of those American dollar princesses if he ever hoped to be rid of debt.

Will grunted in response. He had no real rivals for Lady Gwen's hand. Just a few more weeks of this nonsense and hopefully they could announce their engagement. Yet the thought did not provide the expected—nay, *needed*—relief.

"Did you have a chance to review the draft of the bill I sent over?"

It was the very one that Phoebe had so strenuously objected to. Quite rightly, it turned out.

"I did," Will began. "How exactly are you planning to deal with the 'festering wound of vice' as you put it? I didn't see anything about the specifics." Just a lot of ranting about the moral decay of society accompanied by some heavy-handed metaphors.

"Ah, excellent question. I've given it a great deal of thought and decided it is naive to think we can ever *truly* be rid of the flesh trade, so instead we must cut off the head of the snake as it were, and shutter the bawdy houses. Many of them are owned by women, you know. That endangers both the patrons and the tarts themselves."

Will raised an eyebrow. "How do you figure that?"

"Women may perform the work," he said with an ugly little snort, "but they don't have the capacity to manage it. Especially the money some of them rake in. Besides, it's dangerous. They could be cheated by clients or beaten."

"That may be so, but as I understand it, many women find safety in such arrangements."

"I'm not proposing we close *all* of them, mind you. I know that gentlemen have their appetites. But we must focus on those that cater to the lowest sort."

"Because it's fine if an aristocrat engages in vice, but not a bricklayer?"

"Exactly." The earl did not pick up on Will's sarcasm. "A gentleman may pay a visit to such an establishment after a long, productive day with little consequence, but a bricklayer cannot control his baser urges and thus is likely to become bankrupt."

The man was completely serious. Rather than point out the ridiculousness of the comparison, Will tried another approach:

"But once they're shut down, what will happen to the people who work there?"

The earl shrugged, unconcerned. "They can go to a workhouse."

Will's jaw hardened. "You will only push them out onto the streets, where they will lose what little protections they have."

"Then perhaps they should have made better choices."

"Interesting, I didn't realize you had been given the *choice* to inherit an earldom," Will snapped before he could think twice. Lord Fairbanks stared at him wide-eyed, rendered speechless for once. "Excuse me," Will growled. "I believe I am due to waltz with your daughter."

As he approached Lady Gwen and Lord Whitby, Will did his best to maintain a passive expression, but his thoughts were a riot. Phoebe had been right. The bill would do nothing to actually curb vice or help those in need. It was simply another way to punish the most vulnerable for the sins of the many. He could not be a part of such bald hypocrisy. But that would not put a stop to the bill, either. And though that sharp remark had felt damned good in the moment, he may have just ruined his chance to influence the earl. That wasn't at all like him.

But it was a hell of a lot like Phoebe.

Will gave himself a little shake. He would figure out a way to solve this later. Now he needed to do some wooing.

"My lady," Will said with a smooth bow before nodding to the baron. "Lord Whitby."

"Your Grace," the lad muttered with barely veiled contempt.

Will had long grown accustomed to the superficial deference offered by men like Whitby, who saw him as nothing more than a very lucky upstart.

If only they knew what Will would have done to give it all back.

"Thank you for the pleasure of your company, my lady," Whitby said as he released Lady Gwen. "I hope we can repeat the experience again *very* soon."

Will narrowed his eyes at the bold remark but managed to keep his head this time.

"And I as well," Lady Gwen replied with far more grace than Whitby deserved. Still, the young man didn't even try to hide the wistful look on his face before leaving the floor

"You seem to have made quite the impression on Lord Whitby," Will said blandly as he took Lady Gwen in his arms, all while reminding himself that the ability to make someone feel wanted even when they were being dismissed was a gift—and a valuable skill for a duchess to possess.

She let out a delicate laugh and patted his shoulder. "Not to worry. His lordship is only a friend."

"I wasn't worried," he answered truthfully. The fact that Whitby wouldn't dare act so brazenly in front of her other suitors was another matter.

Lady Gwen preened a little as she flashed him a coy smile. "Your Grace."

But as he stared down at her, Will couldn't help wondering if she thought him beneath her as well. Though he may have inherited a title, for many that still didn't excuse his middling roots. She could simply be going along with their courtship to please her father—or because she didn't have a choice. It was a disquieting realization. And one he should have considered sooner. She certainly *looked* contented enough, but then would he even be able to tell? In any case, Will would need to ascertain the truth before they were betrothed, as he had no desire to force her hand no matter what the earl wanted.

In the meantime he should tell her to at least call him Margrave. Yet the words remained caught in his throat. It was hard to imagine any woman but Phoebe addressing him that way now.

Damn.

"What were you and Papa discussing? He...he didn't look pleased."

Lady Gwen's question was asked lightly enough, but Will noticed the tightness around her eyes. She worried that they had quarreled about her.

"Only some business about an upcoming bill," he assured her.

She immediately relaxed and flashed him a genuine smile half the men in the room would kill for. "Of course."

As Will took her through a turn, he observed several guests admiring her form. She was dressed in a silver gown covered in gold embroidery. The very picture of sophistication and good breeding.

"Do you ever talk with him about his work?"

It could be nice to have a confidant at home. Someone who understood the complexities of Parliament. Someone who would be supportive rather than simply point out all the ways he was wrong.

The image of Phoebe with that disapproving little frown of hers forced its way into his head—and Will forced it right back out.

"Heavens no," the young lady said with another laugh. "I think politics are better left to men like you."

He instantly pictured Phoebe rolling her eyes. "I see."

"But I'm sure my mother has, on occasion, discussed such matters with my father," she hastily amended at the disappointment he had failed to hide. "I'll ask her to advise me."

Will managed a tight smile in the face of her apprehensiveness. "Of course."

Lady Gwen then spent the rest of the waltz complimenting him on everything one could possibly discuss in polite company, while Will did his best to appear flattered, but the look of unease never left her completely. She knew she had erred, but Will wasn't in the mood to reassure her. Perhaps he did want someone who wasn't afraid to tell him when he was wrong, not a sycophant. Someone who challenged him to do better. But only one badger of a woman came to mind. And she was certainly *not* duchess material.

He bid Lady Gwen a good evening and headed for the exit. The ball was in full swing, but Will couldn't spend another minute here. He needed to think.

Will slipped out a side entrance into the cool evening air. Though he had arrived in his coach to keep up appearances, he hardly ever bothered to leave a ball in one. It was far faster to simply walk home.

Higgins, his butler, who absolutely did not approve of this little habit, greeted him at the door.

"Good evening, Your Grace," he said with a bow. "Shall I warm some brandy for you?"

It was his usual ritual after returning from a night out. Something to help relax his nerves before bed.

Will let out a sigh. He had become so utterly predictable. "I suppose."

He then picked up the pile of post and calling cards that had arrived while he was gone and began riffling through them while he walked toward his study.

Then he came to a dead stop at an envelope simply marked *M.* His heart thudded in anticipation as he tore it open.

Margrave,

I owe you an apology, which I would prefer to deliver in person. If you are amenable, meet me outside that disreputable music hall tonight at eleven o'clock.

Yours,
Atkinson

Will's neck craned to read the face of the massive grandfather clock behind Higgins. It was already ten thirty. He let out a curse and thrust the rest of the mail at Higgins.

"Ready the brougham."

He needed something discreet and the landau with the ducal crest would not suffice.

Higgins looked appalled. "Your Grace?"

But Will hurried down the hall. "Quickly!"

Phoebe glanced at the pocket watch tucked into her waistcoat and let out an impatient sigh. Just five more minutes. She couldn't wait for Will any longer than that. It was nearly eleven. Either he wasn't coming or he was out at a ball somewhere too busy wooing Lady Gwen to bother with her. The thought made the edges of her heart curl. But she had no one to blame but herself for the way they had parted.

She shoved aside a vision of Will looking stern and devastating with the elegant Lady Gwen in his arms and leaned back against the cool brick wall. Across the street a group of men entered the bustling music hall. The jubilant notes of an accordion floated through the air, along with raucous laughter. Phoebe swallowed hard. She had never been inside such a place before and the thought was as thrilling as it was nerve-racking.

You'll go in, locate this mysterious Maude woman somehow, and ask her a few questions. Then you'll leave.

Phoebe reached to check the time again but stopped herself. Enough dawdling. She had to do this for Alice. Just as she pushed away from the wall, a coach pulled up nearby. Phoebe hung back and waited as a man descended. As soon as she caught sight of his broad shoulders, the tightness in her chest loosened with relief.

He came.

Will scanned the area, passing over her at first, but then immediately returned when she gave a little wave.

He squinted as she approached. "Phoebe?"

"Hello there," she said cheerfully and touched the brim of her cap.

Will openly gaped at her. "What are you *wearing?*"

Phoebe automatically looked down, though she very well knew the answer. "You've seen me in trousers before."

She and her sisters had worn them often enough in the country, as it made nearly everything easier. Her parents didn't mind as long as they didn't have company, and back then Will hadn't counted.

But he still looked shocked. His gaze traveled down her body before returning to her face. Then he raised an eyebrow. "And how do you explain the mustache?"

Phoebe grinned. She was quite proud of her whiskers. "I help the drama club at school. Last term we put on *Romeo and Juliet*, so there were a few pairs left over."

"Depressing choice for a school play," Will grunted.

"It was, yes. The girls had great fun during the fight scenes though. Our Mercutio was particularly inspired. Here." She rummaged in her coat pocket and pulled out an envelope with his own set of false whiskers.

Will looked indignant. "I'm not wearing those."

"Well, you can't go dressed like that." She gestured at his elegant evening suit. "You look like a duke."

And far too handsome. It was distracting.

"I *am* a duke."

"Not in there." Phoebe pointed across the street. "Remember what the inspector said: you'll stick out. We're trying not to be noticed."

Margrave rolled his eyes. "And you think *you* won't?"

"I fooled you, didn't I?"

"Only for a moment," he grumbled as his gaze tracked down her form yet again, but with more deliberation this time. Phoebe felt oddly exposed. And warm. Very warm. She brushed past him and addressed the coachman, who had been politely pretending they didn't exist.

"Excuse me, sir. May the duke borrow your coat?"

The coachman immediately gave her a bewildered look. "Miss?"

"Come down here a moment," she said as she crooked her finger.

"See? You didn't fool John," Will murmured by her ear as they waited for him to join them on the pavement.

A delightful shiver ran down her neck, but she kept her gaze forward. "Only because he heard you call me Phoebe," she explained as John dutifully shucked his coat and handed it to her. "People see what they expect to see. And in a place like this it does not include a man in a cashmere topcoat. Isn't that right, John?"

He shot a nervous glance at Will. "It's true, Your Grace."

Phoebe then held out her hand expectantly.

"I don't suppose that includes a girl in trousers and a false mustache, either," Will said.

"Exactly. Now stop stalling."

He gave her a dark look before he let out a huff and began unbuttoning his coat.

"Yes, I know this is a terrible inconvenience for you," Phoebe drawled, attempting to lessen the unexpectedly heady effect of watching him undo the buttons with his long, leather-gloved fingers.

"It's a waste of time." Will pulled off his coat and handed it to John. "Here. Wear this."

The man's eyes widened as if Will had handed him the crown jewels. "Your Grace, I couldn't—"

"Just take it, John. It's cold out."

The man obeyed and gingerly placed it around his shoulders. "I won't want to pop a stitch," he explained.

Will huffed in response and put on John's coat, which was both too short in length and too wide in the shoulders. He shot Phoebe an exasperated look. "Is *this* acceptable?"

"Yes. Now your shoes."

Will looked down. "What's wrong with them?"

"They're too nice. You need to scuff them up."

John gave a helpless shrug in response to Will's incredulousness.

"My valet will have my hide," he grumbled, but then set about scuffing up his shoes. "There. That *has* to be enough."

"It is. But you can't wear that." She pointed to his top hat. "It screams toff."

"Fine," he grumbled as he took it off and handed it to John.

"Just one last thing."

Will let out a resigned sigh. "Do what you must."

She reached out and moved her fingers through his perfectly styled hair, mussing the silky strands a little. The rich, woody scent of his pomade tickled her nose. He went quiet as his dark eyes remained on her face, watching her with an intense gaze she couldn't quite meet.

Phoebe wasn't used to commanding the attention of men—both because she didn't want it and they didn't seem much interested in bestowing it. Yet Will always kept his focus solely on her whenever they were together, and she rather enjoyed it.

"There," she said with a slight rasp as she pulled her hand away.

Will straightened and a lock of hair fell rakishly across his brow. "How do I look now?"

Phoebe's breath caught. Like a rogue. Like the kind of man you wouldn't mind meeting in a dark corner. And so much like who he might have been, had the dukedom not fallen to him.

"Very…ordinary," she lied.

"Excellent," he said with a wicked little smile that made her knees wobble. "I've always wanted to be ordinary." Then he swept his arm toward the music hall. "Lead the way, Atkinson."

Ten

Will's lips quirked as Phoebe shoved her hands in her pockets and loped toward the music hall. Though technically he *had* seen her in trousers before, that was ages ago and hadn't made much of an impression on him at the time given how frequently it occurred.

But *this* ... this was an entirely different experience. For example, Will certainly didn't remember ever noticing the way the cut of the trousers emphasized the appealing shape of Phoebe's backside. He tore his gaze away before anyone caught him staring. As they approached the entrance, Phoebe turned back to give him a jaunty wink that he returned with a frown.

Christ, this would never work. How could anyone look at her and not immediately see those full lips or the curves barely hidden beneath her jacket? But, miraculously, as they made their way through the bustling music hall, no one gave her a second glance. Phoebe had been right. People only saw what they expected to see.

Will had never been to this particular establishment but it reminded him of the places he had visited in the Marais during a trip to Paris with his brother and their late friend Ned years ago. It was crowded and dimly lit aside from the small stage backed by a crimson velvet curtain that had clearly seen better days. The accordion player's fingers danced wildly over the keys, moving faster and faster, while the ragtag audience let out a round of cheers. The floor was sticky and the air was thick with the scent of sweat, stale beer, and too sweet perfume. It was the scent of excitement. Of possibility. Will closed his eyes and for a brief moment he was back in the Marais, his arm slung around a stranger and his throat hoarse from butchering Gallic drinking songs. He wasn't a duke then, with the weight of a dozen estates bearing down on him, but just another young man who had come to Paris to get drunk, flirt with women in his terrible French, and look at the occasional piece of art. God, it had felt good.

A swift tap on his shoulder interrupted this little reverie and he opened his eyes.

"Let's talk to the barman," Phoebe said by his ear.

Will nodded, but instead of turning away he was compelled to lean closer, as if someone were tugging on an invisible string, until the lapel of his coat brushed against her arm. Phoebe's lips parted in surprise, her gaze open and inquiring. Will should have drawn back, blamed the movement on someone from the crowd around them, but all he could do was stare into her wide hazel eyes. His fingers tingled with the urge to reach out and wrap around her waist and draw her even closer. To brush the strands of hair that had escaped from under her cap and nuzzle the shell of her ear, but that would most certainly draw attention. Phoebe drew in a breath and began to say something just as someone did shove into Will. Hard. He was forced to step back to keep his balance just as Phoebe grabbed his sleeve.

"Sorry, mate," said the incredibly drunk and quite large man that had bumped into him. He then gestured to the pint in his hand, as if that explained it, and managed to slosh some of it onto Will's shoes before toddling off.

"Stop staring at him like he insulted your honor and slapped you with his glove," Phoebe said. "You're ruining your disguise."

"I wasn't." Will turned to her. "And no one does that anymore."

"If anything, you should have thrown a punch," she teased. "That's how disagreements are settled outside Mayfair."

Will suppressed the urge to roll his eyes. She really did see him as completely inane. "A splendid idea," he said dryly. "But I assume you don't want to get thrown out of here before we even find this woman."

"Fair point."

"Come on," he said. "I could use a drink." Or several.

Will clasped a hand around her upper arm as he led them through the crowd. It had been ages since he had been surrounded by so many people who hadn't a clue he was a duke—or even simply a wealthy man. Will hadn't realized just how used he had become to being fawned over or yielded to, which was highly annoying.

At first he tried saying "Excuse me" and "Pardon," but the beer-spilling oaf had the right idea. Will finally began to shoulder his way through the crowd. A few men cast dark looks at them, but turned away at Will's answering scowl. He straightened a little more, feeling absurdly proud.

Once they reached the bar, Phoebe placed her hands on the counter and stood on her tiptoes to address the stone-faced man behind the bar. "Hello. We're looking for a woman named Maude," she said, deepening her voice. It was about as convincing as that pair of trousers plastered to her rump. "Is she here?"

Predictably, the barman's expression remained unchanged as he continued polishing the pint glass in his hands. "Depends."

She frowned in confusion, but Will took over. "Two ales."

He gave a single nod and went to pour their drinks.

"Oh, good idea," Phoebe said sheepishly.

When the man returned, Will paid him double. "She's over there," he said, gesturing to a far corner of the room. "In the red."

"Thank you," Will said with a nod. They took their pints and sat down at an empty table nearby.

Phoebe leaned across the table. "I can see her," she whispered as she looked over Will's shoulder. "She's alone." He began to glance back, but Phoebe placed a hand on his arm. "Don't!"

He shot her an irritated look. "I can be discreet."

Phoebe sat back in her chair. "Sorry. I'm just nervous."

"We don't have to talk to her."

"No, we must," she insisted. "Or else this whole night will be a waste."

Will knew she meant the search for her student, but that didn't stop the prickle of hurt. He took a sip of his pint and made a show of casually turning to look at the stage, while also casting a glance at Maude. Like Phoebe said, she was sitting alone at a table set back from the others, but there was also a very large man standing close behind her.

"I think that fellow is a guard of some sort."

"I noticed him too. Isn't that strange?"

Will shrugged. "Not necessarily. Her dress looks fashionable. She could be someone's mistress." And there were plenty of men who made sure their asset was protected.

"I didn't know you paid attention to fashion," Phoebe teased.

"I spend a large amount of time in ballrooms," he said sourly.

The light in her eyes faded. "Yes, Freddie says you're practically engaged to Lord Fairbanks's daughter."

"I'm not," he said far too quickly.

Phoebe took a considering sip. "But you will be," she pointed out. "Soon."

Before he could respond, something caught Phoebe's attention. "She's getting up."

Phoebe shoved her chair back but Will caught her arm. "Slowly," he cautioned.

Together they approached the woman as she headed toward the back of the music hall.

"Let me talk," Will whispered to Phoebe as he caught the woman's eye and gave a wave. She let out a huff but didn't protest.

"Excuse me, madam," Will said. "May we have just a moment of your time?"

She was quite striking up close, with dark red hair and generous curves. While her features were too bold to be considered truly beautiful, she possessed a magnetism that commanded Will's attention. Her blue eyes ran down his form in a blatant look of appraisal before returning to his face. "For you I have two," she said with a coquettish smile.

Beside him, Phoebe's shoulders tightened. "Are you Maude?"

The woman raised an eyebrow at the jarring question. "I am. Who's asking?"

"Terribly sorry. But my associate doesn't want to waste your time," Will explained.

"Or ours," Phoebe muttered.

Will gave her a sharp glance, then addressed Maude. "I am Mr. Crispin and this is Mr. Agincourt," he said quickly, while ignoring Phoebe's befuddled look. Perhaps they should have bothered to discuss their aliases but he was in the middle of reading a biography of Henry V and those were the first names that came to him.

Luckily, Maude didn't appear to notice anything strange. "A pleasure."

"Is there somewhere we could talk more privately? I promise it will be worth your while," he added.

She gave them a hard look for a moment, then brightened. "Good. Because my time is quite valuable. Follow me."

As she led them to a back room, Will noticed that the large man was following them. Definitely her guard then. And even larger up close. Will exchanged a look with Phoebe. They would need to be quick about this. He resisted the sudden urge to give her a comforting pat.

The space was much nicer than Will expected. A green velvet sofa took up one wall, while a pair of matching armchairs sat opposite, creating a little sitting area. A large desk was tucked into a corner and a small fire crackled in the hearth.

"The owner of this establishment is a dear friend," Maude explained unprompted as she gave the coals a stir. "He lets me come and go as I please."

"And what do you use this room for?"

But Maude only gave Phoebe a smile as she sat down on the sofa. "Business, of course." She patted the place beside her invitingly and Will sat down.

Though she had made a good show of softening her vowels and refining her movements, it was this easy manner of hers, even more attractive than her physical beauty, that betrayed her lowly roots. For any trace of such vulgar behavior would have been snuffed out of a better born girl.

But not Phoebe, the very unhelpful voice in his head pointed out.

And she was shut out of the most exclusive circles of society for those transgressions. Not that she seemed to care, or was even *aware* for that matter. Will glanced at her. She sat down in one of the armchairs and began to tuck her legs underneath before quickly correcting herself. She spread her legs, placed her forearms on her thighs and then leaned forward, trying to assume a more relaxed posture and utterly failing.

Maude was, quite rightly, staring at her in rapt interest, as one might stare at a dog trying to ride a bicycle. Will clenched his jaw. It would be a miracle if they pulled this off, and if anyone identified Phoebe she would be utterly and completely ruined.

"That is what brings us here. Your business." He emphasized the last word suggestively and she smirked.

"Naturally. So, then," she began matter-of-factly, "how did you hear about the club?"

Club?

Will held her gaze as his mind scrambled for an answer. Thank God he'd mastered the art of bluffing while at Oxford, where he belonged to an underground poker ring. "I was told to be discreet."

Maude seemed amused by this. "I don't normally issue invitations to people I haven't been properly introduced to," she said as once again her gaze roamed down his front. "But I can make an exception for you."

Will hid his surprise behind a smile and played along. "I would be most grateful."

"We'd need two," Phoebe cut in, ignoring Will's glare.

"If that is necessary to guarantee Mr. Crispin's attendance," Maude replied without looking away from him. "However, there is the matter of the fee…"

"That won't be a problem," Will assured.

Her eyes lit up. "Wonderful." She then reached across him for a silver card case on the end table, letting her arm brush languidly against his chest. "Come any time after eight on the second Thursday of the month."

"That's next week," Phoebe said.

Maude reluctantly addressed her. "Look at that. The boy can follow a calendar." Then she turned back to Will, missing Phoebe's murderous glare.

"Please excuse my younger cousin. He's from the country," Will said, as if that explained away Phoebe's behavior. Her glare turned outright hostile, but Will flashed her a look of caution. Better this woman think she was a bumpkin than the truth.

"Ah," Maude said with understanding. "How good of you to take him under your wing. I'm quite fond of a family-minded fellow," she added with a sly smile as she held out her card.

Will returned the smile as he plucked the card from between her fingers. It was made of heavy stock and embossed in glossy ink with a fleur-de-lis on the front.

"It's called Fleur," she explained. "The address is on the back, along with the code you'll need to give the doorman."

Will flipped it over. "Avec plaisir," he read.

With pleasure.

Maude's smile grew. "Perfect." Then she placed a hand on his shoulder and dragged her fingertips down his arm. "I do hope to see you there."

Will's eyes tracked the movement. He then met her gaze. "You will."

Phoebe let out a loud huff and stood up. "We need to leave." She wasn't even trying to hide her irritation now and her voice was dangerously close to her normal pitch.

Maude stared at Phoebe, watching her more closely. That was the last thing they needed.

Just as her eyes began to narrow, Will stood. "Thank you for the invitation," he said.

Maude stood as well, but her attention was still fixed on Phoebe. Will grabbed her arm and pulled her toward the doorway.

For once, Phoebe allowed him to lead her without protest and they brushed past the guard and hurried down the hall.

"I'm sorry," Phoebe said once they were alone. "I don't know what came over me. I didn't even get to ask her about the tenement building."

"It's just as well," Will groused. "She's already suspicious."

"What was that club she was talking about?"

"I've never heard of it before." Will handed Phoebe the card. She studied it a moment before handing it back to him. "But she clearly works for whoever owns it."

It was a common tactic for good-looking women like Maude to entice gentlemen of means to visit dens of iniquity across the city, and be paid a commission for their efforts.

"I'm guessing they own this place as well," Phoebe said.

Will nodded as a voice called out from behind them. Phoebe immediately began to turn around, but Will only pulled her closer. "Keep going."

They entered the main area of the hall, which had grown more raucous in their absence. Will gripped Phoebe's hand to guide them through the crowd, then caught himself and took her upper arm instead.

"Will," Phoebe hissed. "He's coming."

Will dared to look back and saw the intimidating guard pushing through the mass of bodies, his beady eyes fixed on them. Will let out a curse, then another when they reached a particularly dense section right in front of the bar. They were surrounded by revelers all well into their cups. Will scanned the room, looking for an empty space, while Phoebe did the same.

In that short time, the guard made significant progress and was nearly upon them when he shoved aside a burly man who had just taken a sip from a full pint. Beer spilled everywhere and the man whipped around and grabbed the guard by his shirt collar. They were forgotten as the two men began pushing each other's chests. The crowd around them moved toward the action as it quickly escalated to a full-blown brawl. In an instant absolute mayhem broke out. People were punching each other, throwing pint glasses, and jumping behind the bar to grab more. The barman huddled in the corner and the performers deserted the stage, while Maude had vanished.

Someone stumbled against Will, but as he helped him stand up, the man thanked him by throwing a punch. Phoebe screamed, but the man was too inebriated to do more than clip his chin. Will shoved him toward the scrum just as another man lunged at him. Will braced himself for the hit just as someone tugged him backward and out of the brute's clumsy reach. It was Phoebe. Together they scrambled farther away just as a glass sailed past his head. It broke right in front of them and he instinctively drew Phoebe against his chest to shield her from the spray of shards. Their gazes locked and as he saw the flash of fear in her large hazel eyes, his heart clenched.

"Let's go," he shouted over the noise. Together they bolted toward the exit. The night air was refreshingly cool on their overheated bodies. Phoebe stopped to catch her breath, but Will pulled her along. The fight could clearly be heard on the street, which meant the authorities would arrive soon and they absolutely could not be here when that happened.

John had parked the carriage discreetly around the corner and they had just reached it when a paddy wagon pulled in front of the music hall. Will hustled Phoebe inside and watched from the pavement as a dozen policemen ran into the building. He let out a sigh as the tension he had carried since they had first entered the hall finally left him.

"Sir?"

Will glanced up at John, who still had his coat draped gingerly around his shoulders and looked uncharacteristically nervous. "Take us home as fast as you can."

"Right away," he said with a nod.

They quickly exchanged coats and then Will climbed into the carriage. Phoebe had been staring out the window watching the music hall but turned at his entrance. Though her face was only partially lit by the dim coach light, Will could still make out the apprehension in her eyes.

"It's all right. We're safe now."

The carriage lurched to a start and he sat down heavily on the seat across from her. Will then silently cursed himself for using the barouche as his legs tangled with hers in the small space. He pulled back as much as he could, but their knees still bumped together.

Will gripped the hand-pull as John took a hard turn, having taking his instructions a little too seriously. The carriage lamp swung wildly from its hook and Will squinted as the yellow light shone in his eyes.

Phoebe gasped. "You're hurt!"

"I'm fine," Will said automatically just as he felt something warm dripping down his face.

"But you're *bleeding*."

He touched his temple. "It's only a scratch."

"The glass must have grazed you," she explained as she moved beside him.

"That isn't necessary," Will protested as she drew a handkerchief from her pocket.

Phoebe paused and shot him a look. "You don't even know what I'm going to do."

"Well, I assume it isn't a quadratic equation," he muttered.

She let out a laugh. "That would be quite impossible, I assure you."

Will began to smile then hissed in pain as she pressed the handkerchief to his temple.

"Sorry," Phoebe said softly.

"It's fine," Will replied even while the cut throbbed beneath her touch. It was worse than he thought. "You don't share your sister's talent for numbers then?" He needed to distract himself. If he caught sight of his own blood, he was likely to faint right in front of her.

"Absolutely not. To my father's great regret," she added.

Will tried to catch her gaze. There was more behind that offhand remark, but she was focused on tending his wound.

"Do you have any spirits on hand? This should be cleaned."

Will pointed to a small compartment on the seat across from them. "Check there. One can't be a duke without traveling with libations."

"Hold this," Phoebe instructed as she guided Will's hand to the cloth pressed at his temple. She then moved to the other seat, opened the compartment, and pulled out a small bottle of whiskey. Her eyes widened as she read the label. "This is my father's favorite. It's very expensive."

"Just use it," Will said dismissively. "I'm sure I have plenty more somewhere."

Phoebe sat next to him again and took back her handkerchief. She poured a drop onto it, then hesitated. "This may hurt. Perhaps you should have a little," she said as she held out the bottle.

Will could certainly use a drink but for an entirely different reason. He dutifully took a sip and closed his eyes, focusing on the smooth burn of the liquid sliding down his throat.

After a moment he opened his eyes and handed the bottle back to her. "Your mustache is crooked."

Phoebe's hand flew to her mouth. "Oh God, I'd forgotten." Her cheeks flushed as she pulled it off.

Will smiled. "I must say you made a terrible lad."

Phoebe rolled her eyes, though her lips quirked, as if she was trying not to return the smile. "I'm sorry about back there. I don't know what came over me," she added.

It had been many hours since he had eaten anything and between the ale and the whiskey, his head was starting to feel wonderfully fuzzy.

He stared at her lips. "Don't you?" It had looked an awful lot like jealousy to him. He hadn't the chance to reflect on it until now, what with their narrow escape and the general bedlam.

Will lifted his gaze and found Phoebe returning his stare rather intently. Her face had never been this close to his own—not in many years, at least. There was a ring of gold around her pupils, which grew under his inspection. How had he never noticed that before? Or perhaps he had simply forced himself to forget. There was so much about his old life he had needed to leave behind in order to move forward. But now...now he was having a difficult time remembering why.

Just as he leaned closer, Phoebe chose that moment to press the handkerchief to the cut.

"*Dammit*," he bit out as the whiskey seared his injured skin.

"Sorry!" Phoebe cried, but she didn't sound very sincere as she pressed harder. "There, that should help," she said after a few moments.

As she pulled the handkerchief away, Will had the urge to keep her hand there. It would be worth it even with the pain.

"The bleeding's stopped but you may need a stitch or two."

"You are *not* doing them."

Phoebe smiled fully for the first time since they entered the carriage. "Agreed. My sewing skills leave much to be desired." Then the smile slowly faded.

Will blinked. He had gone and done it. He was *pressing her hand to his temple.*

"Sorry." He immediately dropped his hand, but she didn't pull hers away.

"It's all right," she murmured. Then, ever so slowly, she brushed her thumb along his cheekbone in one long stroke. It was the lightest of touches, but Will felt it flicker through his body, setting off the desire he had been trying so hard to keep banked.

Now it flared to life with disturbing speed until Will could do nothing but offer himself up to the white hot flames. Her breath caught as Will leaned toward her, but this time she didn't pull away.

Eleven

*A*s Will gently set his lips against hers, Phoebe could barely leash her chaotic thoughts. He was *kissing* her. *Will* was kissing her. Lord it was even better than she had imagined—and Phoebe had whiled away a significant part of her youth doing just that.

Once she had fully recovered from her shock, Phoebe pressed her hands to his remarkably firm chest. Now was her chance to push him away and let him make some excuse. Blame it on the blood loss. The whiskey. *Anything.*

He was nearly engaged. He was a duke. He wasn't supposed to want this. Want *her.* But all those very reasonable points slammed up against that tiny part of her that had never quite managed to let Will go, no matter how unreachable he became. Phoebe's fingers curled against his cashmere coat and she parted her lips, as she finally relented to the furious storm of desire building inside her. A low moan rumbled through him as he kissed her harder, exuding an authority that would have been irritating in any other situation, but here it only drove her desire higher. It was clear he knew exactly what he was doing—far more than she did, anyhow—so for just this once Phoebe decided to follow his lead.

One large hand cupped the nape of her neck, drawing her

closer and adjusting her head to a more comfortable angle. Something about the movement, the care in his touch, set off a swirl of unwanted longing. It was one thing to lust after him, which she had been doing since the moment he appeared in front of the music hall at her request, but this tenderness was too much. It wasn't something she could contain. An old, familiar ache began to spread through her chest, growing stronger by the second, as the pain of an unrequited girlhood fancy mingled with whatever it was she felt for him now. The pain of lost opportunity and an impossible future. Those reasonable points grew louder and louder, badgering Phoebe to put a stop to this nonsense before she lost all control. Before she gave up her heart once again.

Just as his tongue tentatively touched her own, Phoebe reared back. They stared at each other for a long moment, their heavy breaths filling the quiet carriage.

"Sorry," Will finally rasped as his hands slid down her body to settle at her waist. "I didn't mean to startle you."

"You didn't," she insisted. Though it was quite gratifying to her ego to see he was just as breathless as she was, Phoebe lifted her chin and ignored the mess of emotions battling it out inside her. "Besides, I've kissed men before."

The words were out before she had time to think. His kisses must have muddled her brain.

But Will merely raised an eyebrow at her admission. "Have you now?"

The hint of skepticism in his deep voice caused Phoebe's cheeks to blaze, but she refused to play the ingenue with him.

"Yes. Several. So don't flatter yourself thinking you're the first," she added.

Forget muddled. The man must have *melted* her brain. She was being outrageously rude in response to a few kisses, but he only smiled.

"Oh, I wouldn't dare," he murmured as his fingers flexed at her hips and his eyes grew even darker than usual. He was teasing her. And she liked that *far* too much. She should look away and return to her seat, but Phoebe simply couldn't will her legs to move.

"Well, good," she said flatly. "Glad that's settled."

Phoebe then shifted at the needy ache building between her thighs, and Will glanced down. When their eyes met again, his gaze grew even hotter.

He pushed the cap off her head and tucked a loose strand of hair behind her ear. Phoebe's heart fluttered faster, but she couldn't find the strength to pull away this time. Instead, she pressed her cheek against his open palm. As Will drew his thumb along her bottom lip, his eyes seemed to glow in the lamplight.

"Show me what you know."

Phoebe's heart stuttered at the low command.

It was true, she *had* kissed a few men. But two had been stolen kisses during her London season. Sloppy and, thankfully, quick. The third was from her friend Richard, who didn't even like women. That had been nothing more than a friendly peck at a New Year's party last year.

Will was still staring at her expectantly and Phoebe swallowed, but like hell would she admit to her inexperience. Nor give him the satisfaction of holding such power over her. She wasn't a lovesick girl anymore. Bringing him down a peg was a good enough reason for her. Phoebe pressed her hands against his shoulders and straddled his lap.

His eyebrows rose in surprise, but before he could say anything, Phoebe cupped his insufferably beautiful face and kissed him. It was the kind of kiss she had always imagined giving him: wild and passionate and full of everything she felt but could never say. Will was stunned for a moment but then his arms wrapped around her and he hauled her against him, returning the kiss with even more fervor than before. The flimsy little wall she had managed to erect around her heart was decimated as she leaned into the pure pleasure of the kiss.

This was how she once imagined it would be between them. *This* was what she had once dared to want. And lord, it felt good.

Phoebe felt him grow hard beneath her and she immediately rocked against him. It was instinctual, the way their bodies knew just how to move together. Phoebe shivered from the delicious sensation and Will let out an answering groan. He sounded desperate, like a man on the brink. And Phoebe wanted more. Wanted every last bit of the stuck-up duke that remained within him to crumble under her touch. She ground her hips even harder and he turned his head away, breaking the kiss.

"Christ, Phoebe," he said breathlessly, but the slight censure in his words cut through the dense fog of lust that had clouded her brain.

What was she *doing?*

She shoved off him in one swift movement and sat down hard on the opposite bench, trying to hide her own heaving breaths.

"Are you all right?" His heavy gaze was on her, but Phoebe couldn't look at him just yet. She had revealed far too much. It would be a miracle if he didn't suspect how deep her infatuation went. Now was the time to put him off.

Phoebe crossed her arms over her pounding heart. "Of course," she said, forcing lightness into the words, as if she debauched men in carriages all the time.

Will gave her a long look before he let out a sigh. She watched him out of the corner of her eye as he stared at the floor and pulled a hand roughly through his hair. Phoebe turned to him fully, unable to resist seeing him like this, all rumpled and raw. Because then that pathetic little part of her could pretend that he was still just Will Margrave. And that there was still a fighting chance for something more between them.

But as he glanced up and their eyes met, the vulnerability melted away. Phoebe's heart sank as she watched Will quickly fix his hair and straighten in his seat until he regained the stiff bearing of the duke once again, albeit slightly more undone than usual. He then passed Phoebe her cap and she took it.

Will looked out the window. "We've nearly reached Mayfair. I should have had John bring you home first."

The reason for this lapse went unspoken.

Phoebe nodded. "I'm sorry."

"For what?" He turned to her sharply, his dark eyes now full of challenge, but Phoebe pressed on.

"I meant to say it much earlier, but then everything... happened." She clenched her hands on her lap. God, this was excruciating. "I think I was too harsh with you the other night," she continued. "About your support of Lord Fairbanks's bill."

But Will didn't look at all appreciative. Instead he looked grave. And so very tired.

He shook his head. "No, you were right. I reviewed a draft of Lord Fairbanks's bill and it is purely punitive. There are no provisions for the people who will lose their livelihoods. Only unfairly harsh consequences for those who dared engage in the practice in the first place."

But Phoebe couldn't focus properly on his admission, for at

the mention of Lord Fairbanks she had immediately remembered Lady Gwen. Will may have kissed her first, but Phoebe had pushed things much further. No wonder he had stopped her. No wonder he had looked ashamed. The man was nearly engaged and she had, quite literally, thrown herself at him.

"...and I mean to change it."

She blinked. "Sorry?"

"I mean to change it," he said more urgently. "Or else he'll lose my support."

"Oh. That's good."

He furrowed his brow, clearly expecting her to be more enthusiastic, but Phoebe couldn't focus on anything other than her mortification. She needed to get out of this carriage. *Now.*

Phoebe banged on the ceiling. "I can get a hackney from here," she said as the carriage came to a halt.

"*What?* Phoebe, no—"

But she had already put on her cap and moved to the door. "I'll be fine." She opened the door before John could climb down from his seat. Only once she was safely on the pavement did she look back at Will. He was staring at her with a mixture of confusion and concern.

"And don't worry," she said, then waved a hand between them. "I won't say anything about this. In fact, it is already forgotten."

He began to say something, but Phoebe slammed the door shut and disappeared into the night. It was well past time for her to walk away from Will Margrave.

Will awoke the next morning far too early after falling asleep much too late. After Phoebe bolted from his carriage, Will had

John follow the hackney she hailed. It was only once he watched her enter her home that he could return to Mayfair, but even then he had been completely unable to relax. His mind refused to focus on anything other than reliving those few heated moments in the carriage, when Phoebe had straddled his lap with practiced ease and then kissed him like her life depended on it.

He tried reading, drinking, exercising, and then drinking some more until he finally collapsed into bed from sheer exhaustion and sank into the sweet relief of unconsciousness. But as he sat up with bleary eyes and a sore head, his thoughts immediately— and deviously—returned to Phoebe: the feel of her lush, inviting mouth, the sound of her feather-breath sighs, and the press of her firm thighs as she rocked against his cock.

Dammit. He was as hard as granite. *Again.* He tried recalling her awkward goodbye, but it did little to cool his ardor.

Meant nothing, my foot.

Her words had been a messy act of self-preservation, Will was sure of it. And he understood the impulse, as this entire situation was bordering on farcical. But what he had felt last night was exceptional. Extraordinary, even. And he was quite certain it was the same for Phoebe, though she seemed reluctant to admit it.

Will winced as he climbed out of bed and rang for his valet. It would be a cold bath for him this morning.

After spending a very long time sitting in an Italian marble tub full of chilly water, Will was feeling mostly refreshed. He spent the first half of the morning with his secretary, reviewing reports from his various estates and deciding which pressing problem to throw money at first and which could wait. Such was the business of the duchy.

Then it was on to his social schedule. If given the choice, he would have reviewed a thousand agricultural reports rather than discuss which invitations he should accept, decide who he needed to call on this week and who he could put off, and, most mind-numbing of all, which events he was obligated to attend.

Will hadn't realized he'd groaned aloud until his secretary, Mr. Flynn, raised an eyebrow.

"Would you like me to cancel your afternoon ride with Lady Gwen?"

Will hesitated. Even before he had met up with Phoebe last night, he had decided against pursuing things further with Lady Gwen. She may have been perfect on paper, but it was becoming ever clearer that they just didn't suit. And while there were a great deal of things he was willing to sacrifice to the dukedom, a wife he didn't feel more than a slight attraction to was no longer one of them. Besides, Will reasoned, she might very well have her own reservations about him. It had never been a love match between them, after all. But regardless, it was still the kind of conversation one must have in person, however much one was dreading it.

"No," he sighed. "Do I have anything on for next Thursday evening?"

Mr. Flynn flipped through the schedule and shook his head. "Good. Keep it free."

Once the last invitation had been responded to, Mr. Flynn took his leave. Will leaned back in his chair and stared up at the elaborate plaster ceiling. The room, nay, the entire house was a monument to excess. Nothing but marble, gold, and, occasionally, silver. It may have cost a fortune, but the effect was cold and sterile. Will always felt like he was walking through a museum, not a home. He had wanted to redecorate this house since he first crossed the threshold, but decided it was better to wait until he married so the future duchess could have some input. He then smiled to himself at the thought of Phoebe marching in here and casting one of her withering looks of disapproval around the room. She'd probably suggest they burn it all down and start anew.

And God, didn't that feel right.

A knock at the door interrupted this rebellious little reverie and Mr. Flynn appeared again with a mortified look on his face.

"Sorry to bother you, Your Grace, but... your mother is here."

Will sat up abruptly. "Did we forget she was coming?"

"We did not," his secretary said with just a hint of indignation. Mr. Flynn *never* made a mistake.

"Of course," Will soothed. The last thing he needed was Mr. Flynn in one of his moods. He stood and pulled on his coat. "Better show her in then."

As the man left to fetch his mother, Will rang for tea and began to pace. After a few minutes, the door opened again and Lydia Margrave sailed into the room. Never one to miss making an entrance, she threw open her arms. "Darling!"

"Hello, Mother," Will said as he submitted to a cheek kiss. "Is everything all right?"

She looked affronted. "Do I need an excuse to visit my own son?"

"Of course not," Will said with a tight smile and took her hand. "But I wasn't expecting you in town until next week."

He led her to her favorite chair by the hearth that also looked out over his back garden.

"I thought I'd come a bit early and see how you were enjoying the season," she said as she gracefully took her seat. For the last few years, the front of her dark hair had slowly turned white. But instead of attempting to mask it, she had artfully arranged the long streak to striking effect. Leave it to his mother to find a way to make aging fashionable.

"Ah," he replied as he took the seat across from her. "How was the train?"

Will's mother still lived in his childhood home in Surrey with Cal, but she came to London often.

"It was fine. Uneventful."

Will cleared his throat. "And how is Cal?"

She glanced away and fiddled with her skirt. "Also fine. You know how he is," she added softly.

It had been five years since the carriage accident that took the life of Cal's best friend Ned, Lord Edward Manning, and left him with a broken shoulder that hadn't healed properly and debilitating headaches. It had also effectively ended his budding career as a portraitist.

Though Will had paid for dozens of specialists and all manner of cures, Cal insisted that the peace and quiet of the country gave him the most relief. But Will suspected it was the whispers about the true nature of Cal's friendship with Ned that swirled in the wake of the accident that had led him to largely withdraw from society. Will protected his brother's reputation as best he could, and being out of the ton's crosshairs had helped, but it wasn't enough.

Last fall, after their mother had gone off to bed and they stayed up enjoying a generous nip of port, Cal admitted that the worst thing he could imagine was becoming the duke.

"We both know they would tear me to pieces," he said, unable to meet Will's eyes. "And you wouldn't be there to protect me."

Will had been silent with shock. He had no idea Cal was carrying around this worry, all while Will had been off dallying with widows.

"That won't happen," he finally said. "I'll make sure of it."

So a-bride-hunting he had gone. An arduous task that would become even more difficult once he rejected Lady Gwen.

Will's mother looked past him out the window, lifting up just a bit in her seat. "Your roses are looking well."

"I'll be sure to tell my gardener."

The words came out sharper than he meant them to, but he wasn't in the mood for small talk. His mother was here for a reason and it certainly wasn't to take tea and admire his roses. Just before the moment could grow even more tense, a maid entered with the tea tray.

She visibly perked up and set about pouring their cups. "So then," she began briskly once they were alone again. "*Are* you enjoying the season?"

"As much as any man does."

She gave him a scolding look. "Could you at least try to sound a little more enthusiastic? You're here to find your duchess, the future mother of your children. Why, this should be exciting for you!"

Absolutely *nothing* about this was exciting, but Will managed a weak smile that seemed to satisfy his mother.

"I hear Lady Gwendolyn Fairbanks is very popular," she continued breezily. "Though I always found her rather dull myself. She's too much like her mother. The countess is always blathering on about something tedious, like wallpaper or shoe buttons."

And there it was. He should have guessed that she was here to check up on him. Her casual tone didn't fool Will. His mother may have just arrived in London, but she had amassed a large circle of aristocratic friends in the years since his elevation to the dukedom. Friends who no doubt had been keeping her abreast of all the latest gossip.

He narrowed his eyes as she took a sip of tea. "If you have something to ask me, I'd rather you just come out and say it," he said curtly.

It had been many years since Will had spoken to his mother in a manner that couldn't be described as coolly polite. He really must get some sleep.

She raised a dark brow the same shade as his own and set down her teacup. "Fine." As his mother folded her hands on her lap, the afternoon light caught on her dazzling emerald engagement ring—a pointed reminder that *she* had married for love despite the fervent opposition of his father's family. "Are you going to propose to her?"

It was a perfectly reasonable question, but Will felt the urge to rear back. He rolled his shoulders instead.

"I haven't decided."

It was a bit cowardly of him, perhaps, but it didn't feel right to tell his mother he wouldn't propose before Lady Gwen herself.

Her lips pursed at his evasive response and he had the distinct sensation she knew the truth anyway. "The earl won't like hearing that."

Will was finding it harder and harder to give a damn what Lord Fairbanks thought. "Well, it isn't up to him, is it?"

"No, it isn't." His mother's eyes softened. "I only want your happiness, darling. Whatever you do decide, I'll support you."

Will's cheeks heated. "I know," he muttered and turned away from her sympathetic gaze. They were rarely affectionate toward each other. And certainly not since he inherited.

"I only ask that you let me know once you *do* find your bride. I'd hate to learn about my own son's engagement in the newspaper."

"Of course." He titled his head and took his teacup.

While she chattered away about her circle of friends and her London plans, Will listened politely, offering an "Oh?" and "Naturally" every so often. They were back to their usual routine, and though it wasn't exactly comfortable, it was familiar.

Their relationship had never been the same after Will's father died. She had been too distraught to do anything other than lay abed, so everything had been left up to fifteen-year-old Will. He worked very hard to make sure they could keep the house, even when it would have been far more cost efficient to sell up and move them all to London. But Margraves never took the easy route, it seemed. When she finally emerged from her cocoon of grief months and months later, Will still continued to act as the head of the household.

His mother was generous with her thanks and always deferred to his judgment, until Will was named the heir a few years later and the old duke demanded he come stay with him. She had readily agreed, even *insisted* he go to live with a strange man he had never met in a part of the country he had never visited.

Will had tried to argue, but her mind was made up and he couldn't deny the duke without her support. So away he went, filled with the kind of righteous indignation at her betrayal only the very young could sustain for any length of time. The pain had faded a great deal over the years, settling into more of a muted antipathy, but it never truly went away.

Will absently rubbed his chest. How easily he could still call up that old wound. When he inherited the dukedom, Will made sure she had a lovely summer home in the Lake District, an elegant town house in London, and a generous allowance, but refused to share a roof with her ever again. When he visited her and Cal in

Surrey, he always made sure to return to London the same evening no matter the hour. And if she had ever noticed this pattern of behavior over the years, she never said a word to him about it.

"...Mrs. Atkinson hopes to raise at least fifty pounds."

Will perked up. His mind had been wandering for the last five minutes, at least.

"Oh, really?" He had no idea what his mother had been saying, but this seemed like a reasonable response.

"Well, naturally, darling. Lady Montgomery's garden party used to bring in twice that much. And it's for such a good cause. I'm going over there this afternoon for tea with her and Phoebe to discuss their plans for the bazaar. They need to hold it before the end of the month, so we will have to act quickly."

Will blinked, still lost. "Yes, of course."

"I know I haven't always approved of Alexandra, but what Phoebe is doing is admirable. You can't deny that. Those poor girls have so little. If they lose the school too, who knows what will happen to them."

Will's breath caught. Phoebe's school was in trouble? Why the devil hadn't she said anything? He frowned. "May I help?"

"Of course! I'm sure a donation would be very welcome."

"Certainly, but perhaps more can be done." He wasn't just a bloody checkbook. "I *do* have some sway in Parliament, you know." Will managed a teasing smile that was completely lost on his mother.

Her mouth dropped open for a moment before she recovered. "I...I can ask."

"Actually, might it not be better if I joined you? Then I can find out exactly what is needed."

And Phoebe wouldn't be able to dodge him so easily in her mother's home.

"You want to come to Mrs. Atkinson's," she said slowly, as if Will had spoken to her in Latin. "For tea."

"Yes, if you think she'll have me."

"I'm sure she would be delighted." Then she narrowed her eyes. "Does this have something to do with Alexandra?"

Will let out an impatient huff. "*No.*"

She would probably go to her grave certain that he was in love with Alex.

"All right." His mother didn't look convinced, but she changed the subject anyway.

As Will sat back in his chair and once again pretended to listen, his heart fluttered with anticipation. He was supposed to be finding a duchess, not gallivanting around London with someone who possessed the complete opposite qualities he needed in a wife. But all he could picture was the look of surprise on Phoebe's face when he entered the Atkinsons' parlor. For that moment alone he would suffer through a hundred awkward conversations with his mother. No, a thousand. He smiled and took a sip of tea.

"You're in an awfully good mood all of a sudden," she noted.

For once Will ignored the instinct to hide his true feelings from her behind a stoic facade. "As a matter of fact I am," he replied. "I think it will be a lovely afternoon."

Twelve

Once Phoebe returned from her jaunt with Will, she spent most of the night tossing and turning, too agitated from the events of the evening to sleep. Eventually she drifted off, but even her dreams were filled with him: his skillful kisses, the feel of his commanding touch, and his unrestrained groans. When she awoke with a start just after dawn, her skin was slick with sweat and her limbs were knotted in the bedsheets, while the space between her thighs grew heavy with pent-up desire. She was so unbearably sensitive, wound so tight from this unrelenting tension between them, that she was able to bring herself to release in only a few moments. Phoebe gritted her teeth against the nearly overwhelming urge to say Will's name as she came and settled for a muffled gasp. Then she sank into her mattress while taking heaving breaths and staring blankly at the ceiling.

She wasn't anywhere close to feeling satisfied but it would have to do. Phoebe turned over and screamed into her pillow. She felt marginally better. Enough to actually get on with her day. But then she remembered what that entailed and felt like screaming again. After school she had to rush over to her mother's house to discuss the charity bazaar with some of her society friends. And that meant being on her best behavior to win the support of these matrons. She had to be charming but not vain, humble but not pitiable, grateful but not grating. It was a delicate balance that Phoebe had never quite mastered, but that's what her mother was for.

After dawdling for another few minutes, Phoebe hauled herself out of bed, washed, and donned her version of a suit of armor: a cream-colored blouse, a navy blue skirt with matching vest, a black tie, and a tailored jacket. She always felt especially confident in this outfit. Freddie once said it made her look rather mannish, but perhaps that was why. She then ate a sweet bun and gulped down a cup of tea before heading off to school with Marion. They made polite, impersonal conversation on the short walk. Ever since their argument about Alice, there had been an awkwardness between them that Phoebe didn't know how to resolve. It also didn't help that she hadn't been spending much time in the flat.

When they reached the school and headed off to their class-rooms, Phoebe's relief was swiftly followed by guilt. Perhaps she was behaving cowardly, but she couldn't deal with Marion's judgment over her potentially disastrous personal choices at the moment. Anytime her thoughts dared to stray to Will, she gave the back of her hand a little pinch. But it was not very effective, as by the end of the school day the spot had turned red.

After a brief meeting with the headmistress to discuss a failing student, Phoebe was finally able to leave. She arrived at her family's home later than planned—tired, grumpy, and more than a little hungry. Her mother's friends would be coming in just fifteen min-utes. Phoebe bustled into the house and ran straight up the stairs into her old room. She headed for the dressing table mirror and let out a sigh. She looked like someone who had barely slept and then spent a large part of the day trying to teach a room full of uninterested young ladies how to diagram a sentence.

She quickly fixed her hair and washed her hands and face, but that did nothing to improve the pallor of her cheeks. Perhaps she could slip into Freddie's room and use some of the rouge she kept hidden in a drawer. Phoebe crossed the hall, knocked, and pressed her ear to the door. It didn't sound like Freddie was in. She then opened the door to the empty room and walked over to her sister's vanity. Mother banned Freddie from using any cosmetics, but that only made her very good at hiding them. Just as Phoebe finished dapping her cheeks and lips with the pot of rouge, someone turned the doorknob.

She slipped the rouge back in its hiding place just as *Alex* marched into the room.

"Freddie, did you take my—" She stopped dead when she saw Phoebe, but her usual stony expression didn't register surprise. "Oh. It's you."

"You're back," Phoebe said dumbly.

"Mother didn't tell you? We came home early." Alex then cocked her head and narrowed her dark brown eyes. "I suppose you aren't here to offer an olive branch, then."

Phoebe swallowed, but before she could respond, Alex crossed her arms and looked away. "Father made friends with an American manufacturing magnate and his son," she explained. "And *they* wanted to come to London, so here we are. Father's off showing them the sights as we speak."

While she had been left at home with the ladies. It appeared that Father did have some limits where Alex was concerned.

"Oh Alex—"

"It's fine," she said curtly as she snapped her gaze back to Phoebe.

"They are interested in a partnership that could be very fruitful. And, since according to you all I care about is enriching already wealthy men, I'm *inordinately* pleased." Phoebe bit her lip. This reunion was not going well at all. "So then," Alex continued briskly. "Mother says your school is bankrupt."

Just then their mother bustled into the room looking more harried than usual. She spied Phoebe and threw out her arm. "There you are! Come down at once. Everyone has started to arrive and Lydia Margrave has brought the duke."

"Will is here?" Alex asked at the same time Phoebe bleated, "Her son?"

Their mother shot them an exasperated look. "Who *else* would I mean? Now come on, the both of you."

Alex turned to Phoebe and raised an eyebrow. "Am I allowed to attend?"

"Oh Alex, stop being difficult and *move*," their mother said as she left the room. But Alex remained in place and stared at Phoebe.

"I'd like that," she replied quietly and met her sister's eyes.

More than a few cutthroat businessmen had crumpled under Alex's formidable stare. After a strained moment, she gave a single nod and exited the room. Phoebe let out a breath and followed. But as she entered the light-filled drawing room her parents used for company, her ordeal had only just begun. Will rose from his seat beside his mother, tall, imposing, and irritatingly handsome in his charcoal day suit. His dark eyes immediately fixed on her and Phoebe's stomach fluttered. Beside her, Alex cleared her throat and Phoebe realized the room had gone quiet, awaiting her greeting. She tore her gaze away from Will and cast a smile to the other guests.

"Good afternoon," she trilled. "Thank you all so much for coming today. And Your Grace, what an unexpected pleasure." She curtsied as Will advanced on her.

His expression darkened at her use of his honorific but he dutifully bowed over her hand. "The pleasure is all mine, Miss Phoebe," he said smoothly, with a slight emphasis on her name.

A shiver ran down Phoebe's spine, and she hoped to God no one else noticed the flush working its way up her neck. Will then turned his attention to Alex and Phoebe felt a prickle of jealousy at the fond look in his eyes.

"And Miss Atkinson. You survived your trip to New York, I see."

"More or less," Alex replied. Her tone was only slightly warmer with Will, but he smiled anyway.

"Well, I'm happy you're back."

Just as the prickle began to grow, his mother joined them. Phoebe noticed that Will's smile completely vanished as his mother took his arm.

"When I told my son where I was off to today he insisted on coming along."

"Really?" Phoebe turned to Will with an exaggerated look of surprise. "I had no idea the education of young ladies was of such interest to you, Your Grace."

"I contain multitudes, Miss Phoebe," he said, returning her cloying tone while his dark eyes glinted with amusement.

She opened her mouth to respond to *that* but her mother interrupted. "Everyone, sit please. Let's begin." She then shot Phoebe a significant look.

Phoebe joined her mother on the sofa and launched into her little speech, explaining how the school had greatly benefited from the proceeds generated from Lady Montgomery's annual garden party, but the loss of that funding was felt even more greatly now because the landlord decided to raise their rent without warning. Her eyes inadvertently met Will's and he gave her an encouraging nod that made warmth bloom in her chest.

"So we've decided to hold a bazaar in two weeks' time to generate additional funds," she continued. "My mother has generously offered to help, but we are looking for more volunteers. Admittedly my colleagues and I are not very experienced with planning and executing such endeavors." A few ladies nodded their heads or murmured sounds of recognition. "Any assistance will be greatly appreciated." Phoebe then gave a demure smile as she looked around the room. Hopeful but not desperate. Expectant but not presumptuous.

"And if you fall short?"

The sharp question went off like a gun. Phoebe turned to Alex. Because *of course* it was Alex. "Then the school will have to close until we can find another space," she said calmly.

Alex raised an eyebrow. "Do you *have* another space in mind?"

Her hands tightened on her lap. "No. We do not." Phoebe then addressed the room. "Which is why the success of this event is so important."

"Now then," her mother began. "The floor is open for discussion—*not* you, my dear," she added as Alex leaned forward, ready to strike again. "Let someone else have a turn."

Phoebe's shoulders relaxed as her mother took the lead. Most of the ladies appeared interested, but the greatest surprise was Will, who listened with interest and gave a number of suggestions that were irritatingly helpful. He even offered the use of his own ballroom for the bazaar.

"Thank you, Your Grace," Phoebe said diplomatically. "But we've already decided to hold the bazaar on the school grounds, so the students may easily participate."

Will tilted his head. "An excellent idea."

Phoebe couldn't help blushing at his praise. Hopefully he didn't notice. The discussion continued for another quarter of an hour, after which every guest had pledged either a donation or offered to volunteer at the bazaar.

"I think that went well," her mother said as the guests began taking their leave.

"Yes, thank you so much, Mama. I truly could not do this without you."

Her mother gave her a shy smile. "You aren't mad at me then?"

"For not telling me about Alex?" Phoebe shrugged. "I suppose I can forgive you."

"I just hate to see you fight," her mother said. "And you've been so close for so long."

They'd had the usual sibling struggles when they were younger but had been on good terms for years, until Phoebe had started teaching and Alex became increasingly involved in their father's business.

"We have very different ideas of how the world should work."

Her mother gave her a thoughtful look. "I'm not sure that's true, darling." Then she patted her hand and moved to say goodbye to Lady Kirby.

As Phoebe went to pour herself another cup of tea, someone came up behind her.

"Why didn't you tell me the school was in such financial straits?"

She stiffened at the disappointment in Will's voice. "Because we have a plan." Phoebe then turned to face him. "And I've been relying on your help quite enough lately, don't you think?" Will frowned a little as Phoebe brushed past him. "I hope you didn't come here just to offer your assistance. You've wasted your whole afternoon."

She sat down on an empty chair and gave him an expectant look as she took a sip of tea. Will stood in front of her with his hands clasped behind his back, still frowning. If he thought looming like that would have any kind of effect on her, he was *sadly* mistaken.

"No," he said as he took the seat nearest her.

Phoebe tried not to notice the way his trousers tightened around his thighs as he sat down. The very same thighs she had straddled last night.

She cleared her throat, which had suddenly gone dry, but Will didn't seem to notice, as he kept his gaze fixed ahead and lowered his voice. "I also want your word that you will stay away from Fleur. *I* will handle it."

Phoebe bristled and took another sip of tea to help swallow her irritation. Of all the things she wanted from him, being an over-protective brute was not one of them.

"And what would Lady Gwen think about you going there?"

Perhaps that was a low blow, but it seemed vitally important to remind them *both* of her existence.

Will turned sharply toward her and scowled. "She doesn't—" But then he stopped as if something had just come to him, muttered what sounded like a curse, and stood. "I've forgotten about an appointment."

"Oh." He really did look distressed. "Of course."

Will shot her another look. "Your *word*."

But before Phoebe could respond, her mother and Mrs. Margrave approached.

"Thank you again for coming, Your Grace," her mother said.

Will plastered a smile on his face as he addressed her. "And thank you for accommodating me, Mrs. Atkinson. But I'm afraid I must leave immediately. I'm extremely late for an appointment that slipped my mind."

She nodded graciously. "Oh, of course."

"The carriage will take you home, Mother," Will said, but Mrs. Margrave ignored that bit.

"An appointment? *What* appointment?"

He gave his mother an exasperated look. "Lady Gwen," he grumbled.

It shouldn't have been such a surprise, but Phoebe's stupid little heart still sank.

"Good day, Miss Phoebe," he said with a curt nod.

"Good day," she replied weakly, but Will was already halfway across the room.

Mrs. Margrave stared after her son. "That's not at all like him," she said suspiciously. "I daresay that boy still remembers his school schedule."

Mrs. Atkinson gave her old friend a sly look. "Perhaps he's been a bit *distracted* lately."

"Perhaps," Mrs. Margrave agreed. "Though I'm not sure Lady Gwen is the one distracting him..."

Phoebe turned away from the woman's too perceptive gaze. She didn't agree with her theory, seeing as how Will had just barreled out of the room to meet the lady in question.

"Thank you again for organizing this, Mother. I think the bazaar will be a great success."

"My pleasure. Will you stay for dinner, darling?"

Phoebe's heart clenched at the hopeful look on her mother's face, but she cast a glance at Alex, who was standing in a corner making absolutely no attempt to talk with anyone. "I can't tonight. Sorry."

"All right." Her mother sighed then lifted an eyebrow in question. "You will come on Friday though, won't you? Now that your father and sister are home?"

When Phoebe had agreed to attend Friday night dinner, she thought she would have at least a few weeks respite before Alex and her father returned. But now it was time to pay the piper. "Yes," she said with a reluctant nod. "I will be there."

Her mother broke into a dazzling smile. "Wonderful! I'll tell your father tonight. He will be *so* pleased."

Phoebe wasn't quite sure of that, but she smiled anyway. "I'm looking forward to it."

"That's the spirit," her mother said with a knowing wink. "Now, let's take a turn about the room. There are a few more people you should speak to this afternoon."

"I am at your disposal," Phoebe replied as she took her mother's arm. She was prepared to endure a great deal of inanity if it meant saving the school. But heaven help her if it didn't work.

Thirteen

"Are you certain you don't want a shave, Your Grace?"

Will met the nervous gaze of Peabody, his valet, in the mirror as he buttoned his waistcoat. "Are you trying to say you don't like my beard?"

Peabody's eyes widened. "Oh no, Your Grace! I think it suits you very well. But it isn't...it's not..."

"My usual look," Will supplied, saving the man from further embarrassment.

"Yes," he said with relief. "That's all."

Will returned his gaze to his reflection and rubbed a hand against the dark beard that had grown in over the last week. "I quite like it."

"Change can be a good thing," Peabody replied, though he didn't sound certain.

Will smiled. "Agreed."

Peabody then helped Will into his evening coat and smoothed the fabric across his shoulders and arms with practiced care. Will stood still as Peabody performed his final check. He had never really gotten used to being dressed by a valet, but the old duke had explained that for men like Peabody, this was their life's work, a point of pride and the highest honor to dress a duke. That had sounded a little self-serving to Will, but he had to admit that Peabody did a far better job shaving him than he ever could. Not to mention he kept Will's clothes pristine. Most of the time, though, Will dressed himself unless he had an event to attend that required him to look particularly fashionable, like tonight.

"There," Peabody said. "What do you think?"

Will stared at his reflection in the dressing room's full-length mirror. The beard had seemed a good idea to help further conceal his identity when he attended Fleur later, at least from this Maude woman. If anyone else happened to recognize him, his presence at such an establishment, while unusual, was not extraordinary. He was a duke, after all.

"Excellent, Peabody."

The man beamed and gave a bow before leaving the room. Will checked his pocket watch. He needed to leave in a few minutes.

Or you could stop playing detective and focus on finding a wife.

Will grimaced. This business with Phoebe had turned into a wild, distracting goose chase. He had properly stuck his foot in it with Lady Gwen when he completely forgot about their afternoon ride earlier in the week. The poor girl had been left waiting in Hyde Park with her chaperone for nearly an hour before she gave up on Will. When he arrived at her home breathless and full of regret, she had graciously accepted his apologies, but Lady Fairbanks had been visibly irritated.

Understandable, given that she and Lord Fairbanks were expecting a proposal that Will had yet to deliver. And it hadn't seemed like the right time to explain that one would not be coming, so he stayed for an awkward cup of tea with mother and daughter before making his exit.

Since then he kept his social schedule to a bare minimum and instead focused on the never-ending business of being the duke while trying to tie up a few loose ends. His secretary still hadn't been able to uncover the identity of the owner of that decrepit tenement building and Inspector Holland hadn't made any progress regarding the untimely death of Mr. Felton nor the whereabouts of Alice Clarke. But Will needed to see this through—he *wanted* to.

He felt more invigorated these last few weeks than he had in years. Helping Phoebe gave him a purpose that went beyond simply standing about and looking important. He was actually *doing* things. Not just signing papers or listening as his peers complained about the crumbling state of the world from the confines of their luxurious homes while doing absolutely nothing about it. Will knew his own contribution was laughably small, but he was determined to do more starting tonight.

He planned to stay at Fleur only long enough to discreetly ask about Alice Clarke, as Phoebe was worried the girl was working for Maude. Obviously it would be better if Phoebe herself was with him, but that was absolutely going too far. Then he could stop by Lord Fairbanks's club afterward, as it was nearby. Better to tell him first that an engagement to Lady Gwen wouldn't work. Will's stomach clenched. The earl would not take such news well. Their relationship had already grown chilly thanks to Will's reluctance to support his bill. No doubt it would grow downright frigid once Will revealed his own competing plan and he could no longer rely on the goodwill of his mentor.

Will let out a sigh as he pocketed his watch and left the room. Time to get to work.

Half an hour later, Will's carriage stopped at the corner of a quiet West End street not far from Soho. A remarkably average-looking town house was up ahead. The third in the middle of a row of equally unassuming houses. He checked the card Maude had given him, but this was the correct address. Will stepped down onto the pavement and looked around. The street was as silent as a graveyard, but he had the distinct sensation that he was being watched. Will gave himself a shake and headed toward the house. As he grew closer, someone emerged from the shadows and his heart stopped. They passed under a gas lamp, and he could determine that it was a woman wearing a veil.

"I was starting to think you wouldn't show," the ghostly figure said.

Will blinked rapidly, then hardened his jaw. *Phoebe.* "What are you doing here?"

She threw back the veil and grinned. "I fooled you, didn't I?"

"Only until you opened your mouth."

She shrugged, unconcerned. "Then I won't speak."

"Don't think for even a moment that you can come inside," he growled.

Phoebe drew closer and Will couldn't stop his eyes from tracking down her figure. She wore a dark sapphire gown with a bodice that was surprisingly low cut. He made sure to immediately look back at her face.

"It's Freddie's," she explained unprompted. "And the veil is from a dress-up box I found in the attic."

Will raised his eyebrow. "You kept a *mourning veil* in your dress-up box?" Phoebe began to answer, but he shook his head. "Never mind. Of course you did," he muttered.

"All right. Let's go then," she said briskly and charged forward, but Will grabbed her arm.

"I don't think you understand what goes on in there."

As she turned to him, her eyes caught in the glow of the gas-light, giving her an otherworldly look. "You needn't condescend to me, Margrave." She lifted her chin. "I assure you, I do."

Will tugged her closer and watched her pupils grow larger as he leaned in. "If anyone realizes you're there, you will be absolutely ruined. And not even I will be able to save you."

Phoebe held his gaze. "Then we had better make sure they don't," she said before pulling the veil down over her face.

Will grumbled but dutifully donned the black domino mask he had brought with him. Then he noticed Phoebe staring at him. At least, he *thought* she was staring at him.

"What is it?"

She jolted a little at the question and shook her head. "Nothing. Shall we?"

Will tucked her arm against his side and led them to the town house. The place was tidy and well-kept but looked empty from the outside. All the windows were dark and no sounds could be heard. If this really was a house of debauchery, it was a remarkably discreet one. Will's heart began to flutter as he used the front door's heavy brass knocker.

"I'm sure I will absolutely regret telling you this," he began while they waited. "But I'm glad you're here."

She turned to him as her hand tightened on his arm, but before she could respond, the door swung open. They were met by a positively hulking man with white hair that hung past his shoulders and a pair of rheumy blue eyes. He said nothing as he looked past them with a blank stare, waiting.

After a moment, Phoebe nudged Will and he cleared his throat. "Avec plaisir."

The man immediately stepped back from the doorway and

gestured for them to enter. Will shot Phoebe an apprehensive look even though he could barely make out her face through the heavy gauze, but they dutifully stepped inside. The man led them down a long, dark corridor lit by wall sconces every few feet toward the faintest sound of laughter and conversation.

From the outside it looked to be just another town house, but inside it was deceptively big. They made a sharp turn and proceeded down another hallway going deeper into the house. Will guessed it was actually three row houses combined. No wonder they hadn't heard anything from the street. But the sounds grew progressively louder as they reached a heavy oak door. The old man stopped abruptly.

"Enjoy yer evening," he said in a dull rasp before he turned around and proceeded back down the corridor, dragging his fingertips along the wall.

Will and Phoebe both watched his slow, steady retreat. A blind doorman seemed like a good way to guarantee anonymity.

He faced Phoebe. "Last chance to turn back."

"Absolutely not."

Then she pushed open the door and charged ahead. Will rolled his eyes and followed her into what appeared to be an antechamber but after a few steps, Phoebe halted to a dead stop. As Will came up behind her, he noticed a couple pressed against a wall by another door in the throes of a rather passionate embrace. The woman's skirts were rucked up and the man had hooked her stocking-clad leg around his waist. Whatever else he was doing, she seemed to enjoy it.

"Come," Will said softly as he took Phoebe by the elbow and guided her past the couple, who hadn't noticed them.

The sounds of revelry were even louder now and he opened the door to a party in full swing.

An attractive young lady wearing a silver half mask flanked by two massive men greeted them at the door and asked for the fee.

Will paid the eyebrow-raising sum without reacting, but this club certainly wasn't cheap.

Phoebe reached for his arm and gripped it tightly as he ushered them deeper inside. The room was larger than he expected with patterned wallpaper in a deep forest green and matching sofas in soft velvet. An opulent crystal chandelier hung from the ceiling and a large marble fireplace nearly took up an entire wall.

To his surprise, everyone in this room was fully clothed and simply socializing while masked waiters circulated with trays of champagne. One came up to them, but Will waved him away. He needed to be sharp tonight, especially with Phoebe here. Some of the guests also wore masks, but a number of others didn't. They must be quite confident in the discretion of the other guests.

Will was just about to comment on this when an extremely inebriated man stumbled toward them, leering at Phoebe.

"And who have you brought?" He tried to swipe at her veil, but missed and nearly fell over. "Don't be shy, love. We all share here."

Will wrapped his arm around Phoebe's waist and pulled her against his side. "Not her."

The man pouted. "Well that's not very sporting of you." Then he let out a braying laugh that Will did not return. He gave a shrug. "Fine. You can't hide forever though," he added before toddling off to annoy someone else.

"Who was that?" Phoebe whispered.

"The Home Office's undersecretary."

She let out a huff. "Unbelievable."

"Come." Will took her hand and guided her along the edge of the room. He wanted to avoid any more encounters and only recognized a few other people, none whose attendance here was a surprise. When they reached the other side, he drew Phoebe into a dark corner and leaned over to speak by her ear.

"Did you see her?"

She shook her head. "This can't be all there is."

Will could hear the frustration in her voice. "I'm not sure how freely we can wander about."

Phoebe ignored him and pointed to a door across from where they stood. "There."

"I don't think—" Will began just as she headed toward it. "Christ," he muttered and joined her. As Phoebe tested the knob, he gave a quick look around the room to make sure no one was paying them any attention.

"It's unlocked," she said softly and pushed the door open.

Will held his breath and followed her.

Fourteen

As Phoebe stepped into another corridor dimly lit by wall
sconces, Will let out a huff behind her. "And what exactly is
your plan?"

"Explore every room in this house to make sure Alice isn't here."

It wasn't very efficient, but Phoebe didn't know what else to
do. Ever since Mr. Cartwright had first mentioned this Maude
woman, Phoebe couldn't shake the feeling that she held the answer
to Alice's disappearance.

Will was quiet for a long moment. "And if she is?"

Phoebe gritted her teeth. "Then we get her out."

They reached the end of the corridor, which led to a flight of
stairs. Phoebe had made it up the first step when the sound of a
door shutting came from the floor above, followed by multiple
pairs of footsteps and the murmur of voices. Phoebe turned to Will
as the group headed closer toward the stairs. There was nowhere
else to go and they would be spotted in the corridor.

"Do you mind?" Will asked.

Phoebe shook her head. She didn't exactly know what he
intended to do, but there wasn't time to talk about it. She just had
to trust him.

As the group began their descent, Will led her to a shadowed corner near the stairs and pressed her against the wall. He drew her veil away from her shoulder, making sure her face was still covered. Then, without another word, he nuzzled into the crook of her neck. Phoebe gasped at the sensation of his rough beard rubbing against her bare skin. He began to pull back, but she brought a hand to the nape of his neck and held him there.

She actually *had* intended to keep her promise to him and stay at home this evening. Between school and planning the bazaar, she had been more tired than usual. But while she was going over some details with her mother that afternoon, Freddie had stopped by and made a point of mentioning the latest gossip surrounding Will:

Everyone thought he would have proposed to Lady Gwen by now. I heard he even forgot *about plans they had made to ride in Hyde Park. She waited for him for over an hour, poor thing. Wasn't he here that day?*

Phoebe had ignored her mother's gaze burning into the side of her head and made some vague reply. But afterward, she had gone to Freddie's room and asked to borrow something to wear. Freddie, bless her, hadn't pestered her with too many questions, though she did make Phoebe promise to tell her everything tomorrow.

But as Will's lips tentatively grazed her collarbone, Phoebe wasn't so sure she could keep that promise. She let out another gasp and arched her back. Will responded by pressing his hips against hers. His hand then briefly cupped her bottom before sliding down her thigh and stopping under her knee to lift her leg up, just like the couple in the entryway. The dress was at least an inch too short, given that it was her sister's, but that suddenly seemed an advantage, along with the extra room in the bodice.

"Oh God," she rasped at the sensation this position created. Now she understood why the woman in the hall had been so enthusiastic.

The voices suddenly grew louder and Phoebe froze. She had completely forgotten why they had started this in the first place. Will paused too, his breath heavy and warm on her skin as what sounded like three men descended the stairs directly behind them.

"Capital place Fairbanks has created here," one man said.

Will's shoulders tensed beneath her fingers. Could they mean *Lord* Fairbanks? Her brain felt sluggish but she tried to focus on the conversation.

"Yes," another agreed. "As I understand it, he intends to open more across the city."

"Only if he can pass that bill of his and raze the competition."

"He will," the first man said confidently. "He always finds a way."

"Not without the support of Ellis though."

The other man laughed. "Fairbanks doesn't seem worried. The duke always comes to heel."

Now it was Phoebe's turn to tense. Will still hadn't moved. The first man began to say more, but they caught his attention. "Ah, what have we here?"

Will turned his face away. "Move along," he said gruffly.

Phoebe held her breath, but the men only laughed. "Sorry, chap. Didn't mean to interrupt. As you were."

They laughed again and continued on, their voices slowly fading as they filed down the corridor. Will let out a sigh and sagged against her, but just as her arms came around him, he straightened and tore his mask off.

Phoebe swallowed at the thunderous expression on his face.

"That bastard," he muttered. "That lying, scheming, *hypocritical* bastard."

"I'm so sorry." Phoebe reached for him, but he shrugged away.

"I need to know what the hell this place is and exactly how he is involved," he said. Then he let out a dark laugh. "'Come to heel,' my arse. I'll show him what kind of dog he's trained."

Phoebe threw back her veil. "*Will*," she hissed, but he had already started up the stairs. Phoebe scrambled after him before they lost their cover entirely. "You're going to get caught."

Once he reached the landing, he prowled down the hall toward the nearest door.

"Good," he snapped. "Then perhaps I'll get some answers."

She grabbed his hand just as he began to turn the knob. "Look at me," she demanded. Will reluctantly met her eyes. She could see the anger there, as well as the hurt. "I know you're upset, but that isn't why we came here."

"You don't know what that man has done for me. I always felt so damned indebted to him. And all this time…" Will shook his head stubbornly. "You don't understand."

Phoebe's grip gentled. "Then help me to."

When he met her eyes again, the guilt in his gaze was so startling she nearly stepped back. "I've been so stupid, Phoebe."

But before she could respond, the door swung open to reveal none other than the infamous Maude glaring at the two of them.

"Well, if it isn't Mr. Crispin and Mr. Agincourt," she mocked. "Have you come to take France or just disrupt my evening?" As Will and Phoebe exchanged a look, Maude let out an exasperated sigh. "Come in. *Now.*"

Phoebe hesitantly passed Maude and entered a small sitting room that was decorated just as opulently as the room below, but in shades of pale peach and gold. Across the room, a partially open door provided a glimpse of a similarly decorated bedroom.

Phoebe turned to Maude, who was dressed to match her surroundings in a gauzy blush tea gown barely suitable for company— though perhaps that depended on who the company was. "Are these your chambers?"

The woman had been busy eyeing her outfit and immediately snapped her gaze back to her face. "Only when I'm here."

Phoebe nodded and walked closer to the bedroom. A fire was lit in the hearth and a cream-colored silk dressing gown was draped across the bed.

She looked back over her shoulder. "Is this where you entertain your ... your clients?"

Maude's eyes went cold. "I think I much preferred you with the mustache," she said to Phoebe before addressing Will. "And you without the beard."

Will touched his cheek self-consciously. "I think it suits him quite well," Phoebe said, feeling defensive on his behalf. "And I can't say I don't miss wearing trousers."

Maude began to smile, then stopped herself. "Enough chitchat. Why are you following me? And before you answer, keep in mind that you aren't very good liars," she added.

Phoebe exchanged another look with Will and he nodded his head slightly. If they wanted to get anything out of this ordeal, they would have to tell this woman something. "I'm looking for Alice Clarke."

Maude visibly flinched before her eyes turned to ice. "Why," she barked. It was a warning more than a question, but this woman knew something, and Phoebe wouldn't leave here until she got some answers.

"I am a friend who is interested in her well-being."

Maude let out a snide laugh. "Is that so? A lot of good you've done her."

Phoebe took a step forward. "What is *that* supposed to mean?"

"Phoebe..." Will murmured as he pulled her back, not that Maude seemed the least bit intimidated.

She gave Phoebe a considering look. "You're that teacher, aren't you. Miss Arlington—"

"Atkinson—"

"Whatever. The one giving her a lot of fancy *ideas*," Maude returned, her words dripping with disapproval.

"Alice is smart. I want to help her."

Maude let out a laugh. "Right. Well, teaching her to read Shakespeare isn't going to pay the rent or put food on the table."

Phoebe winced. It was a fair enough point. One she had heard before. But she wasn't here to debate the merits of the humanities. "I know that, but secretarial work is a real possibility for her. She only needs to complete a course. If I could just—"

Maude shook her head. "Alice didn't have time for that."

"How do *you* know her?" Will asked with a narrowed gaze.

But she was not cowed by his tone and merely lifted her chin. "I have a reputation in the neighborhood for my connections. She came to me asking for work, so I found her a position as a maid in a fine house. A *safe* one," she added with a knowing look. "Only a widow and her daughter there."

With no husband to create trouble for a young maid.

"That's a fine story, but I want proof," Phoebe insisted. "And I won't leave until I know she isn't...isn't—"

"Selling herself?" Maude let out a bitter laugh. "No, don't worry. She hasn't stooped to my level. And I'll make sure she *never* has to."

"I didn't mean—"

"Save your words," Maude snapped. "I know what you lot think about women like me. But it's easy to judge when you've never been in my place. And I'm not interested in your pity either. Your school is all well and good for the girls with families that can help them, but Alice needs to be practical."

Phoebe sighed and brushed a hand over her face. "I just don't understand why she didn't tell anyone she was leaving. Could you at least give me her address so I can write to her?"

Maude maintained her steely expression. "She needs to focus on her work."

"Surely she can handle the occasional letter," Will put in.

"That isn't for you to decide." Maude then gestured to Phoebe. "You stick to keeping this lady of yours out of trouble."

"We're friends," Will said just as Phoebe bit out, "I'm not his lady."

Maude's face filled with unexpected mirth and she held up her hands. "Right. My mistake."

Before Phoebe could clarify their relationship, someone rattled the doorknob.

A muffled voice came from the other side. "Why the *devil* is this locked? Maudie?"

"Oh fantastic," Maude grumbled. "You two need to leave. *Now.*" Then she raised her voice and addressed the person on the other side of the door. "Just a minute!"

"That's Fairbanks, isn't it," Will barked. "Let him in so I can give him a piece of my mind."

Maude shot him an odd look as Phoebe tugged on his sleeve. As much as she wanted to see Will take the earl to task, she much preferred to not be discovered in a den of iniquity this evening.

He glanced back at her and his thunderous expression vanished. "Sorry." Then he addressed Maude. "Is there somewhere we can hide?"

"Try the closet." She gestured toward a door on the other side of the room then gave Will an assessing look. "It will be a tight fit with the two of you in there, though. I'll get him out of here as fast as I can."

They scurried over to the closet and Will let out a grumble as he opened the door.

It really was *very* small.

"You go first," Phoebe suggested.

Will had to crouch down just to fit, which meant the only space left for her was between his legs. She took a steadying breath and entered, leaving the door open just a sliver. Phoebe's back was to Will's front and the heat radiating off his body mingled with the woodsy scent of his cologne, invading her senses. He was hunched so far over, he could embrace her if he wished. Phoebe was filled with the urge to press against him, to feel his strong arms around her once more. Her heart thundered in her chest as she leaned back just a little, but Will reacted as if he had touched hot coals and straightened so quickly he bumped his head on the closet's low ceiling.

Well, so much for that.

"Are you all right?" Phoebe had to force the question through her clenched jaw.

"Yes," Will said testily before muttering a curse. "I'm fine."

Then she bent down to peer through the slight crack in the door and ignore how dangerously close their bodies still were. But apparently that wasn't enough for Will and he continued shifting behind her, trying to create as much space as possible.

"Will you stop *moving*?" she hissed after a moment. "I promise I won't touch you again."

"Sorry," he mumbled.

Outside, Maude opened the door to her room and a distinguished-looking man with salt-and-pepper hair immediately strolled in. Lord Fairbanks, Phoebe presumed.

"Why was your door locked?" he demanded.

Maude's entire demeanor changed upon the earl's entrance. She batted her eyelashes and gave a careless shrug. "I forgot. Force of habit, I guess. Still getting used to this place."

The earl stepped closer and gave her a look of such blatant, naked interest that it made Phoebe's skin crawl. "That's a pretty gown. Is it new?"

Maude beamed with pride as she did a little turn. "I bought it just yesterday down at Harvey Nicks. Paid for it all by myself."

A corner of the earl's mouth turned up, but the smile was closer to a sneer. "What a resourceful little madam you are," he murmured as he reached out and rubbed the fabric of her skirt between his thumb and forefinger. Even Phoebe could see her flinch. The earl then pulled her against him and moved to kiss Maude's neck.

"John," she whispered and leaned away. "You promised..."

He pulled back but his grip tightened around her waist. "And so did you," he replied darkly.

Maude turned her head to the side. "You can't blame me for that."

"Only because I can't prove it," he replied in a silky tone edged with venom. Then his manner suddenly lightened as he released her and clapped his hands together. "I'd nearly forgotten why I came up here in the first place." Phoebe and Maude both released a breath. "Lord Harcourt is downstairs. You remember him, don't you? He was in Paris when we—"

"Yes, I remember," Maude replied wearily as she slumped into a chair.

The earl gave her an expectant look. "Well, he's asked for you."

Maude stilled for a moment. "I'm not here to do that," she said with some of her earlier bravado, but it couldn't hide the tremble in her words. "It wasn't part of our arrangement."

The earl nodded as if mulling over her words and casually walked toward her. "Yes, I know, Maudie. But I don't really care. I need his support on a vote and this is his price: another evening in your enchanting company, but without my participation this time."

Phoebe managed to swallow as she grasped what, exactly, had happened in Paris, then felt ashamed by her own naivete. But Will had warned her about what went on in places like these.

Maude began to object, but he grabbed her by the chin and brought her to her feet. "You can buy as many gowns at *Harvey Nicks* as you damn well please, but that won't change a thing about you. Ever. You were born in the gutter, and you will die there. This is just a pleasant stop along the way. And until then you will do whatever it is I ask of you. Unless you want to meet your maker a little bit sooner."

Maude managed to nod even in his tight grip and the earl flashed her an unnerving smile that turned Phoebe's stomach. "That's my good girl."

He then shoved her back down in the chair and looked at his reflection in the mirror by the fireplace. "You have five minutes to come downstairs, or else I'm sending someone up after you," he said calmly as he fixed his perfectly groomed hair. "And they won't be as nice about it as me."

The earl then swept out of the room. After a moment, Maude got up and locked the door.

"It's safe now," she called to them as she sank back into the chair.

Phoebe burst out of the closet and rushed to her side. "Are you all right?" Before Maude could respond, she pulled a blanket off the sofa and draped it around the woman's shoulders. "Here, you're shivering."

But Maude shrugged it off. "I'm fine," she snapped.

"Come with us," Phoebe said impulsively. "We can keep you safe."

As her bright blue eyes met Phoebe's, she seemed to consider it for a brief moment, but then her gaze shuttered. "Just—just go." Then she turned to Will and shot him a fierce look. "And for God's sake, don't let her come back here. The earl is a powerful man with even more powerful friends. And they won't like having anyone interfere with their plans."

Will seemed to consider revealing his own identity, but the urgency in her voice must have given him pause. "Understood," he said with a nod, then turned to Phoebe. "Come on. I think we've taken up enough of this lady's time."

Though Maude had regained some of her earlier bluster, Phoebe still didn't like the idea of leaving her here. "If you ever change your mind—"

Maude gave her a bland look. "I'll be fine, Miss Atkinson. It isn't anything I haven't done before," she added, but her matter-of-fact tone couldn't hide the hollow look in her eyes.

Will then took Phoebe by the elbow and led her toward the

door. Since neither of them had any desire to return downstairs, Maude directed them to the servants' staircase at the end of the hall that would bring them to the mews behind the house. They exited the building without incident and climbed into Will's waiting carriage.

Maude's resigned expression in the face of the earl's callous cruelty would haunt Phoebe for a long, long time. She knew such things occurred with distressing regularity—one only needed to open a London paper to learn of all the horrible ways people treated each other—but seeing it with her own eyes, and feeling so helpless in the moment, was unfamiliar.

"Phoebe." Will's voice cut through her desperate thoughts. She met his eyes in the low light of the carriage. "It will be all right."

She couldn't help laughing at the certainty in his voice. "For whom?"

Will's lips thinned in a grimace, but he didn't answer. Phoebe looked out the window as the shadowy city passed by. "I suspect Maude and Alice have a relationship," she began, desperate to focus on a problem she at least had a chance of solving. "Something more than what she let on. She said that Alice came to her looking for work. But then why did Mr. Cartwright see her coming by the flat more than once? And why did she know so much about me if they were only neighborhood acquaintances?"

Will nodded slowly as he mulled this over. "It's certainly possible. But would that relate to Alice's disappearance?"

Phoebe let out a sigh and leaned her head back against the seat. "I don't know. But why bother to lie about it if it didn't matter?"

Will was silent for a moment. "Well, whatever it is, Maude will never tell you. That much seems clear. I doubt the Inquisition could pry the truth from such a tenacious woman."

Phoebe smiled a little. "I suppose she would have to be to survive in her world. I doubt I could."

Will narrowed his eyes slightly. "It almost sounds like you admire her."

"Perhaps I do, in a way. And she certainly made a good point about the school." Will shot her a questioning look. "We give these girls the kind of education we received, thinking it's part of some noble endeavor on our part. But their lives are so very different. What's the point of reading Shakespeare if you still can't find work?"

"Then do something about it," Will said. "But don't discount the work you're doing in the meantime. Things like literature, music, and art should be for everyone. Not everything has to be commodified."

"That sounds dangerously close to the teachings of Karl Marx, Your Grace," Phoebe said with a wry smile.

Will laughed. "Yes, well, I haven't entirely forgotten my more radical beliefs."

"I still remember the time you came to dinner and got into an argument with Father about the importance of men in positions of power publicly supporting workers' rights across industries."

The subtext being *men like him.*

Phoebe had long considered that evening to be an intellectual and physical awakening of sorts—and was one of the reasons why she had found his new life so distasteful. But oh how she had clung to the memory of a valiant young Will leaning across the table to meet Father's wall of condescension head-on with his razor-sharp insight.

The upper classes are only able to accumulate extreme wealth because there are so many others who earn far less. It isn't the natural order of things. It is the product of a deliberate system.

"There is no one quite so self-important as a young man who has just discovered a political theory," he said with a groan.

"No, you were wonderful," Phoebe insisted. "And what you were saying was true. You taught him something that night." Will let out a dismissive huff, but Phoebe would not relent. "You did. He won't invest in companies that don't allow their workers to unionize. Not all of the workers choose to, of course, but he makes it clear that if management hamper any attempts he will pull his funding."

Will looked dumbfounded. "Oh. Well, I'm very glad to hear that. Thank you for telling me," he added with a modest dip of his head that Phoebe could feel all the way down to her bones. God help her if he kept behaving this way.

As if on cue, Will gave her a penetrating look. "And yet, I got the impression that things are strained between you."

Phoebe let out a sigh. "They are, but that isn't anything new. He's never approved of my occupation. Thinks I'm wasting my time teaching when I could be helping him and Alex make more money."

Will's smile was rueful. "It's not just that, you know. Your sister can be quite egalitarian in regard to the businesses she chooses to fund."

Phoebe managed a reluctant nod. "Yes, I've heard it many times over: 'It's all about the idea.' But it's a business, not a charity, so they only invest in things that will turn a tidy profit."

"Fair point," Will acknowledged. "And you would rather they invested in schemes that improved society in some way?"

Phoebe shrugged. "Not exclusively. I understand the need to generate a profit. But it would be nice if they considered more than the monetary value of a project in their assessment."

Will appeared to mull this over. "Have you said this to your father? Or Alex?"

"No," Phoebe replied as the corner of her mouth curved up. "I've only just put it together here talking with you."

Though the memory of his kisses and caresses would stay with her until the day she died, it was these little moments that she treasured most.

Will returned her smile. "Perhaps you should."

A fierce bolt of longing tore through her and she had to turn away from him to regain her composure.

"I actually haven't even seen my father since he returned from New York," she began. "He's been busy squiring his new American friends around London. I think Alex is upset about it, though of course it's hard to tell."

Will snorted a laugh. "She *is* human, you know. Despite her efforts to appear otherwise."

Phoebe hesitated. "I suspect I hurt her quite badly as well, actually."

"Is this about your quarrel?"

Phoebe nodded. "I made some accusations about her and Father that weren't very fair," she said with a sigh. "I suppose I was being a little self-righteous."

"We all have our faults. It's what we do once they're pointed out to us that matters."

"Well put, Your Grace," Phoebe teased. Will rolled his eyes but there was no hiding the mirth in them. "What are you going to do about Lord Fairbanks?" she asked after a moment.

Will frowned in thought. "I'm not sure. Drafting a competing bill feels far too little now. He should be exposed as the hypocrite he is."

"As much as I agree with you," Phoebe began, "will it matter if he is surrounded by men who share the same secrets? 'Do as I say, not as I do,' etcetera."

"Perhaps not." Will rubbed his bearded chin thoughtfully. "But people like that can be quick to turn on each other at the first hint of blood in the water."

Phoebe leaned forward and placed her hand on his. "Then we must make sure you have an awfully big knife."

Fifteen

For a brief moment Will wondered if he should be concerned by how wildly attractive he found Phoebe's bloodlust, but instead he turned his hand over so their palms could touch. He held her gaze, waiting for the slightest sign of reticence on her part, but as he slowly curled each finger, Phoebe's lips parted and she began to breathe faster. He leaned in toward her and closed his eyes but just as he was about to kiss her, she pulled back.

"You didn't want to touch me."

Will's eyes fluttered open at the abrupt statement. "Pardon?"

"In the closet," she continued. "You kept trying to move away. You nearly took off your own head."

He huffed a laugh. "That's not—that wasn't why." In truth, he had been far more concerned that she would feel his erection and think him a fiend, as it was hardly the time *or* the place, but the idea of actually explaining that was rather embarrassing. "Surely you must know that I'm attracted to you, Phoebe," he said, grateful the dark carriage would hide his blush.

"I wasn't always . . . sure."

She then dipped her head shyly and his heart twisted a little at this admission. "Well, then let me make it absolutely clear,"

Will said as he tugged her onto his lap. His fingertips dug into the swaths of silk around her hips. "There. Does that help?"

They stared at one another in the shadowy light as the carriage swayed back and forth. Then, slowly, the corner of her mouth curved in an impish smile. "Very much so." Phoebe then slid a hand around his neck while her other grazed his jaw. "I do like the beard," she murmured.

Will shivered under her exploratory touch. "Perhaps I'll keep it, then."

Phoebe leaned closer, but just as their noses rubbed together, Will pulled back.

"Wait. There's something I need to say before we..."

Phoebe tilted her head in question. "All right."

"I haven't proposed to Lady Gwen, and I'm not going to."

"I know."

Will paused. "You—you do?"

"Freddie told me," she explained. "Well, just the bit about you not having proposed. I think even she lacks a direct line to your brain," Phoebe added with another one of those coy smiles he wanted to devour.

"Then I suppose I don't mind being the object of society gossip for once."

As Will moved to kiss her, this time Phoebe leaned back. "So...you are unattached then?"

He swallowed. "I am."

But I don't want to be.

The thought flared through him, but he couldn't manage to say the words. Phoebe's casual manner gave him pause. For all his wealth, power, and renown, Will found he was rather desperate. Desperate for her.

This time, when he moved to kiss her, she didn't resist. Will wrapped her in his arms as she melted under his lips, giving herself up to him.

Ever since he walked into that police station, Phoebe had dominated him: his thoughts, his actions, his whole bloody life. It was only during these stolen embraces with her that he felt remotely in control. And even that changed from one moment to the next.

She sighed against his mouth and Will grew rock hard. As he shifted in his seat, Phoebe responded by nestling deeper into his lap. His fingers tightened over her soft thighs and he had to stop himself from digging into her tender flesh. From marking her as his own like some boorish lout.

The carriage suddenly rocked to a halt and they jolted apart. For a moment they simply stared at one another in a daze as they both caught their breath. Will then managed to pull back the curtain and glance out onto the street.

"You're home." He didn't even try to hide his disappointment.

Though every part of him cried out in protest, Will would send her on her way. It was the right thing to do. The *honorable* thing.

Then Phoebe had to go and spoil it all.

"Would you like to come upstairs?" she asked. "My flatmate is away visiting family."

Will slowly turned to her as the blood roared in his ears. He swallowed hard at the innocent look in her eyes. Had he misread the question and did she simply mean to offer him some tea and not herself? Either way, he couldn't possibly accept.

"That is not a good idea."

"Why?"

"Because," he rasped. "I ... I'm afraid I won't be able to control myself."

There. A little brutal honesty to clear the air.

She nodded slowly, as if she was considering this frankly scandalous admission.

"Is that supposed to be a deterrent? Because it isn't working," she said with a seductive little smile that made it perfectly clear just what exactly was on offer. And made him forget time, space, and his own name.

"Phoebe." He tried to sound authoritative but it resembled more of a plea for mercy.

She responded by threading her fingers through his hair. "I know that you must go back to Mayfair to find your duchess, even if she won't be Lady Gwen. But I still want..." Will's breath caught at the partial admission. Then she let out a huff and threw up her hands in frustration. "I've tried ignoring it and failed miserably," she conceded. "So perhaps it's better to simply..."

"Explore it," he finished.

"Just for a night," she reasoned as she shifted her hips. *Deliberately.*

"You're quite ruthless," he said with a weak laugh, feeling like an untried lad again.

"Why thank you," Phoebe beamed before she turned serious. "What do you think?"

Will couldn't look away from her expectant gaze. He had certainly enjoyed dalliances before. Why should this be any different?

Because Alex would castrate him, for one.

And because you never once felt anything close *to this—and you haven't even bedded her yet.*

Yet.

Despite his very real and well-reasoned reservations, Will knew he wouldn't be able to resist her. Whatever she offered, he would take it. Gladly. Caution be damned. His ever-present responsibilities faded to the background when he was around her, replaced by a recklessness he hadn't felt in years. Or maybe it was selfishness. Or maybe it was simply the ghost of the man he could have been had the dukedom not fallen onto his shoulders.

Just for a night.

Surely two consenting adults could give in to their mutual attraction for a few hours. What did they possibly have to lose?

His heart beat loudly in objection, but Will brought his hand to her face and caressed her jaw. Phoebe let out the faintest shudder of breath and he pressed his thumb to her full bottom lip. Her reaction filled him with a dangerous kind of primal greed. He wanted more. He wanted it all.

"Will?" she prompted at his silence.

Will's gaze flickered to her eyes. He had been staring at her mouth.

"You deserve someone who can give you everything. Not just one night," he insisted in one last attempt at chivalry.

She rolled her eyes. "Well now you're just being patronizing. This *is* what I want."

A part of him was rather insulted that she didn't at least *wish* for more from him, even though it was next to impossible. "And a better man would tell you no."

Her mouth slowly curved in triumph. She knew she had him. "But?"

Will let out a frustrated sigh. "But it turns out I'm a bit of a bastard when it comes to you."

Phoebe laughed. "Such a silver tongue," she teased. "Take care, or else I may swoon."

Will returned her smile but couldn't manage an equally pithy response. For anything he said would likely be far too close to the truth.

Phoebe led Will up the back staircase to her flat. It was very late but she didn't dare risk bumping into her landlady, who lived on the first floor. Coming home with a man would get her thrown out on the street. She didn't think Will realized the precarious position she had put herself in, as she was doing an excellent job pretending like her heart wasn't in her throat. She had propositioned the duke of Ellis, and he had *accepted*. But no, she couldn't think of him like that. Tonight he was simply Will Margrave, the man who had once been the object of all her desires. And still was, apparently.

"Here we are," she murmured when they reached her front door.

As Phoebe moved to unlock it, she noticed her hand was trembling. She forced it to still and turned the key. If Will noticed, he didn't comment and simply followed her into the flat. Phoebe silently thanked herself for cleaning up earlier that day, though it was too dark to make out much beyond the threadbare sofa and small table in the common space.

"Come," she said as she reached for his hand and led him toward her room.

Marion's bedroom was closest to the front door, while Phoebe's was at the other side of the common room. She entered and moved to turn on the gas lamp by her bed, while Will hovered in the doorway. As the room filled with a warm orange glow, he looked around the space.

Phoebe was rather proud of her bedroom. She had decorated

it herself with things she bought with her own money. The bed-frame was secondhand brass and made up with a ruffled blanket she found at a Sunday market. She had haggled with the seller before they came to an agreement and she walked away feeling like she had found a trove of gold coins.

Will moved toward a small desk and chair in a corner of the room. Above it hung a corkboard decorated with bits and bobs of things she liked: cutouts from magazines, postcards from school friends, and a few old photos. As Will leaned in to take a closer look, Phoebe hugged her shoulders. She felt strangely exposed, though she was still fully clothed.

"I'd forgotten that day," he murmured after a moment and pointed to a photograph.

Phoebe moved next to him to see. It was a photo taken during a birthday party in Surrey with her sisters, Will, Cal, and the rest of the neighborhood children, though by then some of them had crossed over into adulthood. Will had already been at Oxford for a year and Alex would follow him to Lady Margaret Hall in the fall.

Phoebe stood shyly beside Will squinting in the midday sun with her body turned slightly toward him. Meanwhile, Will stared directly at the camera with a fist on his hip, full of youthful brag-gadocio. She had always treasured this photo, as it was the last time they had all been together. Now it felt like her heart was on display for anyone to see. And painfully obvious that she had been in love with him even then. She glanced nervously at Will. He continued to stare at it with a far-off look in his eyes. Then he slowly reached out and touched the edge of the photograph with great reverence, as if it were a relic of Christ.

"I found out about the dukedom the next morning," he said softly.

"Oh."

Phoebe could still remember the moment Will shared the news. She and Alex had been making paper fans for a picnic they were hosting in a few days. Phoebe insisted they all needed to be labeled, which was really just a poor excuse to write out Will's name. But Alex didn't question it. Phoebe could now see that was a gift on the part of her sister, who usually questioned everything. And then there was Will in their back garden telling them he was to be a duke. Phoebe thought he was joking at first, but then he said he was going to Derbyshire. *Tomorrow.*

He wouldn't be coming to the picnic.

He didn't need her silly fan.

And there was nothing she could do to stop it. *Any* of it.

A desperate sense of helplessness along with a pain so real and sharp crashed over her like a wave. Will already seemed so different, so out of reach, rattling on about all he would own one day without a thought to all he would leave behind. And Phoebe knew down to her bones that the newfound closeness they had been enjoying that summer could *never* grow into something more now.

She had been rude to him that afternoon, though she couldn't remember her exact words now, and hadn't even said a proper goodbye.

"I never wanted it," he said suddenly, and shook his head. Will turned to her, his dark eyes full of regret. "I don't mean to sound so pitiful. I know how lucky I am. But obviously it changed my life."

Mine too.

Yet here he was, despite all that had separated them. And he could be hers once again. For a little while at least.

"Only I...I didn't expect it," he added quietly.

But whoever could expect such a thing? Phoebe's heart clenched with sudden tenderness for that young man thrust into a position, and a world, he knew little about. "And then I had to leave home to go stay with the old duke who made no secret he thought me beneath his very notice, let alone the title," he said with a brittle laugh.

Phoebe placed a hand on his arm. "Will..."

"It's fine," he said, covering her hand with his own. "We found a way to rub along—eventually. And your father was quite helpful afterward in understanding the enormity of it all, especially the business dealings."

"Was he?" She'd had no idea.

Will nodded. "I know he always thought of me as a mouthy little upstart," he said with a smile. "But he was very good to me. I even still employ the secretary he recommended."

"I'm glad to hear that," Phoebe said as she took his hand. "I never really thought how it must have been for you," she admitted. "Especially being sent away. Cal was miserable for weeks afterwards."

And so was I.

Will bowed his head for a moment. "It was...different."

Phoebe stared into his eyes. There was far more he wasn't saying. She tried to think back on what she knew about the old duke, but her mind was a blank. It had been easier at the time to dismiss him completely rather than torture herself over the details of his new life. A life she couldn't really be a part of. Not in the way she wanted most.

And that still hadn't changed, had it? Her earlier bravado faded as Will slowly leaned toward her. This was a terrible idea. And yet, when he wrapped a hand around her waist to pull her closer, Phoebe followed. And when he leaned in to kiss her, she tilted her head back to meet him. And when their lips touched once again, she inhaled deeply, as if she had been holding her breath all these years and now, *now* could finally let go.

She thrust her hands into his thick locks and stood on her tiptoes while Will immediately embraced her. How was it that two people so very different from each other could fit together so perfectly? It felt like one of those incomprehensible equations she had never been able to solve. Or maybe his kisses simply hindered her ability to think properly—or at all. She found she didn't much mind at the moment.

After a few more kisses that syphoned off the last of her reason, Phoebe turned around so he could unbutton her dress, which he seemed to find amusing. Together they made quick work of the rest of her layers until she was down to only her paper-thin chemise and stockings. Then Will gently leaned her back onto the bed and sat down beside her. But as his hungry eyes roved over her body, Phoebe felt the instinctual urge to cover herself. Until he spoke.

"You are so lovely, Phoebe," he whispered as softly as a prayer.

His words should not have affected her as they did. This was supposed to be about pleasures of the flesh. But that mattered little to her heart, which thundered with joy. She had meant it earlier, about not always being certain of his attraction. Because how often did someone get exactly what they wished? It seemed like a dream. Something too perfect to be real. And eventually, she knew she would have to wake up.

"Kiss me," she replied. For she could take no more of his fawning gaze.

"If you'd like," he said with a wolfish smile.

That was a massive understatement.

As he took her mouth in a lush, deep kiss, his warm hands

pressed against her waist. It felt so much better without the layers of clothing between them, but she wanted more. She wanted to feel his fingertips dragging across her bare skin, touching her everywhere. She arched toward him and his hands immediately snaked down her body to ruck up the hem of her chemise.

She broke the kiss to let out an aching groan as his rough palms caressed her overheated skin. The thin fabric felt positively stifling, and Phoebe drew the hem up even higher. Will chuckled at her eagerness but didn't stop stroking her. Phoebe faintly thought it strange that his hands weren't perfectly smooth, but then all other thoughts fled her mind as he began to brush her nipple with the pad of his thumb through the fabric. He stared down at her with single-minded focus, watching for the slightest expression of regret, but he would not find it.

"Yes," she breathed and he answered by gently pinching it. Phoebe let out a surprised laugh. "Cheeky."

Will grinned and lightly kissed her mouth. "But you like it?"

"Very much," she panted as he continued to pluck her nipple.

"Good. And this?"

He put his lips on her other breast and Phoebe gasped as he swirled his tongue around her nipple before taking it into his mouth. She couldn't stop writhing in pleasure as he sucked her through the fabric. He pulled back for a moment and looked quite proud of himself, but given the wave of all-consuming pleasure building inside her, Phoebe decided he had earned the right.

Will then slid his hand leisurely down her body until he came to her drawers. They were plain cotton lawn. Perfectly serviceable. But for once, Phoebe wished she had worn something a little more...interesting.

"Sorry," she mumbled.

He glanced up as he released her other nipple from his lips. "Whatever for?" He began to run his finger along the seam at her waist, giving her a questioning look.

Phoebe's cheeks were burning, but she was the one who had brought it up. "They aren't very nice, is all," she said with a vague gesture toward her drawers.

She couldn't help imagining all the glamorous women he had bedded before, who probably had drawerfuls of lace and silk underthings. And he had traveled, hadn't he? Lord, what if he had slept with a *French* woman? Phoebe couldn't compete with that.

Will, unaware of her compounding worries, simply gave her an amused smile. "I assure you, your drawers are quite alluring." His finger then dipped beneath the waistband and skated over her skin.

"No, they aren't," she blurted out. Good lord, she was making a hash of this.

But the smile never left his face. "They are, because they belong to you." The slow, featherlight touch quickly grew torturous. The lower he stroked, the more sensitive she became until her hips began to shift in jerky movements, trying to chase the teasing sensation.

"Shall I continue?" he asked after an excruciating moment.

"*Yes,*" she practically shouted. To hell with the French woman. She needed more. *Now.* "And you're wearing far too many clothes."

Will flashed her another one of those wolfish grins. "Are you asking me to join you en deshabille?"

"Well, it seems only fair," she said coyly.

He let out a soft laugh. "Ever the egalitarian. How can I resist such a request?"

Oh, she liked that. *Very* much.

He stood to take off his jacket and waistcoat while Phoebe pulled her chemise over her head. Her earlier self-consciousness had now dissolved into a puddle of want. Nothing else mattered at the moment other than Will. He was momentarily distracted in his disrobement by her bared breasts until Phoebe cleared her throat. He then gave himself a shake before toeing off his shoes and stretching out on the bed beside her. There was barely room for the two of them, but Phoebe didn't care. She wanted him as close as possible.

"Is that better?" Will asked as he stared down at her with the kind of tenderness she had once dreamed of. Phoebe force herself to look away and began to run her finger up and down the length of his black braces.

"It is," she replied, attempting a blasé tone. "You may continue."

Will slid a finger beneath her chin and tilted her head up to meet his burning gaze. "Yes, Miss Atkinson," he murmured.

Phoebe's heart skipped several beats as Will pressed his mouth to hers while he found the slit in her drawers and brushed his fingers against her quim, gently at first, but then he slowly began to press more firmly. At the same time his kisses grew deeper and more insistent. When his tongue entered her mouth, Phoebe welcomed it with thrusts of her own. Her enthusiasm seemed to spur him on and he pressed the bundle of nerves above her mons harder and it ached with pleasure like never before. The double onslaught overwhelmed her senses until he was everywhere. She wanted to breathe only him, taste only him. Phoebe gripped Will harder, unable to stop the urgent cries building in her throat, and tugged his braces until his firm chest was pressed tight against her own. She never wanted this to end. But end it did.

Her release rocked through her suddenly, with little warning, and she nearly screamed against his mouth.

Will pulled back, looking surprised himself. "Are you...was that..."

"Incredible," she gasped, still catching her breath as the most delightful warmth flooded through every inch of her body.

He smiled, his eyes nearly black, and cupped her cheek. "I'm glad." Then he turned away and began looking around for something. As she was still basking in a haze of euphoria, it took Phoebe a moment to realize what he was doing.

She sat up and grabbed her crumpled chemise from his hands before throwing it across the room. Will gave her a bemused look but before he could say anything, she pressed against him.

"This isn't over yet. I want more. I want *you*."

"Phoebe..."

"Please, Will," she begged, shamelessly kissing his throat and nipping his earlobe. "I'm a boring little spinster schoolteacher, but let me have this. I know you'll make it good. I trust you."

He let out a pained groan then pulled back. She could see the torment in his gaze, a battle between desire and honor. Phoebe held her breath, unable to keep her desperate hope bottled up any longer. She wasn't sure she could survive his rejection. But then his eyes flashed with a sudden dark intensity and he leaned in close.

"Oh hell," he growled just before kissing her even harder. Phoebe smiled against his lips in triumph. She had won.

Sixteen

A *boring little spinster schoolteacher, my foot.*

Will knew he should stop, or at the very least, slow down, but every time he tried, Phoebe merely urged him onward with an inviting tilt of her hips or the urgent press of her fingers.

I know you'll make it good.

Good lord, how on earth was he supposed to resist that? He should have insisted she put her chemise back on. Perhaps then he would have been able to muster a shred of self-control. But now it was far too late. Phoebe slid his braces down one at a time and together they relieved him of his shirt. Will then stood up.

His hands stilled at the front of his trousers and he waited until Phoebe met his eyes. "You're sure?"

She gave an enthusiastic nod. "Completely."

Well, then.

Will let out a puff of breath and began to release the buttons. He felt Phoebe's heavy gaze tracking every movement and he fumbled more than once, as if he was the virgin here. His trousers puddled around his ankles and he stepped out of them, then returned to the bed in only his smallclothes. He took her in his arms and brushed a strand of hair back from her face, letting his fingers linger at her temple. Her eyes were bright and her cheeks flushed and dewy. She was the very picture of an eager bride on her wedding night. A sharp, sudden desire tore through him so hard his mouth went dry.

He cleared his throat and pushed aside those inconvenient feelings to ponder later. "We'll go slow." She began to protest but he held a finger to her lips. "It will be better for you this way."

She gave him a playful frown. "Your thoughtfulness is most irritating."

Will laughed and kissed her mouth, savoring her full bottom lip between his teeth. She arched into him as her curious fingers trailed down his back. Will moved to cup one of her breasts in his hand. She fit his palm perfectly, so soft and full. He gently squeezed and circled her nipple with his thumb, having already learned what she liked. She let out a gasping sigh and her fingers dug into his hip. God what he wouldn't give to explore every inch of her. To show her all the ways he could bring her pleasure. It would take years.

A lifetime.

But even if Will was tempted to do the impossible and throw his future over for her, Phoebe had made it perfectly clear she had no interest in being his duchess. He could understand that. It was a life of demands and duty, with limitations so very different from the one she had crafted for herself—and clearly loved. He didn't want to take that from her. So if this was all he could have, Will planned to make the most of it.

He moved away from her enticing mouth and kissed down the column of her neck, stopping to worry that sensitive spot at her collarbone he had discovered back at Fleur with his tongue. She let out a rewarding moan and he continued southward, taking the time to lavish each nipple with deep pulling kisses. Phoebe had begun writhing beneath him once again and her mewling cries grew more urgent under his touch. He pulled her drawers off in one smooth motion and then moved on to her stockings. A smile played on his lips as he rolled the economical material down one leg.

"What is it?" she demanded as she pulled the rest of the stocking off and Will set to work on the other.

"Nothing," Will said with an amused smile. He wasn't quite sure how to explain that he found her plain drawers and cotton stockings far more alluring than anything made of silk or lace, so he kissed her instead. Then he dragged a hand to her bare hip and was about to push her thighs apart when she skirted past him and caressed his erection. Will came to a shuddering stop as she continued to rub his aroused flesh.

"Phoebe," he gasped as she reached through the opening of his smallclothes and took him in hand. Her eyes had gone wide with wonder and her lips grew pinker.

"Stop stalling," she said in a breathy voice that made his balls tighten.

He pulled off his smallclothes and fit the head of his cock against her entrance. But the feel of her wet heat nearly overwhelmed him and he had to shut his eyes.

After a moment her hands flexed against his back.

"What are you doing?"

"Thinking about cricket," he mumbled by her ear.

She let out a startled laugh. "Now?"

"Yes," he said tightly. "Unless you want this to be over in less than a minute."

He felt her kiss his neck and smile against his skin. "I don't mind."

The tenderness in her words wrapped around his heart with such dangerous ease that Will gave up on recalling cricket statistics. No, better to get this over with. And safer.

He resumed his movements, making slow but steady strokes into her. At one point he felt Phoebe's entire body tighten and he cast her a wary look.

"Are you all right?"

Her eyes were squeezed shut but she nodded. "Yes. Don't stop now."

He began kissing her neck as he rubbed her nipple with his fingertips and felt her slowly melt. Only when her body began to loosen beneath him did he continue. Then he thrust fully into her and lost his breath. She instinctively raised her hips, angling him even deeper inside her and Will moaned her name, clenching the bedsheets so tightly he worried they would rip.

He felt her hand on his nape, stroking up into his hair. Will arched back into her touch and finally looked at her face. When her eyes fluttered open, it felt like taking a hard punch to the chest. Her lips, the deep flush of a summer rose, parted and she pulled him down for another hungry kiss.

He began to thrust harder, his movements growing faster and more careless as his release began to build. Finally he couldn't take any more of this strange, sensuous torture. Will pulled out from her welcoming heat and grabbed his smallclothes, as he would *not* spend on her sheets.

As a powerful release washed over him, he collapsed beside her. He then immediately pulled Phoebe into his arms. Just as he had suspected back in Maude's closet, her back melded perfectly to his front. But now he could allow himself to enjoy the sensation—at least for a little while. Phoebe let out a contented little sigh as she nestled deeper against his body. Will planted a kiss on the top of her head and together they lay in the near darkness, their heavy breaths filling the room. But instead of the relief that usually followed such activities, Will was left with a gnawing ache.

He wanted more.

He wanted the impossible.

And he was well and truly doomed.

Will was usually up at dawn, his mind already spinning with the tasks that lay before him. But today...today he did not want to wake up. He kept his eyes firmly shut against the midmorning sunshine streaming through the window and enjoyed the sensory pleasures of Phoebe's bed, which smelled of clean linen, warm skin, and love-making. He knew he was supposed to feel like a blackguard for taking her last night, but she had been so absolutely certain about what she had wanted. Who was he to question her?

No, he would not feel any regret. She had reached for him again in the early hours of the morning. Though they had both been in a sleepy haze, they followed the lead of their bodies, already primed for each other. Afterward he had fallen back asleep with his face buried in her hair and their heavy limbs tangled together. It was heaven. Will had never experienced the intoxicating combination of enthusiasm mixed with surprising moments of tenderness. He had felt more himself in bed with her, naked and wanting, than he had in many years. Will couldn't stop the smile pulling at his lips as his cock began to stiffen yet again. He was already going to hell. Why not make it worth it?

But as he reached an arm back to caress Phoebe's sleeping body, he found nothing but empty space. Will blinked and looked over. A piece of paper lay where Phoebe's head should have been. He sat up and grabbed the sheet. As his eyes scanned the irritatingly short note, his heart sank lower with each word.

I went to the school early to plan for the bazaar. Didn't want to wake you.

There were no sweet words, no mention of the earth-shattering night of mutual pleasure they had shared. Only a sterile explanation of where she had gone and not when she would return, as she expected him to leave. Christ, she hadn't even signed her *name*. But that was only sensible, given the risk she had taken with him. Even still, the tips of Will's ears began to burn. He felt like her embarrassing secret.

I find the idea that I would be any man's mistress appalling—let alone a duke's.

Right. He was an idiot. And of course *he* would want the only woman in England who saw his title as a drawback.

Will grimaced. Phoebe had said nothing about her desire going beyond the physical and they had both agreed it would be a one-off. It would be silly to feel used and yet…

What use would I have for a husband?

He threw back the covers and stood. *Enough.* Perhaps it had been a blessing to have awoken here alone. Then he wouldn't have had to face her dismissal whilst being naked. It was well past time for him to get the hell out of here. But first he needed to find his trousers.

After he had slunk out of her flat like a common burglar, Will returned to Mayfair and his fancy life of extreme privilege that held no interest for Phoebe Atkinson. He tried to put her out of his mind by spending the next few days occupied by the tedious work of running a dukedom. And yet, through it all, he could not stop picturing Phoebe at his shoulder like an avenging angel, making little remarks and pushing him to do more, more, *more*.

It was damned irritating—mostly because she was right.

So he gave raises to his steward and housekeeper at the estate in Derbyshire, doubled his annual contribution to a foundling home in Whitechapel, and approved a long overdue scheme to rebuild the roofs of some of his tenants' houses. With every stroke of his pen, Will could picture the old duke on his other shoulder, glowering in disapproval. He had believed in pushing every man, beast, and building in the duchy to the absolute limit, but he was dead. And despite his frequent protestations that Will had neither the brains nor the blood to be the duke, here he was, in the duke's house with the duke's title and all the entrenched power and privilege that came with it. So Will would do whatever he damn well wanted with his feeble mind and watered down blue blood. Or rather, whatever this imaginary Phoebe of his would like.

She also urged him to send a note to Lord Tavistock, asking him to lunch at his earliest convenience. Though he was a member of the opposition, they had been together at Oxford and Will liked him immensely. Whereas Will had all but given up his radical ideals when he became the duke, Tavistock had the advantage of being raised from birth to inherit a viscounty, and thus hadn't felt obligated to prove his suitability to anyone. That meant he had no qualms about embracing progress and publicly chastising his more narrow-minded peers every chance he got. It had earned him the moniker of "Tattling Tavistock" in some of the more ribald papers, but the viscount took it all in stride, for he believed in what he was doing down to the bone.

In short, Fairbanks found him absolutely appalling. But that only made Will more determined to seek him out. He wanted Tavistock's opinion on forming a bill that could actually gain support and put an end to the absolute drivel Fairbanks was spouting. Despite all he had learned at Fleur, Will couldn't entirely rid himself of the guilt he felt for going behind his mentor's back. But he also knew better than most that once the earl set his mind to something, he did not deviate for anyone. All the more reason to join forces with Tavistock.

In the middle of all this came an invitation from Alex, asking him to join the family for dinner on Friday. They hadn't seen each other since the meeting about the bazaar and had some catching up to do. Will asked the footman to wait, as he immediately responded with his acceptance, just as he would have even if he hadn't slept with Phoebe. But as the young man left the room with Will's response, a nagging sense of doubt began to prickle.

It could be horribly awkward if Phoebe was there. What if she assumed he came for her? He would look pathetic. But did he care? Will wasn't even sure anymore. Besides, her attendance seemed unlikely, given the current state of her relationship with Alex. And yet, despite the possibility of an awfully uncomfortable evening, Will couldn't help hoping she *would* be there.

He pressed his forehead to the surface of his desk and closed his eyes. He wasn't used to feeling so out of sorts. Maybe he was coming down with something.

Yes, a case of lovesickness.

He let out a groan at the thought. That was the last thing he needed.

"Your Grace?"

He had entirely forgotten his secretary was still in the room.

Will lifted his head and cleared his throat, as if nothing bizarre had just occurred. Mr. Flynn didn't look convinced. "Have you heard from Tavistock yet?"

The man blinked. "No, the note only went out an hour ago."

"Very good," Will said hurriedly as he pushed his chair back. "Do let me know when you hear from him. In the meantime, I think I'll take a turn about the garden. Get some fresh air, check on the roses. That sort of thing."

Mr. Flynn gave him an odd look, as if Will had just climbed onto his desk and burst into a rousing round of "God Save the Queen." Couldn't a man go look at his damned flowers? "Er... of course, Your Grace."

Will then lifted his chin and hurried from the room before he could say any more ridiculous things.

Phoebe gazed up at the front of Park House. It was a misty spring evening and every window glowed with warm, golden light while the sound of guests enjoying her parents' legendary hospitality could be heard from the pavement. Together, it created an invitingly cozy scene that anyone would long to be a part of and yet a little sigh escaped her. All she wanted was to fill her stomach and fall into bed. The last week had been exhausting, and to her increasing frustration she hadn't slept well since Will spent the night.

It had been cowardly of her to leave while he had still been asleep, but when she had slowly awoken that morning, like a winter fog lifting off the Serpentine, to find Will's warm body nestled beside her own, her heart had cried out to stay with him forever. And that alarming thought had spurred her to her feet.

Since then, she had made sure to stay as busy as possible, preparing for the bazaar and keeping her students on task. And yet, she had still thought of him every day. And every night when she climbed right back into that bed, where she would awake feeling a little more restless and raw each morning.

Though Phoebe had meant what she said about trusting him with her body, she hadn't taken into account her foolish little heart which had burst open for him anew during the night they had shared, and would now have to stitch itself back together once again.

It will.

It *must*.

For she refused to walk that well-trodden path once more. Of wanting what she could never have. So Phoebe was determined to avoid Will as much as possible, but that should be easy enough. They had gone how many years with barely a meeting? Phoebe couldn't remember. She *wouldn't*.

As she entered the house, Alex rose from a chair in the antechamber. She looked her usual stern self but wore a rich green evening gown with a high neckline trimmed in matching lace. A small bustle in a cascade of perfect folds unfurled with her movements, while her dark hair was arranged in an elegant chignon.

Phoebe removed her hat and then cocked her head. "Were you waiting for me?"

"The Americans are here," Alex grumbled in response and crossed her arms, which only emphasized the flattering cut of the gown.

Excellent tailoring, Phoebe observed with a flash of envy.

Alex always insisted she cared nothing for clothing, but that was easy when one possessed her striking natural beauty and a mother who studied fashion plates. Phoebe, still wearing her school clothes, suddenly felt like a hopeless dowd. *No*, she reminded herself. Her clothes were functional, not frivolous. Even still, she couldn't help one last longing glance at the dark emerald beading that ran along the hem of Alex's gown. Perhaps she should take up her mother's offer for an afternoon of shopping. Just for *one* nice dress, so she could stop borrowing ill-fitting gowns from Freddie...

"Did you hear me?"

Alex's sharp voice cut through her meandering thoughts. "Sorry, yes." Phoebe pursed her lips as she unbuttoned her coat and handed it to the waiting footman. "The Americans."

As they headed toward the formal drawing room, Alex filled her in. "They're horribly vulgar, which Father thinks is hilarious. Mother is appalled, but doing her best to be hospitable. The son is already infatuated with Freddie and she is encouraging him, of course."

Phoebe hummed in agreement. Freddie was a terrible flirt— not that anyone needed *more* reason to fall in love with her.

Alex then hesitated right before the drawing room entryway. "And I invited Will."

Phoebe nearly tripped over her own feet before she recovered. "Oh? That's nice," she croaked.

Alex watched her carefully, but otherwise her expression remained neutral. "Yes. Almost like old times, isn't it?"

Phoebe managed a weak hum of agreement. If Alex noticed her reticence, she did not comment on it and tugged Phoebe into the room. The guests all turned to them, but Phoebe kept her eyes on her father. She could not look at Will just yet.

Mr. Atkinson had always been a tall, hulking man with a heavy beard and a full head of hair. And though his figure had grown more portly with age and his hair had long gone gray, he was still a commanding presence in any room. As her mother often said with great fondness, he was the very picture of a lion in winter.

But as Phoebe well knew, a lion had sharp teeth.

"Hello, Father," she said as she rose on her tiptoes to kiss his bristly cheek. "How was your trip to New York?"

"Profitable," he grunted, then immediately turned to the older man beside him. "This is my middle daughter, Phoebe."

The elder man extended his hand. He was a head shorter than her father and his hair pure white, but his blue eyes twinkled with kindness. "Hank Ericson. A pleasure to meet you, dear."

Phoebe smiled as she shook his hand. "Good evening."

"And this is my son, Hank Junior," he added, gesturing to the younger man next to him. He was slightly taller and blandly handsome, with light blond hair, and blue eyes to match his father's. Hank Junior immediately stepped forward and took her hand with another firm shake. "The pleasure is all mine." Phoebe returned his rather forward grin even while the hairs on the back of her neck rose. One could never trust a man who smiled quite so much.

"And how are you enjoying London?"

"Well, it's no match for New York, of course," Hank Junior said with a shrug. "But it has its charms." His gaze then flitted to Freddie, who was by the hearth chatting with Will and wearing a periwinkle gown just as flattering as the one on Alex, though with a much lower neckline.

Phoebe could practically hear Alex trying not to roll her eyes.

"So, Miss Atkinson," Hank Junior began in an overfamiliar tone that had already begun to grate. "Do you work for your dear old dad too?"

"No, I—"

Her father barked a laugh. "Phoebe insists on working as a schoolteacher."

"And we are *all* very proud of her," her mother added with a smile before shooting her husband a chiding look.

"My grandmother was a schoolteacher before she married," Mr. Ericson said approvingly. "A damned hard job it was too. Good on you for doing your part."

Phoebe raised her eyebrows, both at the unexpected curse and the man's admiration. "Thank you."

"I think it's always better for young people to strike out on their own rather than ride on the family coattails into a position they aren't qualified for," Mr. Ericson added.

Alex stiffened beside her while Hank Junior simply rolled his eyes and took a sip of champagne. Phoebe looked at her father, waiting for him to respond to the obvious dig at Alex, but all he did was grunt.

"I assure you, no one in our family is riding on anything," Phoebe said with a dangerous smile. "Especially my sister."

Mr. Ericson's white eyebrows rose. "Oh, of course," he quickly amended as his cheeks turned red. Her father shot her a scowl that Phoebe pretended not to notice.

Will chose that moment to join them. He had shaved off the beard, she noted with a pang of disappointment.

"Good evening, Miss Phoebe," he said politely, as if he hadn't been in her bed only days ago. "You are looking well."

Phoebe swallowed hard as her heart tried to make an escape up her throat. "Thank you, Your Grace."

Hank Junior let out a laugh. "Is that what you're supposed to go by? I get all the rules about your fancy titles confused. In America every man is *mister*, unless you're in the service and have actually *done* something with yourself," he added with that smirk Phoebe was starting to hate.

Will tilted his head. "*Your Grace* is the formal address, yes, but seeing as we are all friends here, please call me Margrave."

Hank Junior grinned. "All right, Margrave it is then. Tell me, are you one of those broke fellows who has to marry one of our dollar princesses to fix the roof of your leaky castle?"

Will took a slow sip of his whiskey. "I am not," he replied, as if the offensive question was incredibly boring. "My predecessor was a forward-thinking fellow, not a broke one. While others refused to give up their bloated properties after grain prices went flat in the seventies, he sold off nearly everything that wasn't entailed and put the profits back into the duchy. The remaining estates are now self-supported."

Mr. Ericson raised an eyebrow. "Impressive."

"I am very lucky," Will acknowledged. "Most men in my position inherit titles that come with massive debts and crumbling estates. But even then, few are willing to make the changes necessary to survive. My father was a country barrister, not a duke, so I do not have the same attachment to the trappings of the aristocracy."

Hank Junior gave a thoughtful nod. "Interesting. I didn't know that could happen."

"Yes," Mrs. Atkinson said. "Will had no idea he was even in line to inherit. It was the most wonderful surprise," she added with a laugh.

Phoebe watched as Will's polite smile tightened slightly. She probably wouldn't have noticed the subtle change if she hadn't grown so familiar with his face these last weeks.

"My God," Mr. Ericson marveled. "How old were you?"

"Eighteen. It isn't a terribly common occurrence, but every now and then a man has a title dropped onto his lap," Will explained, that easy smile returning once again. "I also had the great fortune to know this clever lady here," he said as he raised his glass to Alex. "And she has helped me invest the dukedom's profits wisely."

Phoebe's chest burned with pleasure as Alex tilted her head. When she met Will's eyes this time, she couldn't help giving him a beaming smile.

"I understand you enjoy the theater, Mr. Ericson," Mrs. Atkinson chimed in. "Have you been to Covent Garden yet?"

The lady of the house continued to steer the conversation toward safer waters, until Munson announced dinner. Upon entering the dining room, Phoebe was stunned to find herself seated on her father's left side with Alex directly across from her.

She tried to catch her mother's eye as she headed to the other end of the table on Will's arm, but was pointedly ignored.

Phoebe hesitated a moment before taking her seat.

Into the frying pan, then.

Hank Junior was to her right, but the man was already preoccupied with Freddie to his right. Only one empty seat remained . . . Phoebe's breath caught as Will settled in next to Alex. He glanced over and their eyes met. Phoebe, having blatantly been caught staring at him, looked away only to find Father now eyeing her. He cleared his throat, then addressed Will.

"Haven't seen you at the club this week, Duke."

Ever since he inherited, Father only ever called Will "Duke." Phoebe now strongly suspected Will must hate it. How much he hid from the world behind that polite smile.

"I've been busy with something that has taken up a great deal of my time."

"Well, it's always good to be busy with business," her father replied. "Anything I'd be interested in?"

"No," he nearly barked, then gentled his tone. "That is, this was...personal."

Phoebe immediately looked down at the steaming bowl that had just been placed before her. No one had ever been so interested in cream of celery soup.

"Of course, of course," Father chuckled. "I've heard you're to marry the Fairbanks girl." The warm approval in his voice made Phoebe's stomach turn to ice.

Will choked a little on his water. "I'm afraid not," he said once he had recovered. "That is only gossip."

Phoebe couldn't help the soft sigh of relief that escaped her while Father frowned. "Hmm. The earl won't like that."

"Oh, leave him alone, Philip," Mother said from the other end of the table. "Lord knows no one approved of *you* when we married."

To this he let out a booming laugh. "And I think they've all eaten a sufficient amount of crow ever since, haven't they darling?" He then raised his glass. "To Mrs. Atkinson. The finest woman in London."

Phoebe raised her glass along with everyone else and once again she found herself ensnared by Will's dark gaze. She forced herself to look away and hoped her cheeks weren't as red as they felt.

It promised to be a long, long meal.

Seventeen

The first several courses passed pleasantly enough as Phoebe's mother deftly directed the conversation with the nimbleness of a well-seasoned hostess. Phoebe learned all about the Ericson's life in New York and their business. Every now and then she asked a question to keep things moving, while Alex only spoke to Will quietly, and Freddie was too busy giggling with Hank Junior. In other words, they each played their parts to perfection.

Things didn't take a turn until they were done with the lamb. And Will started it.

When there was a lull in the conversation, he caught Phoebe's eye and gave her a considering look. "How is the planning for the bazaar?"

Before Phoebe could even begin to answer, her father let out a snort.

"Don't tell me *you've* gotten dragged into that school nonsense."

"My dear," Phoebe's mother said to her husband in a cordial voice the family knew was a dire warning.

Will looked genuinely surprised by the comment. "I'd hardly call the education of young ladies 'nonsense,' sir."

"It is for that sort," her father muttered, ignoring the daggers in his wife's eyes. "They're better off spending their time earning coin for their families. Not dawdling the day away in a classroom."

Phoebe set down her fork and glared at her father. She was so blasted tired of this old argument. "Or perhaps their parents should be paid a higher wage, so their children don't need to work."

"Don't give me that look. *I* pay my employees well," he said, tapping a finger to his chest. "I'm only saying that if the poor are going to complain about the lack of food in their bellies, they should be doing all they can to earn more. And sending their daughters off to school is a waste. What are you even teaching them now? More Shakespeare?"

"That was last term," Phoebe said as calmly as she could. "It's Homer now."

Father scoffed and turned to Will. "See? What drivel."

"And yet it's good enough for the boys at Eton or Rugby or, heavens, the local grammar school, but not these girls?"

"*They* aren't complaining about a lack of food," her father responded with exasperation.

"Only because they had the good fortune to be born to a different social class." Phoebe had managed to keep her voice at a reasonable volume but she was nearly out of her seat now. If her father continued, she feared she might lunge across the table.

"I beg your pardon, sir, but Miss Atkinson has a point," Will said crisply. "One can hardly blame the problem of hunger on the education of girls. That is another issue entirely, and one that requires its own solution. I've seen the school for myself and am more than happy to support its mission, however frivolous you may find it."

He then met Phoebe's eyes across the table. "But while I can donate money to good causes, the work of people like your daughter is truly priceless. We owe them all a great debt."

Phoebe stared back at him in open-mouthed shock. No one had ever defended her so boldly before—nor challenged her father on her behalf.

But he merely narrowed his eyes at Will. "You've been to her school?"

"Yes," Alex added as she turned to him with great interest. "When was this, exactly?"

Will blinked at them and shot Phoebe a panicked look. She was about to say that he had come on a tour with his mother, which of course would only lead to *more* questions they couldn't answer, when they were saved by dessert. Or, more accurately, by Freddie.

As the footman placed the enormous apple charlotte on the table, she clapped her hands loudly and let out a delighted squeal. "Oh, my absolute favorite! Mother, you shouldn't have on my account."

"I didn't," she responded, raising a censorious eyebrow at her husband. "It also happens to be a favorite of our *guests*."

Father let out a grumble and slouched in his chair. He had been sufficiently put in his place—for now.

"Is it *really*?" Freddie asked Hank Junior, as if this was the most interesting thing she had ever heard in her life. "How funny!"

"Uh, yes." The young man sat forward with a start. "It is." He would not miss any chance to enjoy Freddie's attention.

"Tell me, do you have an apple orchard by that great big summer house of yours in—where was it again?"

"Newport. And, no. We don't have an orchard there."

But based on the regret in Hank Junior's tone, Phoebe would bet her entire salary the man would put one in before the year was up if it would lure Freddie there. She caught her sister's eye over his shoulder and sent her a grateful look, which she returned with a subtle wink. Sometimes Freddie's unrivaled ability to draw attention to herself was a gift.

After dessert was finished, it was decided that the ladies would not withdraw for tea, given the small size of their party. Instead, they all headed back to the drawing room.

Freddie insisted on playing piano for the room and recruited an eager Hank Junior to turn the pages, while Alex disappeared into a corner with a book. Phoebe's father was busy showing Mr. Ericson his collection of rare maps, while her mother directed a maid on the best spot to leave the tea cart. That left Phoebe and Will alone on the sofa.

"Thank you," she murmured.

"No need," he replied as he draped his arm across the back of the sofa. If she moved over just a little, his fingers could have grazed the nape of her neck. The mere thought of which caused the spot to tingle. "I support subjecting everyone to Homer. I had a schoolmaster who insisted we memorize the opening of *The Iliad* in Greek, no less. It's been nearly two decades and I still haven't recovered."

"How torturous," Phoebe teased.

"Besides," he said as he met her eyes. "Someone needs to challenge your father every now and then. Might as well be me."

Phoebe could only hold his gaze for a moment before she had to look away.

"Have you been well, though? In general, I mean," he added unnecessarily.

Was conversation always this awkward after you had seen someone naked?

"Yes, I'm fine. Busy."

"Business or personal?"

She laughed at the little quip but still couldn't look at his face. Not when he was this close to her. So she stared at his thighs instead. But no, that was a mistake. They seemed to strain against the fabric of his trousers. And now she knew just how well muscled they were. Phoebe shifted in place as she inadvertently recalled the memory of him vigorously thrusting into her. She cleared her throat and forced the inconvenient memory out of her mind, then glanced up to find Will staring at her with the very same heated intensity she had just been trying to forget.

She swallowed hard and his gaze followed the movement of her throat before lingering on her mouth.

To hell with awkwardness.

Phoebe gently bit her bottom lip and Will's fingers flexed against the sofa. When he met her eyes again, the heated look only deepened. Then he raised a playful chastising brow and Phoebe felt an answering throb between her legs. She shouldn't be thinking of such things when her own parents were just a few steps away. And yet it was the very illicitness that seemed to spur her on.

"Although," she rasped. "I've been having trouble sleeping."

"Have you now." Will's voice was deeper than ever.

Phoebe nodded. At some point she had leaned closer and so had he. "My bed has become terribly uncomfortable."

Will gave a slow shake of his head as he clicked his tongue and Phoebe nearly melted into the sofa. "What a shame. Something needs to be done about that."

Phoebe rolled her lips together in a desperate attempt to stave off the silly grin that threatened to ruin the moment. How was Will so good at keeping a straight face?

"Yes, I was hoping—"

"Here you are, my darling."

Phoebe nearly jumped out of her skin as her mother handed her a cup of tea. "Oh, thank you."

As she took it, her hand was trembling so hard that a little tea splashed onto the saucer. Luckily, her mother was too busy handing a cup to Will to notice.

For God's sake, get yourself together.

Phoebe inhaled deeply and recalled her first disastrous day at the school, which had culminated with a student putting a dead mouse in her desk drawer. She had never shrieked so loudly for so long. When her mother took a seat beside her, Phoebe was mostly recovered.

"I'm sorry about your father," she began. "He does mean well, you know. And Will, you were marvelous. I think you made an impression on him."

"It didn't look that way," Phoebe grumbled.

"No," her mother allowed. "But when you've been married as long as I have, you learn to see things others don't." Then she gave Phoebe a significant look before she rose. "Excuse me. I think I need to throw Alex's book into the hearth to get her to mingle."

"Just make sure it isn't a first edition," Phoebe managed to quip even as her cheeks heated.

Her mother pressed a hand to her chest in mock horror. "Never."

When she turned back to Will, he had removed his arm from the sofa and was taking a sip of tea, as if nothing untoward had ever occurred.

Phoebe couldn't help feeling a little disappointed. But that was silly, especially if her own mother had begun to pick up on this...this...whatever this was between them. After all, they couldn't possibly repeat the other night. She herself had insisted it could only happen once. And she'd meant it. Hadn't she?

Before she could examine her confounding feelings any further, Mother dragged Alex over and demanded she tell them about New York. After that, Phoebe tried to concentrate as Alex reluctantly recited her trip down to the most inconsequential detail. Phoebe's rebellious eyes drifted to Will every so often, but he did not look her way again for the rest of the evening.

As the party made their way to the front door to say their goodbyes, Phoebe's heart dragged behind her. The Ericsons left first and Hank Junior nearly fell down the front stairs because he was too busy staring back at Freddie.

"Goodness, you will be the death of that young man," their mother remarked to which Freddie just laughed.

Will then thanked her father and mother for their hospitality, wished Freddie a good night, and made a plan with Alex to meet up soon. When it was finally Phoebe's turn, he took her hand. "Always a pleasure to see you," he said, once again the very picture of the perfectly polite aristocrat.

"You as well," she replied, utterly failing to not hide her disappointment.

But as Will bent over her hand, his fingers tightened slightly. "Meet me in the greenhouse," he murmured. "Ten minutes."

Phoebe's breath caught, but before she could form a response he had already moved toward the door. She stared at his retreating back until Freddie interrupted.

"Why do you have your coat? Aren't you staying the night?"

"Oh you must, my dear," her mother insisted. "It's too late for you to go all that way."

Phoebe blinked. This was too easy. "All right."

"Shall we play cards?" Freddie asked.

Ten minutes.

"I'm actually quite tired. I think I'll just go to bed."

"Suit yourself," Freddie said with a shrug and moved on to find Alex, who had drifted back into the drawing room with their father.

"I'll send someone up to your room with fresh linens," her mother said.

"Don't bother the maids with that now," Phoebe said. "They have enough to do. I'll be fine. Good night. This was lovely." She pressed a kiss to her mother's cheek.

"Thank you for making an effort," her mother said as she gave her hand a squeeze. "It really does mean so much to me. And your father too."

Phoebe returned her smile and made her way up the staircase to her old bedroom. She would take just a few minutes to freshen up and then she would slip out to meet Will. It was as if she was living out a fantasy from her younger days. Only now she knew the reality was far, far better.

Will tapped his fingertip against a pane of glass as he waited in Mrs. Atkinson's greenhouse among her seedlings. The full moon glowing overhead provided just enough light for him to make out his surroundings. It was warm in here and smelled a bit loamy and there was potting soil on his shoes. Not exactly an ideal place for an assignation, but not the worst either.

If she even comes.

He crossed his arms only to start tapping his foot. Why was he so damned nervous anyway? Either Phoebe would meet him or not. And so what if she didn't? They had already slept together. It wasn't as though there was any mystery left there.

Liar.

Will let out a huff. Half the time when they were together she drove him absolutely mad. The other half he was simply mad with desire. He had only gotten the smallest taste these last few weeks, and Will needed more. He wanted to search every inch of Phoebe Atkinson, both in body and mind until he knew her soul like he knew his own.

And dammit, he ached for the chance even though the fallout would be hell. That was what this obsession had done to him. All those years spent examining every move, every thought, every feeling, of making the right alliances, the right friends, being seen in the right places with the right people to prove beyond a shadow of a doubt that he *was* good enough for his blasted title could be undone in an instant by a wild, reckless girl who didn't give a damn about *any* of it.

But at no point over these last weeks had Will actually tried to stop this mad mission of hers. He reprimanded, he scolded, he heartily disapproved, but never anything more beyond that. He had not gone to her parents, nor taken her away somewhere for safekeeping until she came to her senses. Nor had he gone to the authorities. Instead, he encouraged her. Accompanied her. Made *love* to her. Because he liked her relentless determination, even when it put him out of his mind with worry. And he liked who he was while in her company.

No, Will had made plenty of his own choices that led him to

this moment. And there were plenty more that would have led him somewhere else. But he alone decided to come to dinner this evening hoping to see her. And he was the one who had suggested this meeting. Phoebe may have lit the match, but Will held the wick. It was still up to him if the bomb would go off.

Someone tapped on the glass behind him and Will whirled around. His heart pounded harder as Phoebe flashed him a smile and entered. She had changed into a paper-thin ivory wrapper and held a small lamp in her hand. She wore a pair of matching slippers with no stockings and the lacy hem of her nightgown grazed her bare ankles, while her hair hung over her shoulder in a loose braid. Will's fingers twitched with the unholy urge to tug on it, so he shoved his hands in his trouser pockets. God, he was a wreck.

Phoebe breezed past him and set down the lamp on a worktable. "I didn't realize you had such an affinity for flowers," she said with a teasing gleam in her eye. "Mother will be delighted."

Will pushed away from the wall and walked toward her. He was supposed to return her remark with a quip of his own so they could parry a few times in their usual way.

But not tonight.

Will gripped her waist and pulled her against his chest. "Kiss me," he growled without any trace of embarrassment. This is what she had done to him: reduced him to pure animal need.

Phoebe's eyes flashed with surprise in the orange gaslight before softening into another smile edged with affection. "Very well."

She lifted on her tiptoes and pressed her lips to his mouth. It was a kiss of gentle exploration, of tender warmth—and nowhere near enough. After a few searching moments, Will snaked an arm around her waist and hauled her off her feet. He kissed her harder until her lips parted to welcome his demanding tongue. They didn't have time for tenderness. He needed to lose himself in her fire, her sharpness for what little time they were allotted.

She quickly took the lead and met his tongue stroke for stroke. Will grunted as she palmed his stiff cock through the straining fabric of his trousers and he broke the kiss with a gasping smile.

"You're quite ruthless, you know."

Phoebe chuckled and leaned closer. "Does that bother you?"

"Absolutely not. I wouldn't want you any other way."

Her eyes dimmed slightly just before she looked away. Will opened his mouth to question her reaction, but then she stroked him harder this time, with more urgency.

"Will," she whispered in a needy tone he had never heard from her before. Whatever thoughts, whatever self-recriminations faded until he could think of nothing but sating her.

He lifted Phoebe on top of the worktable without any finesse and tore open her wrapper. Her chest was heaving and he could make out the rosy tips of her hard nipples beneath the gossamer fabric of her nightgown. Phoebe began to undo the pearl buttons that started beneath her chin, but her trembling hands kept faltering.

She let out a few adorable curses and managed to expose the hollow at the base of her throat, but it wasn't nearly enough and her progress was far too slow.

Will brushed her hands aside and fingered the lacy neckline. "Is this important to you?"

She gave him a bemused look. "No?"

"Good," he muttered just before he ripped open the front of her nightgown.

Phoebe gaped up at him, but Will simply raised an eyebrow in challenge.

After a moment she dragged her hands through his hair and kissed him with renewed fervor. He then roughly grazed his lips along her jaw and down her throat as she let out a series of urgent cries. Will gently bit her exposed shoulder before nuzzling her décolletage. He paused at the hollow at the base of her throat and gave it a slow, lingering lick as Phoebe shivered beneath him.

"Will," she begged. "Please."

"Not yet. I feel like torturing myself a little more."

He fell to his knees like a weary pilgrim on the steps of a sanctum, ready to worship. Then he pushed up the fabric of her nightgown and spread her legs wide before burying his face between her thighs.

As he dragged his tongue along the seam of her quim, Phoebe let out a startled moan that Will wanted scorched inside his brain so that he might always remember the sound of her surrender. She dragged her fingers through his hair, pushing and tugging as if she wasn't sure whether to stop him or keep him there, but either way Will would not relent. Not until she was screaming his name whilst in the throes of unimaginable pleasure. Consequently, he did not have to wait very long.

Phoebe began to squirm beneath his hands, both relentless and wanting, chanting his name until it nearly lost all meaning and he knew it was time.

"Now come for me, my ruthless darling," Will said as he slowly eased a finger into her lush, pulsing channel. He was rewarded by a fierce tug on his scalp as Phoebe cried out for him.

After a few more moments spent wringing every last tremor from her, Will clambered to his feet. But Phoebe looked wilder than ever. Her eyes had taken on a feral sheen in the lamplight as she pushed his jacket off his shoulders.

"I need you," she gasped.

They were the sweetest words he could imagine hearing from her. This woman who made it a point of not needing anybody, especially not him. Will tossed his jacket on the floor and nearly ripped the buttons off his trousers in his eagerness. Just before he entered her, he paused. Phoebe's eyes were now bright with anticipation, but there was something else in her manner that caught his attention. This unspoken feeling of understanding that sprung between them so easily. She seemed perfectly at ease in his presence, even now. And, come to think of it, so did he. Will slowly drew out his erection, and Phoebe watched with rapt attention as he gave it a long, smooth tug.

She raised an eyebrow. "Are you teasing me?"

"No." Will smiled. "I just want to remember this. All of it."

Her gaze softened and she pulled him in for a long, searching kiss. As she dragged her fingers through his hair, Will swore he could feel the tenderness behind the motion, everything she would not say to him. Yet. But even tender feelings could not stave off the heat between them and soon they were once again desperate and gasping for each other.

Will fit himself at her entrance and slowly pushed inside.

"God, Phoebe," he rasped as she pressed a hand to his backside and urged him in even deeper. She responded by wrapping her legs around his waist and Will leaned forward, gripping the edge of the table with one hand while the other tangled in Phoebe's hair. He found the end of her braid and gave it a gentle tug until she leaned back, exposing her lovely breasts to him. Will took a nipple in his mouth and began to suck in time with his thrusts, which had quickly lost any sense of finesse. She let out another cry and arched beneath him. Will pounded into her harder as he felt her begin to clench around his aching cock. Somehow he had the wherewithal to swirl his thumb around the sensitive nub of her sex and she suddenly jerked against his chest, screaming his name into his shoulder. Will only lasted another few thrusts before he wrenched himself from her and spilled onto her bare thigh.

He let out a breathless laugh at the heady sensation that washed over him and then wrapped her in his arms. Phoebe, his wild, reckless love. How could he ever let her go?

Eighteen

Phoebe laid with Will across her mother's worktable in a sweaty tangle for what felt like an eternity until mutual bodily pain forced them apart. It was also growing late. If anyone caught her sneaking back into the house at this hour in this state, she was prepared with a number of explanations depending on the questioning party, but it was a situation she would still prefer to avoid altogether.

She did her best to button what remained of her ripped nightgown and knotted her wrapper at her waist. Will watched her closely as he righted his trousers and pulled on his discarded jacket. Phoebe could only manage to give him quick, sidelong looks. Now that they weren't acting on their basest urges, she didn't know what to do with herself. But it was Will's behavior that was most puzzling.

My ruthless darling.

Oh how her heart had soared and her belly clenched when he had said those words. And though she did quite like being called ruthless, she most certainly wasn't his darling. But did he truly want that? And, more importantly, did she?

"You're frowning. Is something wrong?"

Phoebe turned to Will and shook her head. "No. Nothing."

But the concerned expression didn't leave his face. "I'm sorry. I know you said before that it was supposed to be just one night."

"You needn't cast yourself as some villainous seducer," Phoebe replied with a lightness she didn't feel. "I came here willingly, didn't I?"

He smiled a little at that. "True."

She then swallowed hard. A part of her rather *did* wish he would seduce her. Then this might all be a little more straightforward. "I should go."

He began to say something, but then stopped. "All right," he finally said.

As Phoebe returned his searching look, the full weight of what they had just done collapsed onto her shoulders. She suddenly felt like a girl again, awkward and out of place like when she would intrude on him and Alex during one of their convoluted discussions about books she hadn't even heard of—let alone read.

"Good night, Will," she said shyly, as if she hadn't just made frantic, passionate love to him.

His brow furrowed, but he gave a short bow. "Good night, Phoebe," he replied, using the stiff, cordial tone that had haunted her for years.

Though she might have a hundred memories of him as the older boy next door with scraped knees and winning smile, he was still the duke of Ellis while she was a humble schoolteacher. All she could have now were these few stolen moments until they came to the inevitable end. Lady Gwen may not be his duchess, but he would find one soon enough. And if Phoebe wasn't careful, she would lose her stupid little heart all over again.

If you haven't already.

On that alarming thought she turned and sprinted toward the house.

After watching Phoebe bolt across the lawn to get away from him, Will slunk home. He should have been relaxed and ready for bed after performing such vigorous activities, but instead he felt more restless than ever. All he wanted was to lock himself in his study and brood over a glass of whiskey. Unfortunately, Higgins was still up and waiting for him in the entryway. That wasn't a good sign.

"Your Grace, Lord Fairbanks is here," his butler said apologetically. "He arrived an hour ago. I told him you were dining with the Atkinsons but he insisted on waiting for you."

Will cocked his head as he took in this information. "Did he give a reason for such an *untimely* visit?"

This had to be about Lady Gwen or the bill. Neither option was particularly appealing.

"No, Your Grace. He did ask for coffee though."

Will sighed. It would not be a short conversation then. "Thank you, Higgins. I can manage the rest. Good night."

Will gathered his thoughts as he made his way toward the study. Lady Gwen was a terrific girl, but they simply didn't suit. And Will could not support a bill that included any punitive measures. Both perfectly understandable reasons. The earl might object at first, but he would come around after more consideration. He must. For Will would not be moved on either issue.

He opened the door and found that Fairbanks had made himself quite comfortable in Will's favorite chair by the hearth. He had also moved on from the coffee and was enjoying a glass of Will's favorite whiskey. At his entrance, Fairbanks turned with a feline smile that sent a prickling sensation down Will's back and scattered his thoughts. It was quite the same way he had smiled at Maude just after he threatened her life.

"Ah. There you are."

Will managed a placid expression. "Good evening. To what do I owe the unexpected pleasure of your company?"

But the earl's smile merely grew at the pointed question. "You surprise me, William."

The prickling sensation increased. Fairbanks hadn't called him "William" since he became the duke. "I beg your pardon?"

"Have a seat first," Fairbanks said as he gestured to the chair across from him.

Will was too distracted to be annoyed at being given such a lordly direction in his *own* home. He sat down while Fairbanks casually swirled the amber liquid in his glass and watched him like a bird of prey. Will raised an eyebrow at the man's continued silence, but it had no effect. The earl seemed to enjoy making him wait. Will shifted his chair at the unsettling thought. What the devil was going *on* here? He was just about to ask, when the earl finally spoke.

"I confess," he began. "I've wondered a time or two about the nature of your relationship with Alexandra Atkinson. The woman is such a cold fish that I can't imagine anyone wanting to bed her unless they enjoy being glared at throughout the act. The middle sister though..." He paused to take a lingering sip while Will's heart ceased to beat. "A surprising choice. Rather mannish for my tastes. I'd have gone for Winifred, personally."

Will's throat had gone dry. "What are you talking about?" he rasped. "And think very carefully about the next words that come out of your mouth," he added with all the dukely hauteur he could muster.

Fairbanks gave him a pitying look. "Come now. Let's not play at that. I know she's your mistress."

Hot shame washed over him. All this time he had been so focused on protecting Phoebe from the perils of the world at large that he hadn't thought to protect her from himself.

"I've had a devil of a time trying to find a skeleton in your closet. I hadn't realized you took all that moral claptrap spouted by the old duke to heart." Fairbanks clucked his tongue. "But I finally found someone at Bow Street who had a very interesting tale to tell about you. I was certain he was mistaken at first, for why would the duke of Ellis dare show his face in such an establishment and for such a woman?" Will's jaw hardened. *Inspector Holland.* Apparently the man did have a price. "You must be quite smitten with the creature to behave so foolishly," the earl continued, his eyes now alight with interest. "I admit, I'm terribly curious to know what she has done to earn such devotion from you. Or is it merely the thrill of ruining an innocent young lady?" The earl then let out a knowing little laugh that made Will's blood curdle. "I've done that a time or two myself, and it is an unrivaled pleasure to be sure."

"You are a disgrace," Will spat. "I would never behave so abominably."

But the earl merely shrugged off the insult. "And yet, your actions paint a much different picture."

Will dug his nails into the heavy fabric of the armrest. "What do you want?" he said coldly. "For me to marry Lady Gwen?"

Fairbanks looked genuinely surprised by the question. "Oh, heavens. I don't think she would have you now even if you asked.

No, my daughter is much too prideful. She was willing to overlook you being a common barrister's son in order to become a duchess, but she will certainly not abide being second in your heart to anyone, let alone a woman so *very* far beneath her. Though I suppose it shouldn't be so surprising that someone with your upbringing would still retain such plebian tastes."

Will gripped the armrest to keep from lunging at him.

"No," the earl continued, unaware of Will's violent thoughts. "You'll need to find some other girl. Though I imagine the pickings will be quite slim when I'm done with you."

"Explain yourself," Will barked. He had enough of the man's insinuations, but the smug expression never left the earl's face.

"Even you won't be able to recover quite so easily from ruining a spinster schoolteacher. Did you know I own a stake in the *London Daily*? It's a terrible rag, but this is just the type of story with mass appeal. The perfect duke leading a seedy double life and dragging a promising young woman down into the muck with him."

"I've done nothing of the sort," Will protested.

"Oh, I highly doubt that. But it won't matter either way. There's enough grains of truth to keep the story in print for the next year, at least."

Will gritted his teeth and steadied his breathing so he wouldn't throttle that smug look off the man's face. "Name your price then," he finally said.

"Your support for my bill. As it is," Fairbanks added.

Of course.

"But you will keep away from Miss Atkinson?"

"Yes, though I should tell you that she remains in a perilous position, especially now that my source knows what his information is worth. If you *really* want to protect her reputation, there is only one thing you can do."

Will gave a stiff nod. *Marriage.*

"It would still be a minor scandal, naturally," Fairbanks continued. "I can't think of a woman less suitable to be a duchess, but then I suppose the duchy can weather another blow. It's survived you, after all. And I'm sure Atkinson will give her a generous dowry, so at least you will get some coin out of it."

"I don't care about that," Will snapped.

Fairbanks gave him an amused look but did not press further. Instead, he finished the last drop of whiskey in his glass and stood. "Allow me to be the first to offer my felicitations, then. I will see you in Parliament."

Will didn't bother to watch Fairbanks leave. When he was finally alone, he emptied the rest of the silver coffeepot into a cup and swallowed the bitter dregs. It would be a late night, and he had a hell of a problem to solve.

When Phoebe awoke the next morning, she blinked in sleepy confusion. It took her a moment to remember that, despite her surroundings, she was not a girl still living under her parents' roof, but a grown woman—one who had enjoyed a passionate tryst in her mother's greenhouse the previous evening. And though that had been a fine excuse for spending the night here, it was time to return to her normal life. Which most certainly did not include illicit liaisons with terribly handsome men. Just as Phoebe's pulse began to race at the memory of Will's warm hands gliding over her skin, she sat up with a start and threw off the covers only to immediately draw them back when she saw the sorry state of her nightgown.

"Good heavens," she muttered. Thank goodness the maids weren't about yet, for she would have a devil of a time trying to explain *that*. Fortunately, it was still quite early. Phoebe was hardly in the mood to speak with anyone, but her parents wouldn't be up for hours and she intended to be long gone by then. Phoebe quickly washed, dressed, and gathered her things, then crept down the hallway. The house was only just beginning to stir and she had nearly made it to the entryway when Alex suddenly came charging out of the library.

Of course her sister was up with the dawn.

Alex came to an abrupt stop when she spotted her. "Oh. Hello." She then nodded to the satchel in her hand. "Leaving already?"

Phoebe lifted her chin. "I've things I need to do. For the bazaar."

"I see." But her sister didn't look convinced. "I don't suppose you know anything about the light that was on in the greenhouse very late last night."

Blasted Alex. Did she *ever* sleep?

"No," Phoebe said with remarkable calm. "I do not."

Alex raised an eyebrow in suspicion. "All right. But if you do happen to recall anything, you can tell me," she said with surprising gentleness, though her thorny expression remained unchanged.

"Oh," Phoebe bleated. "Thank you."

"Have a good day," Alex said with a stiff nod as she swept past her.

Phoebe stared at her sister's retreating back. For a moment she was sorely tempted to chase after Alex and tell her everything, but then she turned down the hall and vanished from sight.

Once Phoebe was outside on the pavement, she let out a breath.

That had been much too close. And while it was one thing for Alex to suspect something, Phoebe would be hard-pressed to explain the situation with Will to her mother. Or, dear God, her *father*. They would need to be much more careful.

Not that it will happen again.

But Phoebe wasn't as quick to dismiss the thought as usual. Last night had been different. It wasn't simply curiosity getting the best of her in a heated moment. No, this was planned. And she had gone to Will with clear intentions that could not be explained away so easily.

My ruthless darling.

She rubbed her chest, though the ache his words caused was not physical, and let out a silent curse at the fates that had conspired to make him a *duke*, of all things. For a girl like her, he may as well be a fairy king. He belonged to another realm. One that she could only visit. Phoebe then headed toward the main road to find a hackney that would take her away from this enchanted land of lords and ladies and greenhouse trysts.

Though her life may not always be easy, it was hers. The misplaced pity and doubtful remarks she had endured from friends and family had only fueled her determination to succeed, and never had she wavered. Had never even felt *tempted* to stray from the odd little path she had chosen for herself. Until now. Until Will. But belonging to someone would mean giving up her hard-won independence—especially to a man like him, to say nothing of the social obligations that came with being a duchess. Goodness, she would have to go to *court*. The very thought of spending the rest of her life traipsing from one ball to the next while enduring the ton's endless disapproval was enough to make her skin crawl.

No. This was what she *wanted*. What she had *fought* for.

So then why did she feel so bloody confused?

Once she was home Phoebe took a much-needed nap in her own bed. She fell into a deep, dreamless sleep. When she finally awoke with bleary eyes and dry lips, it was afternoon. Marion had gone out to do some shopping, leaving Phoebe alone in the flat, so she took her time making a cup of tea to clear the cobwebs from her mind. She had just taken the first restorative sip when someone rang the bell. Phoebe glanced out the window and a messenger boy waved from the street below.

Phoebe grumbled all the way down the stairs and then all the way back up after she paid the boy. She finally sat back down to her tea and absently glancing over the note. But she paused mid-sip as her woolly brain surged to life. She read the note again more carefully and the contents revived her far more than her tea. She gulped the rest down, dribbling some on her chin in the process, then gathered her hat and coat. There wasn't time to fix her hair. Even if she hurried, she would only just make it.

Nineteen

The music hall was mostly deserted at this hour, but in another it would start to fill with patrons. The barman was polishing tables and gave Phoebe a nod. Then he jerked his chin toward the stage, where Maude was chatting with the piano player but her sharp eyes immediately noticed Phoebe.

"Been following me again, have you?" she called out.

"No, I paid the barman to tell me the next time you were here," Phoebe explained as she approached.

Maude looked reluctantly impressed. "Spending your pennies on me? I'm flattered," she mocked before addressing the barman. "But I'll have words with *you* later."

"Don't be too harsh with him. I was very persistent. Alice is important to me. And I think she is to you as well," Phoebe added softly.

Maude's lips pursed as she cast a look around the music hall. "Not here." She then signaled for Phoebe to follow her and they slipped out a back entrance into an alleyway. Maude began to pace while Phoebe waited patiently.

Then she stopped short and shot her a glare. "You won't give up, will you?"

Phoebe gave her an apologetic smile. "I can be quite tenacious. I assume she is a relation of yours. Perhaps...a sister?"

She had been mulling over the possibilities since Fleur, but it was her brief exchange with Alex that morning that had been the most illuminating. There weren't many people who would go to the kind of lengths Maude obviously had for Alice, but a sister would.

She heaved a sigh and leaned back against the brick wall. "What gave me away?"

"It was more of a suspicion," Phoebe said with a shrug. "The way you talked about her, I could tell it was personal for you. I've two sisters of my own and we'd do anything for each other—when we aren't at the other's throats, that is."

Maude hummed in agreement. "Sounds about right."

"Are you protecting her from Fairbanks?" Phoebe then raised her hands in supplication as Maude gave her a hard look. "I won't say anything. I promise you. He is certainly no friend of mine."

Maude crossed her arms as she considered this. "I told him she ran off without telling me and I didn't know where," she began. "He still suspects something, though. He's a sneaky bastard, but he won't find her."

Phoebe recalled the dark look in the earl's eyes the other night: *Only because I can't prove it.*

They had been speaking of Alice's disappearance, and his anger was palpable. But the surety in Maude's voice was a comfort. "How did you meet him?"

The woman huffed and stared past her. "A girl like you wouldn't understand." Then she glared at Phoebe. "Not that I'm looking for anyone's pity."

"No, of course not," Phoebe replied. "I'm only trying to understand the situation. Perhaps then I can be more helpful to any students who find themselves in similar positions."

That seemed to soften something in Maude. She glanced down and scraped her booted foot along the ground. "I suppose. If it could help someone else. Some other girl like Alice. There are so many," she added bleakly. Phoebe nodded in agreement. Maude was then quiet for so long, Phoebe thought she had changed her mind. But then she began: "Alice and I have different fathers. Minc was gone as soon as my ma told him she was expecting, but Alice's da was different. Stephen Clarke was a good man. He treated me like his own. Better than my own mother ever did."

Phoebe's stomach tightened at the sorrow in her voice. "What happened to him?"

"Accident. His arm got caught in some machinery he was trying to fix at the factory where he worked. Bled out on the floor. Never had a chance."

Phoebe inhaled a shuddering breath. "I am so very sorry."

Maude's jaw tightened. "It was pure negligence on the owner's part. Everyone knew. The machine was old and needed to be replaced but why do that when you can have a bloke stuff his hand into the gear shaft twice a day. If I had been the age I am now, I'd have done everything possible to get him before a magistrate. There were witnesses. We had a case. But my ma didn't know anything about that. She was in such a state afterward. Thought the owner was a gentleman because he paid for the funeral and sent over a basket of oranges. As if that could replace a whole person." Maude's voice broke. "I still won't touch the damn things. Ever."

"How old were you when this happened?"

"Ten or so. My mother had to go back to work as a seamstress, so I left school to care for Alice. We carried on like that for a few years until I found work as a maid for a man called Dr. Langtree. It was such a relief. Mother's eyes were starting to go by then and she was losing her speed. That meant less work, less money, and Alice was sickly as a child. I'm not sure if she told you. She never complained, sweet thing, but we nearly lost her more than once." Maude swallowed hard and her bottom lip quivered for a brief moment until she mastered it.

"Anyway, all that's to say I felt like the luckiest girl when I got the position. And in a *doctor's* home, no less." Maude let out a dry laugh. "We had no idea the man was a quack. He provided all sorts of treatments to toffs with too much money and no sense, so there were always gentlemen hanging about. But I quickly realized it was no ordinary household. I'd certainly never heard of maids who danced on tables in their petticoats, nor any who were encouraged to go to bed with houseguests. I tried to come home the first week, but my mother sent me right back. The money was too good."

Phoebe did her best to hide her shock, as if she heard such sordid things every day. "And you met Fairbanks at this house?"

Maude shook her head. "The earl is many things, but he is not one for quacks. The doctor would loan out his maids to friends. I was sent to a bachelor's country house party. We met there. I was already well ruined by then. Becoming his mistress was a great step up in the world for a chit like me, though I couldn't convince my mother of that," she added with a bitter laugh. "She could tell her friends that I was a doctor's maid, but she couldn't tell them I was an earl's mistress. Even she had some standards, I suppose. And Alice was older by then and becoming more aware of the world. Ma didn't want me hanging around, influencing the *good* daughter, so she disowned me. Though she had no issue living in the flat I got for her."

"Fairbanks owns the building, doesn't he?" Phoebe said as the pieces fell into place. "*And* the music hall."

Maude nodded. "When our mother passed, I started visiting Alice again. The poor thing was lonely and needed help. She told me about the school, and you, and your little plan to send her to secretarial school. She was so excited about the idea and I—I got caught up in it. I wanted to help her. To prove that I hadn't thrown my life away like Mother said," she said bitterly. "But in my great wisdom, I brought her to meet Lord Fairbanks. By then our arrangement was over and instead I was helping him with a new venture."

"Fleur?"

"I keep watch over the girls, make sure they're being treated well. That sort of thing. And I'm damn good at it. I thought if Fairbanks saw how smart Alice was, he would pay for her schooling. But then I saw the way he looked at her, the questions he asked, the way he made her blush...and all it did was remind me of how he behaved the first time we met. Then he told me what he wanted with her, and I couldn't let that happen. So I sent her outside the city as soon as I could to stay with an old friend of mine. It was only supposed to be for a little while, until he moved on to someone else, but then things became...more complicated."

"Mr. Felton," Phoebe answered.

Maude gave her a solemn nod. "I went back to the flat to get some of Alice's things and he confronted me. Said he followed us the day before and would tell Fairbanks where Alice was unless I paid him for his silence." Maude's hand tightened in a fist. "He'd always been a snake. He'd sell out his own mother for a bottle of gin if he could."

"What did you do?"

"Told him I'd pay, of course. What else could I do?" She glanced away. "But when I came back later that evening with the money, he took it and demanded even more. I realized then that it would never end. That the bastard would bleed me until I was dry. And I had nowhere else to bring Alice, especially if I was paying him to keep quiet." She looked up and Phoebe's mouth went dry at the starkness in her eyes. "It was an accident," Maude explained. "He had been drinking, of course, and started pawing at me, thinking he could have a tumble as well. But I refused. We began to struggle and I shoved him the first chance I got as hard as I could."

"Then he fell back and hit his head," Phoebe supplied as she recalled the way the body had been positioned.

"Girls like me know how to defend themselves," Maude said coldly. "I've not killed anyone before, but I've certainly had to knock a fellow about now and then. He was so drunk he didn't even try to catch himself. And with a blow to the head like that, he was gone for as soon as he hit the ground. But I won't regret it. He was a horrible man. Caused nothing but pain during his life. And I had to protect Alice. I'd do it again if needed," she added as she lifted her chin.

"I'm not judging you," Phoebe said quickly.

Maude didn't look convinced. "Aren't you?"

"I've had my own encounters with Mr. Felton."

"So I've heard. Detective Inspector Holland," she explained at Phoebe's confused look. "He and I have discussed you and your *friend*. I was shocked when Holland said he was a duke. I've seen a few in my time and none of them act like he does. Don't look like he does either," she added with a lifted eyebrow.

Phoebe blushed and changed the subject. "I didn't realize you and the inspector knew each other."

"Since he was a young constable. He's a good sort. One of the few honest men in the Yard—and the only reason I'm telling you any of this."

"Then, he knows...everything?"

"I went to him as soon as I knew Felton was dead." Maude gave her a cryptic look. "The law would have seen me hang for defending myself. Holland promised he would take care of it. But he hadn't counted on you and your nosy duke."

He isn't my duke.

Phoebe swallowed the automatic rejoinder. "I suppose I should thank him then," she replied instead. "He's done more to keep me out of trouble than I realized."

Maude flashed her a wry smile. "I'm sure he would appreciate that. He was getting tired of you haranguing him over Alice and begged me to tell you the truth."

"And you listened?"

Maude shrugged. "He's a good judge of character. So, then. Now that you have your answer, will you leave me be?"

"Yes," Phoebe began. "But I've been giving a lot of thought to what you said before about not teaching our students the skills they need. And I want to do more to help."

Maude cocked her head. "Is that so?" Her tone may have been skeptical, but she couldn't hide the glimmer of interest in her eyes.

"I'd very much appreciate your input," Phoebe continued. "If you're willing to give it."

The woman was too shocked to hide it. "You want *my* help?"

"You know this area better than I do," Phoebe explained. "And understand what these girls are up against. What they need to succeed."

Maude chewed her bottom lip. "Can I think about it?"

"Of course." Phoebe then hesitated. "There's something else you should know, though I'm afraid it may harm your working relationship with Lord Fairbanks."

"It wouldn't be the first time, believe me," Maude said with exasperation. "What's he done now?"

"He is proposing a bill that aims to close the brothels, and those owned by women will be targeted first. Any violators will be thrown in prison. The rest will be sent to the workhouse."

"That bastard," she bit off. "I *told* him those girls will just end up on the street."

"I don't think he cares if it helps Fleur," Phoebe said. "I know he hides his stake in the club. But if you could give me evidence that proves he is connected to it financially, I can get it in the right hands. Exposing him publicly might be the only way to stop this bill."

Maude's eyes filled with determination. "I'll try." She then glanced behind Phoebe. "You should go. This place will fill up soon."

"All right." Phoebe then stuck out her hand. "Thank you for trusting me."

Maude eyed her for a moment before shaking it. "I suppose Alice was right about you," she admitted before heading toward the music hall. But just as she reached the back entrance, she turned back. "Oh, and Miss Atkinson?" Phoebe cocked her head. "Expect to hear from her soon," Maude said with a small smile, then disappeared through the door.

Twenty

*O*nce Maude left, Phoebe decided to head over to the police station as it wasn't too far. When she entered Detective Inspector Holland's office, the man looked even grumpier than usual.

"Ah, Miss Atkinson," he said, barely looking up from the file in front of him. "Have you come to scold me as well?"

"Beg pardon?" Phoebe asked as she took the seat he gestured to.

"You've just missed the duke reading me the riot act."

"I don't understand."

He smacked the file down and crossed his arms before fixing her with a formidable glare. "It seems that someone earned a very handsome sum for discussing your arrest with Lord Fairbanks—and he assumed that someone was *me*."

Phoebe's stomach clenched. It was distressing to think of the earl knowing *anything* about her, especially her connection to Will. But why had he sought out such information in the first place? Was Fairbanks sour over Will's rejection of his daughter and looking for a way to force his hand? Given what Maude had told her about the earl, he would stop at nothing to get what he wanted and use any means available.

The inspector loudly cleared his throat and Phoebe snapped to attention.

"I'm very sorry, Inspector," she said with genuine remorse even while the worries compounded in her mind.

He softened ever so slightly at her apology. "No matter. I set the duke straight," he grumbled. "And made it clear that I would uncover the leak. But in the meantime, I don't think it's a good idea for you to be here."

Phoebe nodded. "I only came to thank you. I've just spoken with Maude, and I'm sorry I caused such a bother over Alice."

There was a slight twinkle in the man's deep blue eyes. "Not necessary," he said. "You were rightly worried about her. I'm only sorry I couldn't say more, but I had made a promise to her sister."

"Understood."

"Now, as much as I enjoy our little chats, I suggest you head out through the rear entrance before anyone else sees you."

Phoebe stood and headed for the door. Then she turned back. "Was the duke *really* cross?"

Inspector Holland glanced up from the file in his hands and lifted an eyebrow. "Absolutely livid."

As Phoebe returned home, the uneasy feeling lingered though she was fairly confident the earl couldn't know the full truth about her dalliance with Will. But perhaps he had learned enough to hurt his marriage prospects. As much as she didn't like the idea of Will marrying some fresh-faced debutante, she didn't want to be responsible for any difficulties either.

Phoebe was so lost in thought as she entered the flat that she barely noticed Marion until she was standing right before her with an odd look on her face.

"Where have you been?" But before Phoebe could respond, she tugged her aside. "That *man* is here," she whispered. "The duke."

"What?" Phoebe craned her neck but there was no sign of Will.

"He showed up an hour ago and insisted on waiting until you came back." Marion rolled her eyes. "Then I thought he was going to put a hole in the floor with his pacing, so I finally told him to go in your room or else wait on the street."

Despite the nerves fluttering inside her, Phoebe couldn't help smiling at the thought of Marion banishing Will from her presence. "I see."

Most women might look at least a little chagrinned at chastising a duke, but not Marion. "Do you know *why* he's here?"

Phoebe let out a sigh. "There's been a...a misunderstanding of sorts." She didn't know what else to call it. "I'll speak to him."

Her friend's gaze turned wary. "Should I leave?"

"Not unless you want to. I don't think this will take long," she murmured.

"Is everything all right?" Marion asked gently.

Phoebe shook her head. "Not really. But it will be."

I hope.

Marion gave her a comforting pat and left Phoebe to her task. Will was still pacing in the tiny space between her bed and wardrobe. His hands were clasped tightly behind his back and his head was bent down, as if he was deep in thought. She had never seen him look so agitated. Not even when he showed up at Bow Street. Her chest ached at the memory. How much had changed between them since that afternoon. How much *everything* had changed. Phoebe took a steadying breath but her racing heart would not heel. She had effectively lost all control the moment he entered Inspector Holland's office. She was a fool to have ever thought otherwise.

And you won't get it back this time.

As soon as Phoebe stepped into the room, his head immediately snapped up and he halted.

"Where the *hell* have you been?" His scowl nailed her to the spot, but it could not hide the worry in his eyes.

Phoebe closed the door behind her. "I met with Maude," she said calmly.

This appeared to only irritate him further. "Phoebe, you need to stay away from her—"

"She's Alice's sister."

That caught him by surprise as his scowl softened, but only for a moment. "Then where is she?"

"Maude sent her away to keep her safe from Fairbanks," Phoebe explained.

"You can't just take her at her word," Will countered. "A woman like that is used to manipulating people."

"Perhaps, but Inspector Holland vouched for her. He's known everything from the beginning."

Will's dark gaze flashed. "You've seen Holland?"

"Right after you, apparently."

He exhaled. "Then you know why I'm here." At Phoebe's nod, he put his hands on his hips. "Obviously this isn't an ideal situation," Will continued. "But I've gone through every alternative and I think it's best if we see your father directly. I should be able to put a notice in the papers for the end of the week. Do you have a preference for the church? Personally, I'm not keen on a large society affair, but if we had it at St. George's that may effectively silence the rumors that will no doubt spread once the engagement announcement is printed."

Phoebe blinked. "Are you talking about...a wedding?"

"Yes," Will said impatiently. "Ours."

Phoebe didn't consider herself a particularly romantic person, but goodness, he hadn't even *asked* her. "Oh," she managed to say. Her lips suddenly felt numb.

Will crossed his arms. "Did the inspector not inform you that Fairbanks learned of your arrest?"

Lord, how she hated the return of this aloof, condescending manner of his. Phoebe mirrored his stance. "No, he did."

Will raised a haughty eyebrow. "Well, you seem awfully unconcerned for a girl on the verge of public ruination."

Phoebe nearly reared back. *A girl?* He was acting as if she was some simpleminded child.

Or just Alex's annoying little sister.

Her jaw tightened at the ugly thought and the all too familiar feelings that accompanied it. "And yet I don't recall you objecting when the ruination was private," she shot back and was pleased to see him wince a little. "I am not unconcerned. I just never considered marriage to *you* as the solution," she answered honestly.

His eyes narrowed. "Neither did I," he bit off.

Phoebe swallowed around the lump forming in her throat. She already suspected as much, but hearing him say it aloud, and with such derision, was undeniably painful. And to think, only hours ago she had actually dared to consider that he might *want* to marry her.

"But the man is threatening to name you as my mistress and this is the quickest and surest way to protect you," Will continued. "There will still be gossip since you're such an unconventional choice for my duchess, but it will fade in time."

Her heart sank further. *My duchess.* He made it sound like she would simply be another possession: my carriage, my house, my dog. She would be stripped of all individuality. Her purpose reduced to the begetting of heirs and accompanying him to society functions. As much as a part of her wanted Will—desperately so— she could never agree to become his wife under such circumstances.

Her own sense of honor simply wouldn't allow it. She wasn't some inconvenient little mess that needed cleaning up. Instead of treating her as an equal, as someone he *respected*, he thought he could dictate her future all in the name of salvation and she would just accept it.

To hell with that.

Her hands tightened into fists. "No."

Will frowned. "No, what?"

His exasperated confusion only strengthened her resolve. The man really was an *ass*. "No, I will not marry you," she said slowly. "I told you I had no interest in marriage."

"Yes, I know," he huffed. "But that was before—"

"Well, my mind hasn't changed." If he was going to be condescending, then by God, so would she.

He shot her an imperious glare worthy of his title. "You're being very stubborn, Phoebe."

She waved a hand dismissively. "I'm sure you will have no trouble finding someone else to be *your duchess*."

"That is not what this is about and you know it," he growled.

She lifted her chin. "Did you really expect me to be *grateful* that you're willing to lower yourself to marry me?"

"I didn't say that."

"You readily admitted that I'm an inappropriate choice—"

"I didn't say *that* either—"

"*And* that a union between us will cause rampant speculation," Phoebe insisted as her simmering anger now bubbled over.

"Do you expect me to ignore the obvious?" he snapped as he took a step closer. "No, Phoebe. The circumstances are not ideal here. In case you've forgotten, I am a bloody *duke*. And dukes are expected to marry a certain kind of lady. While I admire the life you have made for yourself, we both know you are not exactly duchess material and I will not insult your intelligence by pretending otherwise."

Phoebe flinched as his words tore open an old wound. The one that marked her as different. As not up to snuff in the eyes of society. For she had never been considered elegant or well-mannered enough. At least, not when well-mannered meant smiling at every stupid or offensive remark a gentleman made. No, Will may have played at being an outsider these last few weeks, but in the end he was just as concerned with status as the rest of them. Whatever small kernel of affection she had been holding on to was ground to dust under the heel of his freshly polished shoe.

"And given that you *are* a duke, I'm sure you are not used to being rejected. You are obviously only doing this out of some misplaced sense of honor. So let me assure you, unequivocally, that it is not necessary. Nor is it welcome," she added tartly. "And even if word about us *does* get out, I have a far simpler solution: you can simply deny it. Call it a ridiculous rumor, and all the people whose opinions you care about so very much will believe it was a mistake because they want to. Because no one wants to see a duke marry someone so *unconventional*," she practically spat out the word. "You should go propose to Lady Gwen while you still have the chance. I suspect Lord Fairbanks will be less inclined to spread rumors about his son-in-law. Perhaps you can also discuss your upcoming bill with him."

Will pulled a hand roughly through his hair, disturbing the perfect locks. "That you would think I would have *anything* to do with that swine after all we've learned."

He looked desperate and frustrated and, somehow, even more handsome. Phoebe needed to get him out of here before she lost her conviction entirely.

"But surely even you would not hold his crimes against his daughter."

"Of *course* not," he said, appalled by the suggestion.

"Then it is settled," she replied, trying to appear calm and sensible while inside her stomach churned with nerves. "You will have your ideal duchess and the state of my reputation won't be on your conscience anymore."

Will opened his mouth but then stopped himself. "I'm going to leave before I say something I regret."

Phoebe could only laugh that he didn't think *this* conversation qualified as something to regret.

"This has all come as a shock to you, I'm sure," he added. "I will give you the rest of the day to think this over."

"You can, but my answer won't change," Phoebe said loftily.

Will's jaw hardened as his dark eyes bore into her own. "Is that so?" Phoebe nodded, but it was weak. Distracted. He took a step toward her. Then another. "And you are certain there is nothing left between us?" he murmured as his gaze dipped to her mouth. "Nothing else worth...exploring?"

Phoebe inhaled sharply before she could catch herself. His nostrils flared as his gaze returned to hers and that blasted heat swiftly raged to life between them. He leaned toward her then and Phoebe's traitorous heart stuttered as she breathed in his familiar scent of shaving soap.

She hated just how much she longed to feel the press of his firm, commanding mouth on hers. How easy it would be to fall back into bed with him and hope things would somehow magically sort themselves out. In another moment he would gather her in his arms and even though she had rejected his offer of marriage, she didn't trust herself to resist the offer of his body quite so easily. But while she had no doubt it would be a highly enjoyable diversion, in the end nothing would change. And it would only make their inevitable parting that much harder.

"Y-yes," she rasped, forcing the word past her lips, and took a stumbling step back. "I am," she added, a little more firmly now. "We're done here."

Will slowly straightened as a light faded from his eyes. One she hadn't noticed until it was gone.

Wait.

"I see." He blinked and that bored look of aristocratic indifference returned. She hadn't seen it for weeks. Not since he stepped into the inspector's office and turned her decent little life upside down.

Come back.

He tugged on his cuffs and then reached for her. Phoebe's eyes fluttered and for one ridiculous moment she thought he might caress her cheek in goodbye. But just as his beguiling scent filled her nose once again, he retrieved the hat from the top of the chest of drawers beside her.

"Then I won't make the mistake of repeating such an objectionable proposition to you ever again." He gave a short bow and placed his hat on his head. "Good day."

Phoebe stood there dumbly for a moment until she moved out of his way. He brushed past her without another word. She heard him murmur a goodbye to Marion before firmly shutting the front door behind him. Phoebe stood frozen in place, unaware of how much time had passed, until Marion appeared in the doorway with a look of concern on her face.

"Did you just reject a proposal of marriage? From a duke?"

The question broke through Phoebe's daze and she lifted her chin, trying to muster her outrage once more. "It sounded more like an order to me."

Marion let out a laugh of disbelief. "Well, he wasn't spouting poetry, I'll give you that, but Phoebe, my God. You could have been a *duchess*."

We both know you are not exactly duchess material.

Phoebe turned away as her eyes began to prickle. "He would have regretted it."

And she couldn't bear to watch his disappointment grow once he realized his mistake. Perhaps her reputation would suffer, but he would see in time that she had saved them both. Her heart, however, was another matter.

Marion placed a hand on her shoulder. "Are you sure about that?"

The gentle question was like a lance through her chest, melting whatever numbness still remained. "No," she said miserably as a hot tear slipped down her cheek. "No, I'm not."

Twenty-One

The next morning Will locked himself away in his study as soon as he awoke. Luckily, there was always work to be done. Work that would occupy his mind. Work that would give him what Phoebe could not.

Would not.

No. She'd made it perfectly clear that ruination was far preferable to being his wife. In his mad dash to protect her, Will hadn't considered for even a moment that she would reject him. It had both sorely wounded his pride *and* called attention to it, which nearly rankled as much as her rejection. He tore open another letter with relish and scanned the note. It was from Lord Tavistock, asking to meet the next day. Will quickly jotted a response and rang for his secretary.

"See that this is delivered directly."

"Yes, Your Grace," Mr. Flynn said as he took the missive.

Will looked around his desk. "What else is there to do?"

The man shook his head. "Nothing, Your Grace."

Damn.

"Are you certain?" Will couldn't be left alone, otherwise he might brood. And he was so damned *tired* of his own thoughts marching relentlessly through his brain. Of combing through every single moment of the disastrous encounter with Phoebe.

Mr. Flynn glanced at the clock on the mantel. "You've been working for the last five hours."

Will sat back in his chair. The entire morning had slipped away from him.

"Perhaps a light repast? It's also lovely out."

Will gave his secretary an arch look. "I do not need to take a turn in the garden like some wilting maiden."

"Of course not, Your Grace."

"But I could use something to eat," he admitted as his stomach roiled with sudden hunger.

"I'll go tell Cook," Mr. Flynn said with a bow and left the room.

Will slowly rose from his chair. His body had grown stiff from sitting for so long. He then meandered over to the window and stretched his arms over his head. It did look awfully nice out. Perhaps some fresh air would do him some good.

The door opened again and Will let out a huff. "What now?"

All he wanted was something to eat, but when he turned around *Alex* was charging into the room. Higgins had long-ago relinquished his gatekeeping duties when Alex showed up, much to everyone's benefit.

"I've something I need to discuss with you," she said by way of greeting, not at all put off by his sharp tone.

"Alex—I didn't know you were coming."

She took a seat on the sofa by the hearth and folded her hands on her lap. "How could you? I only decided this morning."

Though he was used to Alex's straightforward manner, he could certainly understand why others found it perplexing. "Right. Well, then," Will said as he sat down in an armchair across from her. "To what do I owe the pleasure of your company."

"Marry me."

Will blinked. "I'm sorry?"

"We don't have to actually *get* married, but an engagement at least would be very helpful," she said with a nod.

Perhaps Will had started to hallucinate in his famished state. Where the hell was Flynn?

"Why?" He drew the word out.

"Thanks to that blasted Mr. Ericson, Father has gotten it into his head that no one will approve of me taking over the company as a single woman and we'll lose all our clients. And you *know* how stubborn he can be."

"Yes," Will replied diplomatically. Alex was just as stubborn as her father, if not more so.

"Father is keen to make a deal with these Americans and he's insisting I make an effort to find a husband, so I only need the engagement to last until the papers are signed and they return to New York," she went on as that agile mind of hers spun a plan. "Hopefully by then I'll have shown my mettle and convinced Father and the board I'm up to the task, with or without a *man*." She wrinkled her nose as she said the word. "And since you won't propose to Lady Gwen, I thought you might be willing." Her eyes then narrowed slightly. "Unless, of course, there is someone else."

Will shifted in his chair as alarm bolted through him. Her comment was subtle, but then that was just how Alex did things. There was no doubt that he had been found out. "You know I would do anything for you…"

"But not this," she finished.

As unlikely as it was, a very small, very silly part of him still hoped for the chance to reconcile with Phoebe. And an engagement to her sister, even a fake one, would not help his cause. Perhaps Will was a romantic after all.

"I'm sorry, Alex."

She shrugged. "It's fine."

"You don't seem terribly concerned," he noted.

"I'm sure I can find someone who would be interested in entering a mutually beneficial arrangement." Before Will could press on this point, she fixed him with a sharp look. "So then. When will you propose to Phoebe? Tell me what you plan to say first. But if you need help with a ring, you should ask Mother or Freddie. They all look the same to me."

Will cleared his throat. "Ah, well..." He had skipped over the actual proposal a bit yesterday, hadn't he? "It might be too late for that."

He then explained the situation with Lord Fairbanks, his threats against Phoebe, and Will's plan to save her via marriage— along with her immediate, and unyielding, rejection. Alex listened patiently while he relayed the details with a studious expression on her face, but when he finally finished, she raised one lone eyebrow.

"Well. You certainly mucked that up."

He let out a dry laugh. "Yes, I can see that."

She then turned thoughtful. "I had no idea you still felt so beholden to the dukedom."

Will's shoulders hunched. That was not the reaction he had expected. "It's a little hard not to, given that it has occupied my *entire life* for nearly a decade."

Alex waved his concern away as if it was a dust mote. "I suppose, but you would hardly be the first duke to make an unconventional match. Why you ever considered Lady Gwen in the first place was a mystery to me. She would have bored you to death before the wedding breakfast was over, poor thing."

Only Alex could feel pity for someone like Lady Gwen, who lived a life of luxurious comfort and was adored by everyone. Well, *nearly* everyone.

"But she knew what was expected of a duchess," Will said, defensive. "And she would have excelled in the position."

Alex looked unmoved. "You sound like you're talking about an employee, not a wife."

Fair point.

Will pulled a hand down his face. He suddenly felt very, very tired. "I just wanted Phoebe to be prepared for what would happen if we married."

"By insulting her?"

"Of course not," Will groused. "But you know the gossip would have been relentless: her teaching, her failed season, your father's family connections, *everything* about her life would have been henpecked to death. Would you rather I said nothing about it? Paint some fairy-tale picture that would never come to pass?"

"No," Alex admitted. "Not at all. But you make it sound like you were only proposing to her out of obligation. No self-respecting woman *would* accept. Frankly, I'm rather proud of her for rejecting you."

Will pressed the heels of his hands against his eyes and let out a groan. "Oh God. I really did bungle this."

"There, there," Alex said as she attempted to give him a comforting pat. His valet's clothes brush was more soothing. He sat up and Alex immediately withdrew her hand. "Do try to have a little faith in her. Phoebe can manage a bit of scandal."

Will let out a dark laugh. "You're assuming she would even *want* to now."

"Well, I admit that you've dug yourself an awfully deep hole, but I'd imagine she would endure far more than a botched proposal for you." Alex studied him for a moment. "Do you really not know she's been in love with you for ages?"

He stared back at her as a flash of heat washed over him.

In love.

It was a shock to hear those words spoken aloud. And yet, it was like finding a missing trinket one had lost long ago. Will couldn't ignore the strange relief that flooded his heart—nor the terrible longing that pulsed even harder. How much he had wanted that once. How much he wanted it still.

"That's a 'no' then," Alex added with a smug smile. "Goodness, and everyone says *I'm* terrible at understanding people. But it's been clear to me since we were children."

Will sat back in his chair, dazed. *All that time.*

"I guess I never really considered it," he said. "She was always so much younger. But then that last summer, before I left, I began to want…"

Something. Anything.

Everything.

He let the unfinished confession hang in the air between them.

"You never told me."

"Because once I found out I was the heir, it didn't matter," Will insisted.

Alex scoffed. "Hogwash."

"It didn't seem like that at the time. And I haven't made a decision without first considering how it would affect the dukedom since," he admitted, as pathetic as it sounded. "I think that's why these last few weeks with Phoebe have been so…so exhilarating. I've felt more like myself in her company than I have in years." Then he shook his head. "But she's made it very clear the prospect of becoming a duchess holds absolutely no appeal to her."

"Isn't that preferable though? Someone who actually wants *you* and not the title?"

Will let out a sigh and stared up at the study's ornate painted ceiling of Zeus on the throne surrounded by all the lesser gods and goddesses. It was meant to reflect the late duke's political ambitions, but the painter had possessed more vision than talent. A chubby cherub with bulging blue eyes stared down at Will. Lord, he really did hate this room. "I'm not sure who I am anymore without it."

"Oh, rubbish," Alex groused and moved to stand. "If you're going to be dramatic, I'm leaving."

"Please don't." He managed a weak smile. "I'll be good."

"Well, then. What will you do now, Your Grace?"

"I have no idea," he said. "My plans have all fallen apart. I haven't a bloody clue what comes next."

But perhaps he'd start by getting that hideous ceiling painted over. Will let out a gasping laugh. Why had he waited so long to do something so simple?

Alex, unaware of this train of thoughts, looked appalled. "I can't think of anything more horrid."

"I'm sure. But even you can't control everything."

"I know *that*," she snapped. "That's why I came here to begin with. But might I suggest you start by being true to yourself, instead of worrying so much about that blasted dukedom? Your fellow aristocrats certainly don't worry half as much about how their actions reflect on their legacies."

"It's different when you're born to it," Will grumbled.

"Yes, and *you're* different because you weren't. So stop trying so hard to be like them and embrace who you are."

Will's mouth curved. "You're quite clever, you know."

"Yes, I do. And everyone would be much better off if they'd only listen to me. Shall I speak to Phoebe?"

Will shook his head. "No, she was right to reject me like you said. I need to become someone she'd actually *want* to marry first. At least one who knows his own mind."

Alex rose. "Then you've got some work to do."

"And you have a fake fiancé to find. Just be careful you don't break some innocent young man's heart."

She scoffed again. "I highly doubt that."

"You've always underestimated your appeal."

Alex avoided his gaze as she tugged on her gloves. "You know why."

"He was an idiot."

Alex shook her head. "Only you would call an Oxford don an idiot."

"Well, he isn't one anymore." Will recalled the stormy evening she had turned up at his rooms at Christ Church College soaked to the bone and pale as ivory. It was the only time he had ever seen Alex cry. And only a little. Even when her heart was utterly broken by a careless man. "And he has you to thank for all his success."

Alex pursed her lips. "He would likely debate that," she murmured before giving him a weary smile. "I do hope you can make things work with Phoebe. She deserves happiness. And I think she could find it with you."

Will glanced down. "I need to get reacquainted with myself first, as it were."

"A fine idea. And don't worry too much about Lord Fairbanks," she added with sudden gravity. The gleam in Alex's eye was unsettling. "I'll take care of him."

Twenty-Two

The front hall of the Langham Place School was filled with fine ladies milling about the tables where students had put together demonstrations showcasing their academic accomplishments. Phoebe stood in the corner watching them all and bursting with pride. There was also a silent auction being run by her mother and sisters while a food and beverage area was staffed by both students and volunteers. Miss Sanderson, the music teacher, was organizing a group of students in the corner to sing a short program. They wouldn't know until much later if they had raised enough money, but Phoebe felt certain the bazaar was a success.

"I must commend you, Miss Atkinson," the headmistress said. "You've done a marvelous job here. You should be proud."

Phoebe dipped her head at the praise. "Everyone worked very hard to put this event together."

"But not as hard as you," Mrs. Richardson pressed. "I know it takes strong leadership to pull off an event like this. And you've demonstrated that you possess the necessary qualities."

Phoebe blushed. After her argument with Will, she had thrown herself into planning the rest of the bazaar—at the expense of nearly everything else in her life. But that had only proved just how little she had outside of the school. It was quite sobering. "Thank you, ma'am."

The headmistress scanned the room and let out a heavy sigh. "A pity it will all be for naught."

"Pardon?"

"I heard from the landlord yesterday. Even if we raise enough money, he will not be renewing our lease. I didn't want to say anything until the bazaar ended."

Phoebe gaped. "Can he do that?"

"Oh yes," Mrs. Richardson said matter-of-factly. "It's all perfectly legal."

"But...but *why?*" It felt like the room had shifted beneath her feet.

"He got a better offer," she replied with a shrug. "Someone wants to turn this entire building into one of those ghastly department stores." The headmistress wrinkled her nose. Not everyone was enamored of the one-stop shopping behemoths that had taken over central London.

"In this neighborhood?"

"It's changing, and swiftly. I worry that our girls will be forced out once rents rise. And they certainly will if a department store is built."

Phoebe shook her head in disbelief. "How can you be so calm about this?" She was boiling with anger at the gross injustice of it all.

"You don't reach my age without being knocked down a dozen times over. But then you get up, shake the dust off, and start again. Whatever we raise today will help us find another property."

But the thought only made Phoebe's shoulders sag with the great weight of it all.

"It feels like every time we reach the top, the mountain grows another foot."

Mrs. Richardson turned to her with a gentle smile. "And yet, that is how most progress is made, isn't it? Not in great leaps and bounds, but in tiny, diligent steps. It isn't until you look back that you see how far you've come. Don't let this break you, my dear. Let it inspire you to do more."

But Phoebe could only nod. She needed to grieve this loss first.

"You should also know that the duke of Ellis pledged to match whatever we raise today."

The headmistress was watching her closely, but Phoebe managed to tamp down the thrill trying to burst through her. "His Grace is very generous," she said with a bland smile.

Will had to have made the pledge long before she rejected him. And yet, she couldn't make herself ask. Because it didn't matter, either way. This wasn't about her. It was about the school. The school she had now lost.

Mrs. Richardson was quiet for a moment. "Indeed. I understand you have known him since childhood. Your mother told me," she added in answer to Phoebe's surprised look.

"There isn't anything going on between us," she said quickly. Hardly subtle, but, essentially, the truth.

"Of course." The headmistress gave her a diplomatic nod. "Not many know this, but I was engaged once. Years and years ago."

"You were?" Phoebe couldn't hide her shock. It was hard to imagine the headmistress as anyone other than the woman before her.

Mrs. Richardson smiled. "He was a teacher too. At the London Polytechnic. That's where we met. But he expected me to give up my career when we married. Understandable, especially in those days, but I refused. I enjoyed my work and didn't see the need to stop until we had children."

"That sounds...very reasonable," Phoebe replied as she flushed with embarrassment. She had always assumed Mrs. Richardson expected complete dedication from her teachers, but perhaps that had just been a convenient excuse for her own single-mindedness. Phoebe had given her far too little credit.

"I thought so too," Mrs. Richardson continued. "But he disagreed. So we parted ways and he married someone else not long after. A colleague of mine, actually," she said with a little laugh.

"I'm sorry."

"Oh, don't be. I don't regret it. But sometimes I wish we had been able to come to an understanding. Or rather that I had found someone who hadn't asked me to choose in the first place." Then she gestured to the tableau before them. "This school has been the work of my life, and I'm proud of it so very much. But I'm getting on in years and sometimes the nights can be lonely," she admitted.

Phoebe worried her lip. "I'm not sure why you're telling me this, ma'am," she said.

"Because I know how much this school means to you, and all that you have given up for it." Her brown eyes softened as she placed a gentle hand on Phoebe's arm. "Your dedication to the students is admirable. But if you find yourself luckier in love than I was, make sure you take it. That's all."

Phoebe stared at her dumbfounded, but before she could respond, the headmistress tilted her head to address someone approaching them. "Inspector Holland! I'm so glad you were able to come."

Phoebe turned to find the inspector beside her. "Mrs. Richardson, Miss Atkinson," he said, acknowledging them both with a nod. "I can never refuse a summons from a schoolmistress."

Mrs. Richardson let out a girlish laugh Phoebe had never heard from her before. "Have Miss Atkinson show you around. I see that Lady Beckinwith has just arrived and she'll pout if I don't greet her immediately."

Once they were alone, Inspector Holland handed her an envelope. "I confess I did not only come here because of the headmistress. It's from Maude," he added. "She said she found what you were looking for."

Phoebe's head was still whirling from the headmistress's confession, but she had to put it out of her mind for now. She pressed the envelope to her chest and met his questioning gaze. "I think we may be able to bring down Lord Fairbanks with this."

"Good," he said with a stern nod before he scanned the room. "But I'm going to pretend I didn't hear that."

Phoebe smiled at his profile. He was a terribly handsome man, and yet she was not at all moved. It appeared her stupid little heart still belonged entirely to Will.

"Would you like some lemonade?"

He cracked a rare smile. "I'm not one for sweets usually, but I suppose I can make an exception for a charitable cause."

"Very good."

Phoebe then led him to the refreshments table and they had just taken their cups when Freddie bustled over, her sharp brown eyes decidedly fixed upon the inspector.

"Phoebe, you know it's quite rude not to introduce your *friend* to your own sister."

She huffed a laugh at Freddie's complete lack of subtlety. "Detective Inspector Holland, this is my younger sister, Miss Winifred Atkinson."

Freddie wrinkled her nose. "No one calls me Winifred," she explained to the inspector. "Dreadful name, really. It sounds like someone's aged spinster aunt."

"Otherwise known as your namesake," Phoebe put in. "Though I think Great-Aunt Winifred would strenuously object to being described as 'aged.'"

"No doubt the old battle-ax would, but I still prefer Freddie," she said with a cheery smile.

Inspector Holland raised a sober brow at their exchange but even Phoebe could see the flash of amusement in his gaze. "I like Winifred."

"Well, we all have our faults," Freddie quipped and the inspector let out a short, rasping laugh. Freddie then broke into the beaming smile that usually appeared only when she bested Monsieur Laurent in a fencing match. Interesting.

Phoebe left the two of them and walked over to the silent auction table where her mother was chatting with another volunteer while Alex was organizing bidding slips.

She handed her sister the envelope. "Can you make sure Will gets this today? It's important."

Alex raised an eyebrow. "Then why don't you do it."

Phoebe bit her lip. Only Marion knew what had happened with Will.

At her silence, Alex let out a resigned sigh and pocketed the envelope. "Let's go have a chat." She then addressed their mother. "I'm stepping out with Phoebe for a moment. Don't touch *anything* until I return," she said with an arch look.

"Yes, darling," their mother said with a distracted wave and returned to her conversation.

Alex came around the table and hooked her arm through Phoebe's. It was the closest they had been in months. "Everything that woman touches instantly turns to clutter."

Phoebe laughed. "And yet somehow she knows exactly where everything is."

"Yes, but *I* don't," Alex huffed as they turned down a quiet hallway. She then released Phoebe's arm and faced her. "So then, what's happened between you and Will?"

Phoebe narrowed her eyes. "Why do I have the feeling you already know?"

Alex deftly avoided answering the question. "I want to hear it from you."

Phoebe automatically crossed her arms, feeling like the petulant younger sister once again. "He came to my aid while you were in New York. My student was missing and he offered to help…" Phoebe then gave a shortened version of the events of the last few weeks, leaving out the more salacious details for both their benefits.

A long silence ensued as Alex mulled over the information. "So," she said abruptly. "Despite all that occurred between the two of you, when Will did propose you turned him down."

Phoebe's cheeks burned. Of course Will told *Alex*.

"He never actually proposed," she corrected, desperate to keep this petty jealousy at bay before it consumed her. "He just assumed I'd accept. That I'd be *grateful* he was willing to lower himself," she added, unable to keep the bitterness out of her voice.

"Phoebe—"

"It's over, Alex," she insisted. "We both agreed."

And you are certain there is nothing left between us?

She rolled her shoulders against the wave of doubt swelling inside her.

"All right. I won't push you to talk about it." Alex sighed. "But if you change your mind—"

"I won't. As it turns out, I have something more pressing to deal with at the moment anyway. The school is closing. Mrs. Richardson heard from the landlord yesterday that he won't renew our lease. So this was all for naught," Phoebe added, gesturing to the bazaar.

Alex frowned in concern. "I'd hardly say that. If anything, you've proven to a group of people with too much money how valuable a school like this is," she said. "We'll think of something. Don't worry."

At Alex's decided nod, Phoebe felt the smallest flicker of hope in her chest. But even under the best circumstances, reestablishing the school would take time. Which meant that once the bazaar ended, Phoebe would be left with nothing.

It was a sobering prospect.

"Come." Alex took her arm. "You could use another glass of lemonade. And we should probably check on Freddie. I saw her cornering a large mustached man."

"That's the inspector I told you about," Phoebe explained. "I think he can handle her."

But Alex shook her head at the lighthearted quip. "She's been spending time with the younger Mr. Ericson. Father is hoping it turns into something."

"Really?" Phoebe was shocked. "I can't see them together at all."

Alex kept her gaze fixed ahead. "It would be good for the company." She parroted the line Father always used to justify, well, everything.

And what about Freddie?

But Phoebe kept that thought to herself. For now.

Later, long after the last guest left and the final chair was packed away, Phoebe made her way to her classroom. Mrs. Richardson wouldn't make the announcement about the closure until Monday but after that they would need to be out of the building within the week. The summer holiday would have to start a few weeks early, but God willing they would find another space before the autumn term. She couldn't think what might happen if they didn't.

Phoebe entered her silent classroom and collapsed in the chair behind her desk. The sun had just begun to set and golden light filtered into the room. She touched the cover of her well-worn copy of *The Odyssey* and felt a bit like screaming at the gods for seemingly thwarting her at every turn.

Now it appeared that she was to go on a journey of her own, but without an Ithaca to guide her. For the first time in years, she didn't have a plan. Didn't know what the future would hold. She could see nothing ahead but blankness. Phoebe waited while the golden light slowly faded from gold, to orange, to a deep dusky violet. Only when darkness threatened did she force herself to her feet and step into the unknown.

Twenty-Three

Six weeks later
A village in Surrey

I read all about your defection in the paper," Cal said as he poured the tea. "Hard to ignore it, really," he added with a chuckle before turning apologetic. "Sorry. That isn't funny."

"No, it's fine," Will said on a sigh as he accepted the teacup. Though he was weary from traveling down from Derbyshire on such short notice, he knew he had made the right decision as soon as he stepped off the train. "It was long overdue."

Ever since Will had declared his intention to switch parties on the floor of Parliament last month, the papers had been full of him, though few had bothered to mention his plan to cosponsor a new bill with Lord Tavistock aimed at funding more public housing for women and children, with preference given for those who left the flesh trade.

Will had plodded along in a fog for another few weeks, but left for the ducal estate in Derbyshire as soon as Parliament was in recess. With his marriage plans put on hold indefinitely, there was no good reason to stay in London for the summer and be harassed by journalists hunting for a story.

But he realized his mistake moments after he entered that dreary front hall. Will didn't want to be alone in this empty mansion full of dusty relics to a family he felt no connection to. He wanted to go *home*.

Now he sat with his brother in the cozy back room they jokingly called the library while a soft Surrey rain fell outside.

As Cal took a sip of tea, Will surreptitiously studied his younger brother and was relieved to see the hollows beneath his cheeks had plumped and the purple smudges under his eyes had nearly vanished. For the first time in years, Cal looked well rested. Happy, even.

"So then," he said as he set his cup back on the saucer. "How did Lord Fairbanks take the news?"

Will arched a brow. "Suspiciously well."

Fairbanks had never brought his bill to committee for reasons Will was still trying to uncover. The man had paled as soon as he caught sight of Will in the halls of Parliament but tried to keep up appearances. Until Will opened his mouth: *I have spent far too long neglecting my own beliefs in order to appease sanctimonious little men like you. But that ends now.*

Strangely, Fairbanks made no attempt to bully him into rescinding his defection even as a crowd of their peers began to gather. Will hadn't meant to create a sideshow, but perhaps it was better this way. For there would be no doubt in anyone's mind that he was no longer Fairbanks's lapdog.

Then Will leaned in close, so the others could not hear: *And if you so much as* think *about slandering Miss Atkinson, I will make sure all of London knows about your connection to Fleur and what a raging hypocrite you are.*

But this too was met with absolutely no resistance. Fairbanks immediately held his hands up and swore he had no intention of defaming the young lady. He had been mistaken. Of *course* she wasn't his mistress. A thoroughly preposterous idea.

The man's immediate repentance was unexpectedly irritating, as Will had come ready to trade words backed by the proof Alex had given him. But even more irritating than Fairbanks's spine-lessness was seeing Phoebe proven right:

People will believe it was a mistake because they want to.

For one dangerous moment, Will felt the urge to declare the truth. That he was absolutely in love with an odd bluestocking schoolmistress, and damn anyone for suggesting that she wasn't fit to be his duchess. Phoebe Atkinson was far, far better than he would *ever* deserve.

Instead, he simply walked away.

"But that's good, isn't it?" Cal asked, pulling Will back into the present. "You should have stood up to him ages ago."

Will grunted in reply, still half-lost in his thoughts. As much as he would like to take all the credit for the earl's acquiescence, it seemed far more likely that someone convinced Fairbanks to retreat first. But Will hadn't had the chance to uncover anything before he left London.

"In any case, I don't think he'll be much of a bother." At least for now. And Will still had the damning documents from Fleur to use if needed.

"Well, I'm glad to hear it. Mother will be too."

Will's gaze snapped to his brother. "What do you mean?"

Cal shrugged. "She never liked those men: the old duke and his friends. She thought they had too much influence on you."

Will let out a dark laugh. "Yes, well, she only has herself to blame for that seeing as how she was the one who happily sent me away in the first place." His chest was so tight with the memory of that old betrayal that he could barely get the words out.

"But Will, what was she to do?" Cal asked as he leaned forward. "Did you really expect a country widow alone in the world to go against a man like him?"

Will's nostrils flared as he stared into his brother's pleading face. Cal, despite a heartbreaking loss that would have soured most people, still managed to see the best in everyone. Will had always envied that about him, especially now.

"Yes, actually. I did," he snapped. Then he sat back in his chair and crossed his arms. Nothing like a visit home to make one feel like a child again. "I don't want to talk about this anymore. It's done."

"All right," Cal said softly and offered him a plate. "Here. Have a biscuit."

Will took one and bit into it with relish. As he chewed, he looked around the room to avoid Cal's sympathetic gaze. But everywhere he turned, another memory surfaced, then another. His father's law degree still hung on the wall alongside a portrait of their mother a teenaged Cal had painted as a birthday present. The collected works of Charles Dickens in red Moroccan leather, which his mother insisted they each read in full, were proudly displayed in the bookcase next to a bell jar that contained the first model ship Will had successfully built by himself. How could one small space filled with such ordinary things hold so much joy? These were the exact opposite of the treasures he now owned: a world-class art collection, artifacts stolen by far distant relations, and more books than a man could read in a dozen lifetimes. But if he had to choose, Will would trade it all in a heartbeat for anything here. For the reminders of all he had left behind.

His mouth suddenly filled with a bittersweetness that couldn't be blamed on the biscuit. It was a longing for the past. For the afternoons of his boyhood spent in this room, when his father was still alive and dukes only appeared in fairy tales and newspapers from London—not real life.

Will cleared his throat. "Thank you again for accommodating me on so little notice," he said stiffly. He had managed to send a message only a few hours before his arrival, but Cal met him promptly at the station full of smiles.

"Of course," his brother replied. "This is your home too. And with Mother still in London it's nice to have some company."

"I don't like you being out here all by yourself."

"I'm not," Cal insisted. "I have friends in the village. And the Atkinson girls call every now and then when they come to stay. That Freddie is something, isn't she?"

Will tried to return his brother's grin. "Does…does Phoebe ever come?" He hoped the question didn't sound as desperate as he felt.

Cal furrowed his brow in thought. "Not since last Christmas. I think she's too busy with that school of hers to get away much."

"Right."

"There's also a new vicar in the village," Cal said hesitantly. "Father Lloyd. He's been coming for supper every Saturday and likes Coleridge even more than I do. We've started a little Romantics reading group."

Will genuinely smiled at the blush staining his brother's fair cheeks. "I'm so glad." He then reached out and touched Cal's arm. "And don't worry. I will be sure to find a bride by next season."

Though Lord Fairbanks had kept his promise not to slander Phoebe, Lady Gwen decided all on her own that she had had enough of Will's dithering and accepted the heir to a viscountcy. They quickly wed in time for Royal Ascot and as she was the first debutante to marry that season, it helped distract from her failure to capture a duke. Will saw her not long after, holding court in Hyde Park accompanied by a passel of young ladies all dressed alike in pastel walking gowns. If she noticed him, she gave no indication. Just held her golden head up proudly and laughed at something a friend said. Will continued on, shouldering the snub as he deserved, but he could not feel an ounce of regret for not marrying her. She was a lovely woman who should have every happiness, but the version of himself that had focused on her in the first place felt alien to him now.

But unfortunately, he was still the duke and still needed to find a wife. Perhaps he could wed one of those mercenary American girls who would be perfectly happy with only his title and not his heart.

Cal cocked his head. "Whatever do you mean?"

Will blinked. "Last time I was here you said your greatest fear was becoming the duke. So I'm making sure that won't happen."

"Oh, God. I forgot all about that." Cal pressed a hand to his chest, his brown eyes wide with mortification. "Tell me you haven't been bride-hunting on *my* account."

Will pinched the bridge of his nose. Sometimes being the elder brother was harder than being a duke. "Christ, Cal. Do you have any idea how *worried* I've been?"

Cal bowed his head in regret. "I'm very sorry. I shouldn't have burdened you with that. I mean, it's true, but I was feeling rather pitiful that day. And it certainly shouldn't be why you get *married*."

"It was time to find a duchess anyway," Will grumbled.

Cal gave him a considering look. "You deserve to be with

someone you love, and who loves you back. Forget all the duchess business."

Will let out a grim laugh. "A bit hard to when the chance to become a duchess is your biggest draw."

"Then those women aren't for you," Cal insisted. "And you're far more than that blasted title."

Will gazed out the window at the green meadow that led to the Atkinson's property. How many times he had crossed it as a boy. Always with a sense of anticipation for what lay ahead. The excitement of the unexpected. That feeling had been lost to him for so long, until Phoebe came barreling into his life again.

He swallowed against the lump building in his throat and met Cal's gaze. "I think I'm beginning to realize that, as foolish as it sounds."

"No, it's honest," Cal said as he reached over and patted Will's hand. "And that, dear brother, can never be foolish."

Twenty-Four

*P*hoebe hurried down the platform of Snug End's little station. The train had been delayed leaving London and she was nearly fifteen minutes late. Luckily the village high street wasn't very large. Just a few shops, a pub, and her destination: Mrs. Graham's Tea Room.

A bell tinkled as she entered the establishment. At a quarter after noon, the cheerfully decorated tearoom was filled with customers occupying tables, peering at the large pastry case, or simply milling about chatting with one another. The friendly atmosphere instantly set Phoebe at ease as she scanned the room. It appeared that this Mrs. Graham had a penchant for lace doilies given that they covered nearly every available surface.

"Miss Atkinson! Over here!"

Phoebe turned to the speaker and broke into a broad smile as Alice Clarke waved from her seat at a table in the back corner. Phoebe weaved through the tables and embraced her former student.

"Oh, Alice. It is wonderful to see you."

"You too, miss. I'm so glad this worked out."

Alice's first letter had come only a day after the bazaar, and it had been a much-needed balm for Phoebe's crushed soul. They had written back and forth over the next few weeks until they were able to find a time to meet.

Phoebe pulled back and was pleased to see that the girl's cheeks were full and rosy. "You look well. And happy."

"I am, miss," she said. "It's been nice to be out of London. Get a bit of fresh air."

"I'm sure." Phoebe managed to smile even while her heart ached at the thought of Alice staying in this little village indefinitely.

Once they took their seats, a girl about Alice's age came over to take her order.

"Millie, this is the lady I was talking about," Alice said excitedly. "My old teacher."

The girl's eyes rounded. "Oh, I've heard so much about you! I wish we had a school like that around here."

Phoebe's cheeks flushed. "You're very kind."

The smell of something freshly baked wafted through the air and her stomach rumbled.

"*Everything* is delicious," Alice said. "But I'm partial to the lemon scones." She gestured to her empty plate.

"Then I'll have that," Phoebe said to Millie. "And a pot of your strongest black tea."

"Right away," the girl said and scurried off.

"You come here often?" Phoebe asked once they were alone.

Alice nodded. "Mrs. Druthers, the lady I've been staying with, takes in sewing and I help. Nothing too fancy, mind, but it gives me a bit of pocket money."

"That's good. It's important to have a skill like that. I wish I did."

"You teach."

"I used to teach," Phoebe corrected.

Alice's eyes softened. "I'm so sorry about the school. But surely Mrs. Richardson can find a new location."

Phoebe shrugged. "It's taking longer than expected. And I'm worried that the longer it takes, the more students we'll lose. So for now I am without employment."

And it had been the worst two months of her life—though she couldn't blame it all on the school's sudden closure.

Millie returned with her tea, scone, and a fresh pot for Alice. Phoebe fixed her tea while Alice peppered her with questions about everything she had missed at school while she was away.

"The girls must have taken the news about the school very hard," she said when they had exhausted Phoebe's gossip stores.

"Yes," Phoebe said as she absently stirred her tea. "It's funny, the girls who seemed the least interested in my lessons were the most upset."

"Perhaps they only realized what they had once it was lost."

Phoebe's smile was rueful. "Perhaps."

Alice's gaze turned serious as she set her teacup aside. "I'm sorry I never told you about Maude. My mother acted like she was some terrible family secret and we'd be ruined if word spread. But that always seemed awfully unfair to me since my sister did so much for us. And when Mother fell ill, Maude took care of everything without a word of complaint."

"Don't apologize." Phoebe waved a hand. "You certainly weren't required to tell me all the intimate details of your life."

Alice shook her head. "I should have told Maude to contact you when I left London though. Then you wouldn't have worried about me. But it all happened so fast and Maude was adamant."

"That's all right. She had her reasons. Besides, I had an adventure," she added with a small smile. That was how she should think of her time with Will.

I once spent a spring galivanting around London with a handsome duke.

It would be a fine story to tell her nieces and nephews one day—with a few tactful omissions, of course.

Alice raised an eyebrow. "So I heard."

Phoebe deftly changed the subject before her cheeks could heat even more. "Did your mother and sister make peace in the end?"

Alice shrugged. "When Maude came to see her, Mother refused at first. Stubborn woman. It wasn't until I insisted that nothing Maude ever did was unforgivable that she gave in. I told Maude that too. I'm not ashamed to have her as my sister."

Phoebe patted her hand. "I'm sure that meant a great deal to her."

"She's finally cut ties with Fairbanks, you know," Alice said softly. "For good."

"I'm very glad to hear that." Phoebe let out a sigh of relief as the earl's ugly words from that night in Maude's room came back to her. "I don't think he treated her well."

"Not at all. It's men like *him* that should be ashamed of themselves. Not girls like Maude. They're the ones that made the world this way. And then they claim to have some moral objection to it?" She shook her head in disgust. "None of it makes sense to me."

"No, it doesn't," Phoebe agreed. Though she had read about Will's defection in the paper, there hadn't been a word about Lord Fairbanks' bill—or her. Hopefully the evidence Maude procured was enough to keep him quiet. "What will she do now?"

"I'm not sure. She has no real schooling." Alice looked thoughtful. "It'd be nice if there was some kind of training for women like her. To help them start fresh."

Phoebe nodded as an idea began to take shape in her mind.

"There's something else," Alice added, then paused to take a breath. "I've decided against that secretarial course."

"Really?" Phoebe couldn't hide her disappointment. "If it's about the money—"

"No." Alice firmly shook her head. "It's not that." Phoebe tilted her head expectantly. "I want to teach like you. In a school like ours," she said in a great rush.

Phoebe was stunned. "You . . . you do?"

Alice bowed her head shyly. "I know I'll have years of schooling ahead of me, but it's what I want. And I can take in more sewing to pay the fees. I'd darn a thousand shirts to do it."

"That won't be necessary," Phoebe said. "You're a brilliant girl, Alice. And I will do *everything* in my power to help you succeed."

The girl looked up with hope in her eyes "Really?"

"Of course. It would be an honor. Truly."

They spent the next hour discussing teacher training colleges. Phoebe made up a list of possibilities and promised to do more research.

"I can't let you do all that," Alice protested.

"You can. Besides," she said with a tight smile. "It will give me something to do."

Though Phoebe had insisted on paying the full rent on their flat since the school's closure, Marion accepted a governess position with a family outside London for the summer. She fully intended to return as soon as a new school was opened, but in the meantime that left Phoebe alone with far too much time to spend *thinking*.

"When does Maude think it will be safe enough for you to return home?"

Alice quirked her brow. "Well, that's no longer an issue. Obviously Fairbanks wouldn't dare try anything now."

Phoebe stared at her. Why did it feel like she was missing something? "You mean...because of the information that connects him to Fleur?"

But that didn't make sense, as Fairbanks didn't know that had been Maude's doing and as far as she knew, the mere threat of exposure had done enough. He hadn't moved forward with that bill of his and there had been nothing in the papers connecting her to Will—the odd disappointment she felt at that was something she tried not to dwell on.

"No," Alice said slowly. "Last I heard he had to pull out of the club anyway. Because of your sister, Alex." At Phoebe's confused silence she continued: "She bought up his debts, and said if anything happens to any of us, she'll ruin him."

Phoebe sat back in her chair, dumbfounded.

"She didn't tell you? I would have sworn you were behind it," Alice marveled.

Phoebe let out a short laugh. "I'm not nearly so ruthless as that. And I don't have Alex's money."

Though each sister had access to a healthy trust once they turned twenty-one, Alex had amassed a sizable fortune all on her own. Still, it must have been a considerable investment.

"I can't believe she did that," Phoebe murmured.

"Can't you?" Alice prompted. "She is your sister, after all. Look at what mine did for me."

"That's true." Phoebe bowed her head. She was being unfair again. Alex would likely do far more, if called upon.

They chatted for a while longer until Phoebe had to leave or else risk missing her train. By then they were the only two customers remaining in the shop. Alice walked her back to the station just as the train arrived. They embraced on the platform, with both promising to write again soon.

"Take care of yourself, Alice."

"You too, Miss Atkinson."

"I think you can call me Phoebe now."

"All right. Phoebe." Alice smiled shyly. "And tell your sister thank you. Though I hope to do it in person soon."

"I will."

Phoebe then boarded the train and took a window seat in second class. She waved to Alice as the train pulled away and watched her grow ever smaller until she was just a faceless figure in the distance. Then she sat back in her seat and let out a sigh. For the first time in the months since Alice had disappeared, Phoebe felt certain she was safe.

Twenty-Five

*O*nce Phoebe returned to London, she headed straight for Atkinson Enterprises. It was after five, but everyone knew Alex never left before six on work days. As Phoebe stepped down from the hackney, she paused in front of the handsome brick building in a prime location just outside the City. Atkinson Enterprises had occupied the same ground floor since her grandfather opened the original accounting firm forty years ago. But it was Alex and her ingenious knack for spotting the next big idea who had helped their father expand the business into investments. Now the firm's offices took up the entire building.

The lobby was deserted at this hour and the click of Phoebe's heeled boots echoed across the pristine marble floor. She hadn't been here in years. When she was a young girl, her mother would occasionally drop her and Alex off while she did some shopping and together they would play in their father's office for hours. Phoebe was more interested in the butterscotch candies he kept in a drawer especially for her, but Alex was already fascinated by his work even then. The memory rubbed against a raw spot in Phoebe's heart as she passed by her father's closed office door. How much simpler things had been between them back then. When all she needed from him was a kiss on the cheek and a handful of sweets.

As predicted, Alex was still in her office at the end of the hall, the warm glow from her desk lamp lighting the way like a beacon. Phoebe knocked on the open door as she entered.

"Hello, there."

Alex barely glanced up from the portfolio she was studying. "Hello."

If she was surprised by Phoebe's sudden appearance, she didn't show it. The small space was decorated with various odds and ends Alex had laid claim to over the years, like some kind of furniture-hoarding magpie. None of it matched, but it was rather charming in a way. It was the exact opposite of their father's lavish office, where the museum-quality art, the sofa covered in watered silk, the matching Louis XIV chairs, and fine Aubusson rug were meant to impress perspective clients. But this space, with its unadorned walls and bare wood floor, was meant only for Alex. And she didn't care what it looked like as long as she could get her work done.

Phoebe took the only other chair in the room besides her sister's: a high-backed Baroque-inspired monstrosity she recognized from their late grandmother's house. Once seated, she was noticeably lower than Alex. But the effect was likely intentional.

Phoebe craned her neck. "Where's Father?"

"He left hours ago," Alex replied without looking up from the page in front of her. "He never stays past four these days."

"You shouldn't be here all alone."

"Why not? I do my best work when no one else is here."

Phoebe ignored the pointed remark. "What are you reading?"

"A business proposal. What else?"

"Anything interesting?"

"It could be, if they agree to my changes." Alex sighed and

closed the portfolio. She sat back in her chair and met Phoebe's eyes. "All right. Out with it."

"What do you mean?" She added an innocent blink, but unsurprisingly this did not work on Alex, who crossed her arms in response.

"You've obviously come here to say something, so get to it."

"Can't I visit my sister without an ulterior motive?"

"Of course. But you wouldn't set foot in here without one."

Phoebe laughed. "That's a tad dramatic, Alex."

Her sister's expression remained. "Is it? By my count you haven't come here in at least three years."

Well, she had her there.

"I met with Alice Clarke today," Phoebe began. "She told me about Lord Fairbanks. How you bought all his debts."

Alex softened ever so slightly. "Oh."

"And I came here to thank you—"

"No need."

"Alex," Phoebe said with exasperation. "What you did was... was above and beyond what anyone else would have done. And so very generous."

"You're my sister. Besides, it was time someone brought Fairbanks down a notch."

"I'd say you brought him down far more than that."

"Yes, well." Alex glanced away and Phoebe noted the slight blush coloring her pale cheeks. Goodness, she was *embarrassed* to have her good deed revealed. But when Alex met her eyes again, she merely shrugged. "I'm charging him a healthy interest rate. And it's more than I would get having the money sitting in the bank."

Phoebe couldn't help smiling at her explanation. It was just so very *Alex*. "Well, I'm still incredibly grateful. I only wish you had told me what you were planning."

"There wasn't time," she insisted. Phoebe was tempted to contradict that reason, but let it pass. "It seemed the best way to guarantee the earl's silence quickly, and Will was so distraught—"

"What?" Phoebe asked before clamping her mouth shut. She didn't *want* to know. Because it didn't matter.

Alex raised an eyebrow. "Surely that isn't a surprise. The man *had* threatened to publicly ruin you."

"Yes, but…" Phoebe hesitated. Her stomach churned as she searched for the right words. "Will was annoyed by the whole business, and what he thought it required of him."

"You mean the proposal?"

"If you could call it that," Phoebe muttered. "I know he had already decided against marrying Lady Gwen, but I was not the alternative he had been considering before the earl's threat."

Even now, after all these weeks, she still couldn't think of that afternoon without her shoulders hunching with embarrassment. Will's aloof manner as he dictated his plan to save her reputation via marriage certainly hadn't read as *distraught* to her. Formal, cold, clinical, even. But never distraught.

Alex was quiet for a long moment. "Speaking as someone who is not entirely comfortable discussing their feelings in delicate situations, or ever, really," she began. "I suspect that what he actually felt went far beyond annoyance. And you must know that he didn't propose to you simply because he thought he was required to," she added in a disbelieving tone that got Phoebe's back up.

"He made it perfectly clear that was *exactly* why he was proposing," she said tartly.

"But, as I said to him, it was hardly the only option," Alex pointed out. "Yet that was the first one he suggested. And I know how you've always felt about him," she added.

Phoebe pressed her fingers against the wood of the chair as her defiant mind recalled the look on Will's face just before he stormed out of her room. His visible disinterest had struck her heart as fiercely as a prizefighter's fist, and she could still feel its echo even now.

I won't make the mistake of repeating such an objectionable proposition to you.

"Why are you doing this?" Phoebe couldn't hide the desperation in her voice. "I already told him no. It's done."

Alex's dark eyes bore into her own. "Not until he weds someone else."

Phoebe flung herself out of the chair and began to pace. "I can't listen to any more of this."

"In all that time you spent together, did you really never consider it?"

"Of course not." Phoebe shot her a glare. "He's a *duke*, Alex."

"He's also Will. You know him."

Phoebe shook her head. "Which is why I *know* I can't be the kind of duchess he wants. I'll be a pariah and he'll regret it within a week. And...and I won't be able to bear it."

Alex's face lit with sudden understanding. "You're afraid."

Phoebe halted. "No."

Yes.

"I always thought you didn't care about society. About the gossip," Alex marveled.

Phoebe gripped the back of the chair. "I don't," she insisted. "But...it's easier to not care when you are removed from that world. And a duchess isn't. She is expected to lead it."

Just saying the words made her want to hide under the very chair she clung to.

"I understand your reservations," Alex said. "And I can't pretend it will be easy for you, but you won't have to do it alone. You'll have us, and Will of course."

"But he wanted someone like Lady Gwen," Phoebe said miserably. "The woman was born and bred to be a duchess."

"Oh, to hell with that," Alex broke out. "You can be whatever kind of duchess you want. And yes, Will thought he needed someone like her for far too long, but what he *needs* is someone who makes him happy. Someone who wants him for who he is, not that damned title."

Phoebe smirked. "I don't think I've ever heard you curse before."

"I only do it when someone is being particularly dunderheaded." Alex punctuated this with a glower.

"A good policy," Phoebe said with a laugh.

Alex broke into a small smile before she turned serious once again. "The point is, I can't imagine Will being much bothered by petty society gossip, especially *now*. The man did just willingly ruin any chance he had at becoming prime minister," she added and gave Phoebe a knowing look.

"That wasn't *my* doing."

"No, but I think you gave him the push he needed to be truer to himself," Alex said. "I know the social obligations of a duchess aren't very appealing, but instead of focusing on all the worst bits, why not imagine all the good you could do together?"

Your sister is *human, despite her efforts to appear otherwise.*

Phoebe's mouth reluctantly curved at the memory of Will's words. She blew out a breath.

"You're quite insightful, you know."

"On occasion," Alex said with a brief smile.

Phoebe thought of Alice worrying about Maude's future, and the crestfallen looks of the girls when they were told that the school had to close. She thought of Millie, wishing there was a school near her, and Mrs. Richardson, valiantly pushing on despite setback after setback. Phoebe's heart sank with the heavy weight of regret. How much had she lost simply by being afraid? Alex was looking at her with the slightest hint of compassion in her gaze—a commiserating pout on anyone else—and Phoebe's lip began to tremble.

"I don't suppose you know what Will is up to now that Parliament is in recess?" she croaked.

"Last I knew he went to Derbyshire for the month."

Her heart sank even further. It was one thing to travel to Mayfair for a mea culpa, but Derbyshire would take a little more planning. "It's just as well," she sighed. "Better I have time to think this through."

Besides, even if Will hadn't proposed merely out of obligation, his feelings could certainly have changed after her cold rejection.

You are obviously only doing this out of some misplaced sense of honor. So let me assure you, unequivocally, that it is not necessary. Nor is it welcome.

Phoebe cringed. She needed to do this right. But first she needed to figure out just what it was she wanted.

"Why don't you go to Surrey for a bit," Alex gently suggested. "It would be good for you to get out of the city."

Phoebe thought about her lonely little flat and the long, aimless days that stretched ahead of her. "Yes, I think I will."

"I'll tell Father tonight. I know he's been thinking of taking the Ericsons there for some shooting at the end of the month, but it will be empty until then."

"Perhaps you and Freddie could come and stay too," Phoebe said shyly. "It would be nice, us all together."

Alex broke into a wide smile. "That's a marvelous idea. Come back to Park House with me. Then we can tell everyone together."

Phoebe rose from her chair. "All right." For the first time in ages, she looked forward to going home. Phoebe clung to that warm, comforting feeling while she waited for Alex to gather her things. Then they walked down the hall arm in arm. As they passed by their father's dark office, Alex turned to her.

"You know," she began. "He still keeps those candies you always liked in his desk."

"Oh? I didn't know he liked them too."

"I've never seen him touch the stuff," Alex sniffed. "No, I think he keeps them there for you. Just in case you ever come to visit."

Phoebe swallowed against the lump that had formed in her throat. "Well, then I will," she rasped. Out of the corner of her eye she could see Alex smile.

"Glad to hear it."

Twenty-Six

*A*fter a few days in Surrey, Will found his rhythm in the slower pace of the country. He still awoke at dawn, but now instead of hurrying to get dressed and prepare for an onslaught of activities, Will enjoyed a simple meal of tea and toast while leisurely reading. Since the London papers didn't arrive until the afternoon, he began starting his day with a bit of a novel instead. He had fallen out of the habit of reading fiction years ago, but Cal had practically forced the first Inspector Dumond novel into Will's hands and he quickly devoured it before moving on to the next.

Cal was usually up by nine and they breakfasted together while discussing their plans for the day, after which they each retreated to their separate areas of the house: Cal in the library and Will in the upstairs sitting room, as there was a small writing desk underneath a window that looked out over the back garden. Will often lost himself gazing at the lawn below, his thoughts floating between business, Cal's future, his mother, and the remnants of his personal life.

Sometimes they had luncheon together, but not always. Then once Will had caught up on all the work he had neglected in the morning, he would take a rambling afternoon walk. Back in London, he spent most of his days cooped up inside various elegantly appointed rooms, but they couldn't compete with good English countryside.

Upon returning, he would wash up and join Cal for supper followed by a quiet evening in the parlor.

"Perhaps you should spend more time here," Cal replied one morning when Will announced that he couldn't remember the last time he felt so at ease, nor slept so soundly.

But that was impossible. Aside from the never-ending demands of the dukedom, the Atkinsons' property bordered their own. More than once he had inadvertently wandered to the top of the small hill that overlooked the inviting Georgian manor house, with its heavy boughs of wisteria framing the main entrance and curling lengths of ivy growing up the walls. It was nearly as familiar to him as his own childhood home. But even gazing at it from a safe distance still caused his heart to lurch.

No. He could not stay here.

Besides, Will had a country home of his own—several, in fact. Though none of them really felt like his. They were full of dusty antiques and family heirlooms that held no meaning for him. Will was simply the guardian of these properties and this title until it passed on to the next duke. But by God if he had a son Will would do everything in his power to keep it from becoming an albatross around the boy's neck.

"Perhaps," Will replied before changing the subject to the weather. It wasn't the subtlest of responses, but Cal didn't press him on it.

Later that day Father Lloyd, the new vicar, came to luncheon. He was a nice, quiet chap with a thin frame and hair as pale as cornsilk who put a gleam in Cal's eye that Will hadn't seen in years. It seemed a good idea to give the two of them time to visit alone, so once the plates were cleared, Will excused himself and went off on his daily ramble. This time he made sure to head in the opposite direction of the Atkinsons' house, least his rebellious feet carry him there again.

Though spending more time at home was out of the question, Will did like the idea of being closer to Cal. Perhaps he could find a little place away from the London fishbowl and without the hefty ducal expectations that came with visiting his estates. A tidy cottage that had no need for a dozen servants to keep it running. A place where he could have true peace and privacy. A place where he could just be... himself. The thought spurred him onward and for the first time in weeks, he felt genuinely excited about something. Will crested another hill and stopped to catch his breath. As he scanned the verdant swells and dales before him, his eyes lit on something below.

The brook.

Will tugged on his collar and let out a sigh of envy. Would he were still a lad with the freedom to take an impromptu swim.

So do it, then, an appealing voice whispered. *There's no one about.*

This vantage point gave him a clear view of the surrounding area, which was enticingly empty of people. No one to happen upon a naked duke. Will shifted on his feet. He could already feel the cool rush of water on his overheated skin. Before he could talk himself out of it, he was hurrying down the hillside, unbuttoning his shirt as he went.

Afterward, feeling quite refreshed and just a little bit naughty, Will lay on the bank to dry out. He closed his eyes against the warm sun and inhaled the dusky scent of ripe wildflowers and summer grass.

The Atkinson girls used to come here to make daisy crowns. Once, Phoebe had shyly given him her crown and he proudly put it on his head, hoping to make her burst into a fit of giggles. Instead, she beamed up at him with those big hazel eyes until he returned it and carelessly moved on to something else.

Only now did he realize she had meant it as a gift. And he had just tossed it aside.

Alex had been right. He *was* an idiot.

Will sat up and pulled on his damp shirt. His wet hair still clung to his scalp, but he couldn't lay here any longer. He needed to move. To outrun these blasted memories. By the time he entered the house and stalked past the open parlor door toward the staircase, he was so lost in his own thoughts that he didn't hear Cal until he practically shouted his name. Will paused on the first step. Father Lloyd was probably still here. It would be incredibly rude of him not to say goodbye, even in his current state of dishevelment. Will swallowed his sigh and headed back toward the parlor.

It was only once he had entered the room with no hope of escaping unnoticed that he realized it wasn't the vicar sitting with his brother, but Phoebe herself.

As Will stopped dead in his tracks, he belatedly remembered that his damp shirt hung open at his throat and his sleeves were rolled to nearly his elbows, while his jacket was folded across his arm. In other words, he was scandalously undressed.

She's seen you naked.

Unsurprisingly, the reminder didn't help.

For her part, Phoebe's cheeks had turned a particularly fetching shade of rose that suggested she had been equally caught off guard.

"Isn't this a lovely surprise?" Cal grinned, blissfully unaware of the undercurrent of tension running between them. "Phoebe is staying next door for a few days and came by to say hello."

Will blinked rapidly but the apparition did not fade. Phoebe was *here*. In the parlor. Looking like an ethereal maiden in white muslin, while a droplet of brook water slid down his back.

"Hello," he replied. It felt as awkward as it sounded.

"I didn't know you were home," she said quickly—and accusingly. Then she stood up and the napkin on her lap fell onto the floor. "I should go." Phoebe then turned to Cal. "It was so good to see you again."

"You're leaving?" Cal was obviously confused, but Phoebe was already headed for the doorway.

"Wait," Will called out weakly as she rushed past him and exited the room, a delicate scent of fresh linen trailing in her wake. He couldn't help the deep inhalation that followed and his eyes fluttered closed.

But Cal was too busy staring after her with open-mouthed astonishment to notice this pathetic display. "I don't know what's happened," he said to Will. "We were having the most lovely chat." Then he frowned in horror. "I hope I didn't say something to *offend* her."

"You didn't," Will said as he tore his gaze from the now empty doorway. "What is she doing here? In Surrey," he added.

"Her school closed, poor thing. So Alex suggested she come home for a bit of rest."

"What?" His mind whirled at the news while his heart ached for what she had lost. All that work had been for naught. She would be devastated.

But Will didn't wait for Cal to respond. Those rebellious feet of his had already gone after Phoebe. And this time, Will would not stop them.

Phoebe raced down the front steps and cut across the lawn, propelled entirely by her own blinding sense of mortification. If she had any idea Will was there, she never would have set foot on the Margraves' property, let alone their *parlor*.

Cal had been thrilled by her surprise visit and they quickly got lost catching up until his eyes suddenly lit at the sound of footsteps storming down the hall.

"Oh, that must be Will now."

Will? *Here?*

Phoebe had been too stunned to respond, then desperately hoped she had misunderstood, until the man himself strode into the room and looked at her as if she was a ghost, so great was his shock. Entirely understandable given the remarks she had hurled at him during their last encounter. But now she was in his own home holding a biscuit and gaping at him like an idiot.

Somehow he had grown even more handsome over the last two months, though that could have been on account of how little clothing he was wearing. His shirt was open at the throat, revealing a glimpse of his naked chest, tan from the summer sun, and his hair was appealingly tousled—just as it had been the night they investigated the music hall, or the morning he lay asleep in her bed. In any case, he looked healthy and well rested and *very* surprised to see her.

Cal was asking him something about his walk, but Will's dark eyes were solely fixed to her with alarming intensity. Phoebe didn't care to wait to see his expression change to outrage once he recovered from his understandable shock, so instead she bolted.

My God, what must he *think* of her?

Though Will deserved her apology, that at least meant sending over a note first. Not showing up in the man's *home*. She had nearly made it to the footpath that connected the two properties when someone called out her name. Phoebe glanced back and saw Will stalking down the lane. Her first instinct was to break into a run, but he would overtake her in another moment. Rather than make this even more awkward, Phoebe stopped and turned around to accept his ire. She owed him that much.

His gaze narrowed as he drew closer and Phoebe instinctively shut her eyes.

"I'm sorry," she blurted out. "I had no idea you were home."

Her explanation was met by an excruciating silence.

"I know," he finally murmured. Phoebe cracked one eye open, then the other. Well, he didn't *look* angry.

He also hadn't bothered to button his shirt. As he stepped closer, Phoebe noticed it was damp. Damp enough to show the outline of his chest. Which she had touched with her own hands.

"I came to see Cal," she explained while forcing her gaze to meet his own.

One corner of his mouth pulled back, as if he were trying not to smile. "I know." Then he swallowed and Phoebe was riveted by the movement of his bronzed throat.

Lord, she needed to get out of here.

"He said your school closed?"

Phoebe glanced up at the question, but the sympathy in his eyes was even more than she could bear. She had to look away. "The landlord got a better offer. It will be a department store."

"I'm very sorry," Will said. "What will you do now?"

Phoebe let out a grim laugh and turned back to him. "Not a clue. Alex said I should come here to clear my head and decide what to do next."

Though that was not working out so well at the moment.

But Will gave a thoughtful nod. "I've found it can be helpful to break out of one's routine now and then."

"Oh?" That was surprising to hear. She couldn't imagine Will ever feeling unsure about anything. He always seemed so certain, so secure about his place in the world. But then he looked down with a sheepish expression that squeezed her heart.

"London had become...too much. I needed to leave for a while."

Understanding dawned on her. "I read about your actions in the papers."

It had been impossible to avoid, given how much ink had been spilled in the papers both decrying and extolling his defection from the ruling party.

"It was long overdue," he added dismissively, as if it weren't the political scandal of the summer.

"Even so," Phoebe said gently. "I think the bill you and Lord Tavistock proposed will do much good."

Will met her gaze and his dark eyes flickered with an emotion she was dangerously tempted to call hope. "You do?"

Phoebe couldn't stop from smiling at his eager tone and nodded.

"I appreciate that." He returned her smile but then quickly sobered. "I've also spoken with Lord Fairbanks. He shouldn't cause you any trouble, but please let me know immediately if he does."

Phoebe tilted her head. "Did Alex not tell you? No, of course she didn't," she muttered at Will's look of confusion. "She bought up his debts and threatened to ruin him if anything came out about myself or the Clarke sisters."

His eyes widened as he processed the enormity of what Alex had taken on. "My God. That is...impressive."

"And a little terrifying."

"Two words that most certainly describe Alex," Will added with a knowing smile Phoebe liked far too much. She glanced toward the footpath and he immediately noticed. "I'm sorry for keeping you," he said, taking a step back. The instinct to reach for him was so strong that Phoebe had to force her hand into a tight fist. "I only wanted to make sure you didn't leave on account of me. I won't bother you."

"No," she said quickly. "It is I who should apologize. Coming into your home after..."

She couldn't make herself say the words. *After I rejected you.*

But Will shook his head. "I haven't been here in years. It belongs to Cal now. And he can welcome anyone he likes."

Phoebe stared at him as he shifted in place. This man, who had the entire country at his beck and call, wasn't even comfortable in the place of his birth.

"It's still your home too, Will." She then blushed again as his eyebrows rose in surprise. That remark had been far too overfamiliar. She didn't deserve to say such things to him. Not anymore. Goodness, she was stepping in it today. "My sisters are coming tomorrow," she added briskly, attempting to retain some degree of neighborly cordiality. "Perhaps...perhaps we will see you again."

She made sure to say *we*, as she didn't have the right to assume *I*.

He studied her for a moment before nodding. "Yes. Perhaps," he said haltingly followed by a short bow. "Have a good evening."

"You as well," Phoebe replied, but he had already turned away. She stood in place as he strode toward the house and watched until he disappeared inside.

But he never looked back.

Twenty-Seven

*A*re you all right? You've been awfully quiet ever since we got here."

Alex's words roused Phoebe from her thoughts. She shifted in her chair by the hearth and faced her sister.

"Sorry. I'm fine," she said with a smile that felt as forced as it must have looked.

For the last day, Will had barely left her mind. The regret that had been gnawing at her for weeks had reached a violent crescendo once he was standing before her in the flesh. Phoebe could see so clearly how her own misgivings had drowned out the very real feelings she had for him. Feelings she was now utterly incapable of ignoring.

Alex immediately frowned. "If you didn't want us to come, you should have said so." She and Freddie had arrived that afternoon and they had all retired to the cozy parlor after an early supper.

"No, it's not that at all. I'm so glad you're both here. Truly."

"For goodness' sake, go easy on her, Alex," Freddie chimed in from her place sprawled on the chaise, where she was sipping her second glass of sherry. Or was it her third? Phoebe had been too distracted to keep track. "She's *obviously* still heartsick over Will," Freddie added with a dramatic sweep of her arm.

Definitely a third sherry.

Alex narrowed her eyes at Phoebe. "Is that it?"

Freddie let out a sputtering laugh. "Considering she's actually in possession of a full range of human emotions, yes."

Phoebe shot her a chiding look as Alex crossed her arms. Freddie had been in an unusually prickly mood that evening, which wasn't helped by the wine she'd imbibed at supper. Phoebe suspected Hank Ericson was the culprit, but hadn't had the chance to ask.

"I *have* emotions," Alex insisted. "But last time we spoke you only said you needed time to think. Has something changed?"

Phoebe picked at a loose thread on her skirt. "You could say that." She then explained about her visit with Cal yesterday, along with Will's unexpected appearance.

"Oh God," Freddie said with wide eyes. "How mortifying."

"Now look who's being insensitive," Alex crowed.

Phoebe let out a groan and slumped in her chair. "It's true though. I looked like an idiot. A *fickle* idiot, at that."

"But he did come after you," Freddie pointed out. "Surely that means something good."

"It means he was being polite," Phoebe replied. "To save us both any future awkwardness."

After going over their brief conversation a hundred times at least, that was her most indulgent interpretation. The worst was Will thinking she was a self-important little harpy and needed to be sure she had left the property—Phoebe couldn't torture herself with that one anymore.

"No, I agree with Freddie, actually," Alex said with a decided nod. "He didn't have to do that. Rather dramatic, if you ask me."

Freddie let out a snort. "You think any kind of expression is dramatic."

Alex sat forward in her chair. "Running out of the house in a wet shirt *is* dramatic!"

"And romantic," Freddie said with a dreamy sigh. "Oh, I'm excited for you!"

Phoebe crossed her arms against the flutter in her chest. "Why? Nothing has happened." She said it as much for herself as her sister.

But Freddie simply held up a finger. "Yet."

"Perhaps we can all go for a picnic tomorrow," Alex suggested. "Remember that spot where we used to pick daisies?"

"They don't need a picnic," Freddie cut in. "They need to be *alone.*" She then waggled her eyebrows.

"You truly are a master of subtly," Phoebe remarked.

"The we can suggest they go for a walk just the two of them," Alex tried again, but Freddie let out an exasperated sigh.

"That is *so* obvious!"

Alex lifted her chin. "Well, I wouldn't suspect anything."

"Because, again, *you* aren't normal."

"All right, that's enough," Phoebe said as Alex's mouth fell open in offense. "Freddie, none of us are anywhere close to normal. If you manage to think of a not painfully awkward way to get us alone, do let me know. But for now I'm off to bed. And a picnic does sound like a lovely idea, Alex. With or without the Margraves."

"I'll send a note first thing tomorrow," Alex said, resolute.

"Sleep well, sisters," Phoebe replied as she rose from her chair. "And *try* to be nice to each other once I leave."

Freddie mumbled an apology while Alex gave a begrudging nod.

But hours later, despite her exhaustion, Phoebe was still wide awake. She had been tossing and turning since the moment she laid her head on her pillow, as every time she closed her eyes, all she saw was Will standing before her on the lane while Freddie's words echoed in her mind:

Surely that means something good.

With her sisters' encouragement fresh on her mind, Phoebe forced herself to examine their exchange with new eyes. Though he had every right to coldly dismiss her from his home, he did the exact opposite. He was courteous and apologetic and, most baffling of all, kind.

But that wasn't fair. Will had always been kind to her, even when he was also being insufferably stuffy. Phoebe smiled in the darkness as she remembered the priggish duke who had barged into Inspector Holland's office. How much he had changed since then. How much *she* had changed. But her feelings for Will remained stubbornly, achingly consistent.

Freddie was right about one thing: they did need to speak alone. But with her sisters here already creating havoc and their parents following a few days later, her options were quickly shrinking. Tonight could be her last chance to say everything she had been mulling over since he followed her out onto the footpath.

Phoebe sat up and pushed back the covers. If he rejected her, so be it. He had every right to do so. But even still, she had to know. Had to be certain whether all was lost between them or if there was the slightest chance to have her heart's deepest desire. The tiny flicker of hope her sisters' words had sparked grew into a guttering flame as Phoebe quickly dressed and stole out of the house. Luckily, the moon was full and lit her way through the woods. But even if it had been pitch dark out, she would have found the way. Phoebe could always find her way to Will.

Will turned onto his back and let out a sigh. It had been a good two hours since he'd retired and the house had long gone silent, but he still couldn't sleep.

Though he had been relieved to learn that Phoebe and the Clarke girls were entirely safe from Lord Fairbanks, a small, selfish part of him was disappointed. For it meant he was absolutely useless to her now.

He had just resolved to get a book when there was a rustling outside. Will sat up and waited, just in case he was hearing things, but after a moment, the sound came again. Something was *definitely* outside—and getting closer. Will frowned as he threw back the covers and stepped lightly across the room. It had to be some kind of bird or animal. What else would it be at one in the morning? He paused for a moment, then pushed open the window, hoping the sound would scare off whatever was out there. But instead the something fell *inside*. Not something, he immediately realized, but *someone*.

Will swore as the intruder toppled directly against him. They both hit the floor hard, with Will taking the brunt of the landing. He let out a groan while a pair of small hands pressed onto his chest.

"Good lord," the intruder hissed. "You aren't wearing a shirt."

He blinked at the dark mass as a familiar scent cut through his confusion. "Phoebe?"

She threw off the hood of the cloak she was wearing and looked down at him. Her eyes sparkled in the low light. "Or trousers."

Will immediately pushed her off him and launched to his feet. Then he wrapped the heavy velvet curtain across his torso, as it was the only available piece of fabric within reach. "Well, I was abed. And wasn't exactly *expecting* anyone," he huffed.

"I'm not criticizing you," Phoebe said as she stood. "I'm just surprised."

For some reason he found this insulting. Will raised an eyebrow. "I suppose you thought I wore an ankle-length nightshirt and a cap?"

"Not a *cap*." Phoebe laughed. "But definitely a nightshirt."

"Sorry to disappoint," he said crisply.

"I never said I was disappointed," she murmured and moved deeper into the room.

Will pressed the curtain even tighter across his hips as this strange mixture of humiliation and arousal coursed through him. He cleared his throat in an attempt to sound somewhat controlled. "Would you mind telling me what you're doing here? And why you didn't use the front door?"

Phoebe glanced at him over her shoulder. "At this hour? I was trying to be more inconspicuous to protect my reputation," she explained, though it sounded like she was teasing him. "I thought you'd approve. Besides," she added as she began studying his room. "I didn't know you'd be naked."

Will let out a cough. "Yes, well." He didn't finish the thought. She had moved to the large bookshelf in the corner that held various knickknacks, and Will suddenly felt even *more* naked—if that was possible.

"You have an awful lot of poetry books," she observed.

Good. Poetry. A completely innocuous topic they could discuss whilst he hid behind a drape.

"I fancied myself an heir to the Romantics at one time."

She threw him a scandalous look. "Even Lord Byron?"

"In my younger days," he admitted. "I'm not proud of it."

Then she gave him a smile that made the drape feel even more inadequate and he had to clear his throat again. "Would you mind handing me my dressing gown?" He pointed to where it was slung over the back of a chair near her.

Phoebe tossed it to him. Then returned to her perusal of the bookcase to give him a bit of privacy. Will knotted the dressing gown tighter than usual. She seemed remarkably at ease while standing in a man's bedroom in the wee hours of the night.

"Do you make it a habit of climbing through windows?" Lord, he hated how priggish he sounded.

"No," she said measuredly and continued to scan the shelves. "Only with you."

His heart seemed to miss several beats, but before Will could respond to this admission, Phoebe came to an abrupt halt. Something had caught her eye. As soon as she reached toward the right-hand corner of an upper shelf, Will remembered and his heart came stuttering to life.

Dammit.

She pulled down the pencil drawing slightly yellowed with age and stared at it for a long moment while Will's stomach became well acquainted with the floor. He had completely forgotten about the drawing.

"I didn't know you kept this," she said, her voice understandably full of astonishment.

Will swallowed. This... would be difficult to explain. It was a relic from that long-ago summer. Alex and Phoebe had come to visit him and Cal one evening and they all sat in the back garden enjoying the long, later hours of daylight.

In just a few weeks Will would learn about the dukedom, but that evening he was blissfully unaware of what fate lay in store. Instead it was Phoebe, with her long hair and sly wit, who kept his attention. Cal was always sketching in those days. His fingers never seemed to stop moving, and as they all chatted he drew. First a blooming shrub, then a happy little mouse dressed in a suit, and finally Phoebe in all her sun-kissed summer glory.

When he showed her the finished portrait, she immediately declared her chin too sharp and made Cal put it under the sketch pad out of her sight. But later, after the sisters had left and Cal had gone inside, Will went back for it. He thought it a marvelous likeness. Cal had expertly rendered her heart-shaped face, which Will thought was perfectly proportional, along with the mischievous gleam in her eye.

"I liked it," he said simply, for that was the truth.

She let out a short, baffled laugh and ran a finger along the edge of the yellowed paper. "I was so embarrassed when Cal showed this to me, though I can't remember why now."

"It is a very good likeness."

Phoebe began to turn toward him and paused. "I barely dared to hope back then that you . . . you saw me like that."

The firelight danced along her profile, illuminating the delicate slope of her nose, her parted lips, and, yes, her perfectly pointed chin.

"I've always seen you, Phoebe," Will breathed. It was a relief, in a way, to say the truth aloud.

As she met his gaze, Will was beyond grateful to see the desperate hunger in her eyes. His was probably worse.

"Why did you come here?" He forced the question past his lips and paired it with a tentative step forward. It felt like he was standing barefoot on a bed of nails as he awaited her answer.

Her eyelids fluttered, as if she had just woken up. "I . . . I wanted to speak to you," she murmured.

Will inhaled deeply in a futile attempt to control the erratic beating of his heart and took another step. "About something that couldn't wait till morning?"

She shook her head slowly. "No." The word was softer than a whisper.

Will opened his mouth to speak, but his words were lost as Phoebe suddenly ran to him. He wrapped her in his arms without a thought and pulled her to his chest.

"I'm sorry," she said against his neck. "I'm sorry I was so awful to you back in London when you were only trying to help."

He stroked her hair and it slid under his fingertips like silk. "You weren't awful, I behaved like a pompous ass." He could feel her answering smile. "I deserved it."

"Even still, I shouldn't have spoken so harshly," she said. Then she pulled back and met his eyes. "I came here to ask for your forgiveness. And your friendship."

Will cupped the side of her face with his palm and gently stroked her cheek with his thumb. "You never lost it."

But Phoebe shook her head even while she pressed her hand to his, as if there was any chance he would have pulled away. "Well, I *should* have. The things I accused you of—"

"Phoebe, please," Will urged. "We both said careless things we didn't quite mean in the moment. I know that." Then he let out a breath. "But I should have been more understanding about your reservations instead of deluding myself into thinking you need me." He let out a dry laugh. "But that was only because I wasn't ready to accept the truth—that it was I who needed you."

She gaped at him. "You...you do?"

"Most ardently," he said with a decided nod. "You've had my heart since that summer," he said, gesturing to the drawing. "And then I wasted an awful lot of time thinking I needed someone to fit into my life. A life I was forced into. But I won't do that anymore. I want to fit into yours."

She pressed her forehead to his chest. "What's left of it, you mean?"

Her morose tone set his teeth on edge. "This is just a setback. You're meant to do great things, Phoebe. And I want to be there while you do them. That is, if you'll let me."

She huffed a laugh that fanned out across his skin and tilted her head up. "You say that as though there's any doubt even while I stand here."

"Well, you weren't so keen on it before," he reminded her.

"True," she said with a nod. "It wasn't until I talked to Alex that I realize how scared I was."

Will raised an eyebrow in question. "Of me?"

"God, *no*," she said fiercely. "About being a duchess," she admitted. "And the expectations that come with the title. It sounds so silly now, but I let that overrule everything in the moment." She paused for a breath. "Even the love I felt for you."

Will's chest warmed at her words. "My darling," he breathed as he cupped her cheek once again. "But it *is* scary. I understand that. Believe me. Perhaps more than anyone."

Phoebe's eyes fluttered shut and she leaned her forehead against his chest once again. "I've been such an idiot."

Will smiled as he began to rub her back. "May I get that in writing? Preferably engraved on a plaque of some kind?"

Phoebe grinned up at him. "It can be your wedding present," she quipped.

"An excellent idea. I accept. But only if you kiss me first."

She pressed a much too chaste kiss to the hollow at the base of his throat. "Does that count as me proposing to you?"

Will tucked a lock of hair behind her ear. "Let's call it a draw and say we *both* did."

"Oh, I like that idea," she said brightly.

"I thought you might." He gave her a sly smile as he leaned in. "Duchess."

Phoebe broke into a laugh just before he pressed his lips to hers. "You know, that doesn't sound half bad when you say it."

"I'm delighted. Now for God's sake, let me kiss you properly."

Phoebe ran her fingers through his hair and gave him a teasingly apologetic look. "Yes, Duke."

Will let out a growl as he pressed her back against the bookcase. Phoebe immediately curled her arms around his neck and heat surged below his waist. Neither of them would be leaving this room until she said that again in earnest.

Will began to drag his lips upward along the curve of her neck, enjoying the way she shivered beneath him.

"You weren't hoping for a long engagement, were you?" he murmured by her ear.

"Hmm," she began in mock consideration while her fingers dug into his hair just the way he liked. "I suppose it depends on how convincing you can be."

Will pulled back to find the glint of friendly challenge in her eye. "Oh, I can be *very* convincing."

She leaned in until their noses were touching. "Good. Let's see."

Will then took her mouth in a lush, demanding kiss, and set to work doing just that.

The bookshelf proved delightfully sturdier than expected. And even though a few volumes of poetry were sacrificed to the floor in the process, Will felt certain Byron would approve.

"All right, I'm convinced," Phoebe said afterward rather breathlessly as he collapsed beside her. They had been forced to move to his bed, lest the entire house awaken from the rhythmic thudding of the bookshelf against the wall. Will was absurdly proud he had even managed such a position in the first place, but he wouldn't attempt it again unless they were truly alone.

He pressed a kiss to Phoebe's cheek. "Happy to hear it. Now we just need to tell your family."

Phoebe groaned. "Must we? I'd much rather elope to Gretna Green and tell them afterwards."

He turned on his side to face her. "Can't. They make you wait a week now even there."

Phoebe let out a surprised laugh. "How do you know that?"

"Cal's been giving me his lurid novels to read while I'm here."

Her eyes lit with excitement. "Oh! He has the most *marvelous* taste."

"And to think they let you shape young minds," he said with a teasing kiss.

Phoebe let out another laugh. "Those girls would probably never stop reading if I could teach them penny dreadfuls."

Will stroked her hair. "Perhaps something to think about."

"Along with everything else," she added with a sigh.

"There really is no rush, Phoebe. We can find a way. I just want to be with you. Though we might need to be more careful, unless you're ready to start a family."

She gave him a shy smile. "Not yet. I'll talk to Alex about precautions we can take."

Will blinked. "Oh."

"It's one of her pet projects, funding free contraception to women—though Father doesn't know. Even *that* may be too eccentric for him," she added quickly, then turned thoughtful. "I do think I've been too hard on her."

"It seems to be the natural course for indulged younger siblings."

She gave him a friendly pinch. "But you and Cal get on."

"We do," Will acknowledged before revealing their conversation last fall that had spurred his decision to bride hunt. "I suppose I can't be too cross with him though," he said as he pulled Phoebe into his arms once more, "since it led to this moment, however winding the path may have been."

"Yes, let us be grateful for our meddlesome siblings, older and younger alike."

Will chuckled and kissed her nose. "And let us never tell them so, lest they take all the credit."

"Agreed." Phoebe then pressed Will onto his back. "Now no more talk of family. I want to try that last thing we did again, but with me on top this time."

Will clasped his hands behind his head and let out a mock-sigh. "All right. But I must say, you are very demanding."

Phoebe leaned down until their noses touched. "Oh, you have *no* idea," she murmured.

A grin split his face as he pulled her in for a kiss, quite certain he was going to enjoy finding out.

Twenty-Eight

The next morning Will headed for the breakfast room much later than usual. Cal would have finished hours ago, but Will didn't mind the thought of having the room to himself as he couldn't stop smiling like an idiot. Phoebe would be his *wife.*

He had spirited her out of the house through the back entrance hours ago before immediately returning to bed for some much-needed sleep. But he had every intention of repeating their activities tonight. Perhaps in her bed this time. He could surprise her, much like she had surprised him. But rather than falling through the window, Will preferred something more subtle, like kissing her awake.

It was on that thought he entered the breakfast room. And found his *mother* seated at the table.

"Oh, good morning, darling," she trilled, setting down her teacup. "Cal's gone into the village, but I've been waiting for you, sleepyhead." Will was rendered speechless. "Here, take a seat," she said as she patted the spot beside her. Will was so stunned he obeyed without question. "Would you like me to make you a plate? I had Cook make a tray of creamed eggs for you."

Will managed a nod. "All right."

She flashed him a smile and set about gathering his breakfast from the sideboard while Will eyed her.

"I thought you were in Sussex with the Hoxtons," he said.

"I was, but then Mrs. Hoxton wasn't feeling well, poor thing. So I returned to London early. Then Cal sent me a message saying you were here." She cast him a glance over her shoulder. "Do you still hate kippers?"

"Yes."

She clucked her tongue and glided over with his breakfast. "Just like your father," she said with a smile. "They're good for your brain."

Will's mouth quirked. They had been having this debate since he was a boy. "I don't care. They taste like low tide."

"Nonsense!"

She returned to her seat as Will picked up his fork. "Thank you for remembering the creamed eggs, though."

"Of course."

Will attacked his plate with relish. He was far hungrier than he realized. His mother watched him with rapt interest.

"Oh my," she marveled. "Cal said you had been keeping active here."

Will grunted in reply. Better she not know exactly *how*.

"It's good for you to get outside in the fresh air," she continued. "You spend too much time behind a desk."

"That's not really a choice I have, Mother," he said tartly. "Managing a dukedom is rather a lot of work."

"I know that. But you have very competent people working for you. I only meant it needn't consume you so," she added.

Will set down his fork, but the sympathy in his mother's eyes took the bite out of his temper. "You're right."

Her eyebrows rose. "I don't think I've ever heard you say that to me before."

"Mother," he warned. "In my defense, you haven't given me much advice. It's usually the other way round."

She glanced down at the decorative tablecloth and began running her finger along the stitching. "I know," she murmured.

Was his mother nervous? The thought was rather unsettling.

"You've had so much put upon you," she began. "First your father died and you had to make sure we were all right. Then all the nonsense with the dukedom."

Will raised an eyebrow. She had never once uttered a cross word about it before.

"And you've borne it all without complaint," she continued, meeting his gaze. "But I think...I think it must have been very hard."

Her voice grew thicker on those last words and Will had to clear his throat before he could speak. "Why did you come here?"

"Because Cal asked me to. He thought it would be good for you. For us," she amended.

Will stiffened automatically. "I see."

Her dark eyes searched his face. "I know you're punishing me for something. I just wish you would *tell* me."

Will stared past her out the window. What he would give to be with Phoebe right now. He was his better self with her. He let out a heavy sigh. "I don't mean to punish you, Mother. Truly. But I've never been able to understand why you sent me away that summer. After I inherited."

She looked genuinely surprised. "I didn't *send you away*. His Grace summoned you, and it seemed like the best thing."

"But you didn't even ask me. Just shipped me off to Derbyshire."

"Well, of course I did. What did *I* know about becoming a duke? There was so much for you to learn. And by then you had already been at Oxford a year," she pointed out. "You weren't a boy anymore, Will."

He sat back in his chair and crossed his arms, feeling like a petulant sixteen-year-old again. "I hadn't been since the day Father died."

She bowed her head. "I know I relied on you too much back then, and I'm sorry for that. It wasn't fair to you, all that responsibility. I suppose I thought it meant the inheritance was easier for you to navigate. But maybe that was just convenient thinking on my part," she added. "And then Cal had his accident and he was so ill for so long…"

She looked up and her face was etched in such pain that Will felt it in his chest. That had been a terrible time for all of them.

"I know," Will said, reaching for her hand. "I'm sorry. I—I hadn't thought of it like that."

Her fingers tightened around his palm. "Don't be. That's a mother's job. And you're right. I should have protected you more."

With her words, the heaviness over his heart began to lessen. Will had grown so used to carrying that weight he hadn't noticed its presence until now. Though it would take more than one morning for that old wound to fully heal, this was a promising start. "I appreciate that. Very much."

She gave his hand another squeeze before letting go to take a sip of tea. "So then," she began without preamble. "Cal said you made Phoebe Atkinson run out of here yesterday."

Will nearly choked on a bite of creamed egg. "Did he now," he rasped. Given that he and Phoebe had reached an understanding only hours ago, Will hadn't told Cal the truth about their relationship. That hadn't stopped his brother from peppering him with increasingly pointed questions last night. At the time Will thought he had successfully deflected Cal's suspicions, but the smirk on his mother's face told a different story.

"He also said that you spent the rest of the evening in a foul mood, though that doesn't appear to be the case this morning."

Will blew out a breath. Best get this over with as quickly as possible. "Phoebe and I are going to marry."

But the amusement on his mother's face immediately turned to shock. She pressed her hands against the table. "*What?*"

Will shook his head in confusion. "Well, what did you think I was going to say?"

"Not that!" She rocked back in her chair and squinted past him as if trying to understand a difficult math problem.

"You don't approve." Will was surprised by how devastated he felt.

But his mother finally looked at him and her eyes softened. "No, no. It isn't that at all. Only I . . . I would have *sworn* it was Alex you were after."

Will leaned his head back in relief even as he rolled his eyes. "Mother, we've been over this—"

"I know—"

"Again and again. And *again*—"

She laughed and held up her hands in supplication. "I *know*. I know." Then she tilted her head, considering something. "Phoebe, eh?"

Will gave a decided nod. "Phoebe."

"I'm happy for you. And, not that you need it, but I wholeheartedly approve," she said, returning his nod. "That girl has a good head on her shoulders and a generous spirit. Excellent qualities in a partner."

"Thank you," Will said, noting that she hadn't said *duchess*.

"And I know you've been worried all this time about finding someone who would make a good duchess," she continued, as if she could sense his thoughts, "but I think it is better this way. You shouldn't have to sacrifice everything to the title. Life is short, my boy. And happiness can be so fleeting. When you find it, you must grab hold of it tightly for as long as you can."

Will had to look away from her shimmering eyes, lest they both become overwrought with emotion. "I intend to."

"Well then," she said with a watery smile. "I suppose you had better take yourself over to the Atkinsons next."

Will waved a hand. "I'm sure Phoebe already told her sisters. I'll head over there later."

But his mother gave him an arch look. "Actually, I was referring to her parents. I came down with them on the early train."

Will must have made some kind of verbal response, but he would be helpless to repeat it. Mostly he was *very* glad Phoebe hadn't slept in. He threw down his napkin and pushed out his chair. "I'll be back."

"Should I tell Cal the news?" his mother asked as he headed for the door.

"No, wait for me," he managed to call back. "Let me tell him."

Will didn't want to miss the gloating look on his brother's face. He smiled at the thought and hurried even faster to the Atkinsons' house.

Twenty-Nine

I'm deliriously happy for you, Phoebe, but if you even think of putting me in a lavender bridesmaid's dress, I'll scream."

"Freddie!" Mother admonished.

"Only because it makes me look like the undead," she added.

Phoebe's grip on Will's arm subtly tightened. They had only just told them the news and the wedding talk was already starting.

Her parents had arrived a day earlier than originally expected to prepare for their guests. When Phoebe had slunk back to the house at daybreak after her reunion with Will, she had been greeted by Alex, who broke the news of their parents' impending arrival along with her own decision to return to London on the early train, using the vague excuse of *a business development.*

Phoebe guessed it had more to do with a desire to avoid the Ericsons, but before she could ask, Alex congratulated her on her engagement.

How did you know?

Alex raised an eyebrow. *Well, you came in with a ridiculous grin on your face. And I assume you weren't gone all this time playing checkers.*

Phoebe's answering blush had confirmed it.

"You will wear whatever color your sister decides and look happy about it," Mother pronounced.

"Even orange?"

"Honestly, Freddie," she scoffed. "Of course she wouldn't choose *orange*. Why would you even suggest that?" Then she turned to Phoebe. "You won't, will you, darling?"

"No orange. Or lavender. I actually haven't thought about it yet."

"Good," she said, visibly relieved and continued to debate the merits of different dress colors with Freddie.

Phoebe exchanged a glance with Will, one she hoped communicated her desire to abscond to Scotland immediately rather than endure months of wedding planning.

He gave her a fond smile in return and patted her hand. "They're just excited," he murmured by her ear.

"Or still in shock," she replied.

Phoebe's father hadn't managed to wipe the surprised look from his face since they announced their engagement. It was becoming rather irritating.

"Well, this is a very unexpected development," he said for the third time in ten minutes.

"But a welcome one," her mother added with a warm smile.

"Most definitely," he said with a vigorous nod before turning thoughtful. "But to be honest, I'd have thought Freddie the most likely to marry a duke."

Freddie let out a loud snort. "As far as I am aware, the only other duke currently without a duchess is Dartmoor, and he must be close to sixty."

"And still swarmed by fillies eager for the title," their father added. "Besides, you've Hank Junior now."

Freddie didn't reply but her eyes noticeably dimmed.

"Have you settled on a wedding date?" her mother said, deftly changing the subject.

"We haven't decided yet. *I* suggested we elope," Phoebe began, pointedly ignoring the choking sound her father made, "but Will talked me out of it."

"I want to give Phoebe some time to adjust to her new role," he explained. "And I want the whole of London society to see her become my wife."

"Good," her father said with a decided nod. "As it should be." He then raised a bushy eyebrow at Phoebe, who couldn't hide her surprise at this reaction.

"What about just before Christmas?" her mother suggested. "Oh, wouldn't that be lovely. Think of the greenery!" She then launched into various details to consider, all of which Phoebe would leave up to her. This continued for several long minutes until her father leaned over to Will.

"I'd like a word with your betrothed in private," he murmured.

"Of course," Will said with a bow.

Phoebe gave him a confused shrug as she followed her father into his study.

"You're angry Will didn't come to you first," she said as soon as he shut the door.

"Why must you always assume the worst of me?"

Phoebe's mouth fell open. "I don't!"

"You do," he insisted. Then he shook his head. "Your mother was absolutely right. As usual."

"What does *that* mean?" Phoebe asked hotly.

Her father let out a sigh and gestured to a chair before his desk. "Sit down, my dear."

Phoebe hesitated for a moment before obeying.

Her father took his place behind his desk and clasped his hands. "Did you know I worked for my father's biggest competitor before

I went to work for him?" She shook her head, dumbfounded by this revelation. Her father put nearly all of himself into Atkinson Enterprises, often at his family's expense. "I needed to prove something to myself," he explained. "Or maybe to us both."

Phoebe's mouth curved to one side. "Did Grandfather see it that way?"

He had been a stoic, intimidating man who rarely smiled, except for Freddie. She could get a smile out of anyone.

Her father let out a sharp laugh. "No. He was not pleased, to put it mildly. But I was very young and very stubborn. I got to see what it was like not to be the boss's son and how another firm ran things. Both invaluable experiences that I brought back to the business when I was ready, which he allowed without question. Because he was a good businessman, and an even better father." His voice warbled on the last word and Phoebe's fingers twisted in her skirt. It would be so very difficult to remain cross with her father if he began to cry.

But then he blinked and met her gaze. The corner of his mouth lifted. "Your mother has always insisted we're more alike than we realize. I can see it now."

The dismissive snort was out before Phoebe could stop it, but her father was unmoved.

"I have only ever wanted what is best for you, yet you have challenged me at every turn. When I offered you a job at the company, you refused and struck out on your own. You even *lived* on your own—"

"Lots of girls do these days."

He shot her an arch look. "Not girls raised like you. I suppose it was some kind of cosmic retribution for what I put my own father through. And I am man enough to admit now that I found all of it...hurtful," he said. "And because of that, I did not always react in the best way. But I want you to know how much I admire you and the life you have built for yourself."

Phoebe's fingers twisted ever tighter. This was unexpected, to put it mildly. "Would you think that even if I wasn't about to be a duchess?" She said this lightly and with a wry smile in a desperate bid to maintain her own composure, but her father remained distressingly sincere.

"You know I don't give a damn about any of that, Bee," he murmured.

He hadn't called her that in years. "Father..." she said softly as her eyes prickled.

"There's something else," he interrupted, as he pulled out a file from his desk drawer. When he turned away, Phoebe was quite certain he was blinking back tears. "It took longer than expected, but I found a building not far from your old school. It's a little smaller, but Alex and I toured it and she says it has more windows and a larger yard for the children to play in. She said the old one was very small."

Phoebe managed to nod as she took the file from him. "It was."

"In any case, the rent is paid for the first three months—though I suspect that bullheaded headmistress of yours will insist on paying me back."

"She will," Phoebe agreed as she looked over the papers. Then she glanced up when she saw the owner: Atkinson Enterprises.

"You *bought* the building?"

Her father shrugged. "That wasn't the plan at first, but the old owner was a shifty fellow and it seemed the best way to ensure the school wouldn't have to move again. Ever."

Phoebe was stunned. "I—I don't know what to say. 'Thank you' seems woefully inadequate."

"Well, that's good enough for me," he said with a smile. "I'm proud of you, Bee. I'm sorry it took me so long to say that."

She came around the desk and threw her arms around him in a tight hug. "Thank you, Father," she whispered as her throat tightened with emotion. "Thank you, thank you."

"You'll need to thank your sister, too. It was her idea."

"I will."

Phoebe pulled back, then hesitated. She didn't want to ruin this new accord, but she had to say something. "Why are you forcing Hank Junior on Freddie?"

Her father frowned in confusion. "I'm most certainly *not*. The lad asked to court her and when I told Freddie about it, she agreed. Enthusiastically, I might add."

Now it was Phoebe's turn to look confused. She certainly hadn't seemed enthusiastic yesterday.

Her father sighed and gave her a fond look. "Freddie isn't like you or Alex. She doesn't have the same ambition."

"Freddie is massively talented," Phoebe argued. "She could do anything she wants to."

"But that's just it, Bee," her father implored. "I think she's finally grown bored of society and is feeling a little lost because she doesn't really know *what* she wants."

"Oh," Phoebe said weakly. "That...that makes sense."

"Your mother thinks marrying and starting a family would be good for her, and I agree."

"And even better if the marriage can benefit the business."

"Well, yes," he admitted, a tad sheepishly. "A connection with a family like the Ericsons would open doors a little more easily in New York."

"But really, Papa. *Hank Junior?*" Phoebe couldn't help wrinkling her nose. "He's so dull."

"If she finds a better offer, so be it. But I don't see that happening," her father added.

"What do you mean? Freddie's the most popular girl in London."

He gave her a pitying look. "Lots of men *like* Freddie, darling. But that doesn't mean they want her for a wife. Hank Junior is an American and seems more accepting of her eccentricities." Phoebe bit her lip. She hadn't considered that. "And Freddie does seem taken with the idea of living in New York."

Phoebe started. *"What?"*

Her father's eyes widened. "Perhaps you should speak to her about this," he said hastily. He never did like getting involved in their sisterly business.

Phoebe crossed her arms. "Yes, perhaps," she murmured distractedly.

Though if Freddie was seriously considering moving across an ocean without bothering to mention it to her, there was no *perhaps* about it.

Once they rejoined the others, Will suggested they walk over to his home and tell Cal their news. Freddie immediately offered to come, which would provide the perfect opportunity to confront her about New York.

Not confront. Ask, Phoebe reminded herself.

But as soon as they reached the footpath, Phoebe whirled on Freddie. "Is it true you're going to marrying Hank Junior and move to New York?"

Freddie stopped short and turned to her. In the strained silence that followed, Will looked between the two of them.

"I... I think I'll just go on ahead," he mumbled and hurried along without waiting for a response.

"So, you and Father are each other's confidants now," she said once they were alone. "That was fast."

Phoebe ignored the jab. "Why didn't you say anything?"

"I didn't realize I was supposed to tell you every thought in my head. Especially when you haven't been very forthcoming with *me*."

"But Freddie—"

"No," she insisted. "That isn't fair. You've said barely a word about Will for all these months and now you're getting *married*."

"I'm sorry. You're right. And I wish I had confided in you about Will more—"

"At all, you mean," Freddie snapped. "And to be perfectly honest, I didn't tell you because I didn't think you'd care. You've been wrapped up in your own life for years now."

"Freddie, *of course* I care," Phoebe said thickly. "I know it was difficult because of my quarrel with Father, but I never meant for you to think I didn't care about you."

Her sister squeezed her eyes shut and took a breath. "Sorry. That was too harsh." She then took Phoebe's hand and met her gaze. "You have your teaching and Alex has her uncanny ability to make money, which has left me feeling like a dolt in comparison."

"That's not true."

"What am I good at?" she demanded with a sudden intensity far removed from her usual breezy manner. "Flirting with men? Being charming at parties? Making sure rich people feel important?"

"Well, I can barely do any of those things," Phoebe pointed out. "And Alex wouldn't even try."

"Because you don't need to," she countered. "You have abilities and accomplishments."

"What about the fencing," Phoebe said weakly.

Freddie rolled her eyes. "The fencing is a pastime. And it doesn't even have any practical use, as I have yet to find myself in a duel. I'm talking about meaning. About passion. A life's work. So, yes. The idea of moving to New York and starting anew sounded exciting. That's the whole point of America, isn't it?"

"Sounded? Then...you aren't considering it anymore."

But despite the hopeful note in her voice, Freddie only shrugged. "Hank Junior hasn't proposed yet. I guess I'll decide when and if he does. And now may we please focus on your *actual* engagement? Really, Phoebe. Can't you enjoy being the center of attention just this once?"

Phoebe managed a smile and patted her sister's hand, though that did little to assuage her worry. "If you insist."

Yet she had every expectation her sister would find herself in a similar position very soon. But it remained to be seen what she would do from there.

Chapter Thirty

Three weeks later
London, England

This really has been a remarkable success, Your Grace," Mrs. Richardson said as she scanned the busy front hall of the Richardson School for Young Ladies. "I can't thank you enough."

It had been Will's idea to host an open house to welcome the neighborhood to see the school's new building—along with its new name. Though it had been a bit of a trial convincing the headmistress that the school she had founded should bear her name, she finally relented and today wore the honor with pride.

"And as I said before," he replied. "There is no need. I'm just happy to make myself useful."

Mrs. Richardson huffed a laugh and patted his arm. "Oh, don't worry. We will find *plenty* for you and your soon-to-be-duchess to do," she said, giving Phoebe a conspiratorial smile.

"We certainly will." Phoebe nodded.

"I suppose I should make another round," Mrs. Richardson said as something caught her attention. "I see some new arrivals. I'll be back."

The headmistress then hurried off to greet the newcomers.

They had been at the school for hours and Will had lost count of the number of times excited young girls ran up to Phoebe to say hello. It warmed Will's heart to see the joy spark in her face each time—and he would do everything in his power to keep it there.

Phoebe pressed her shoulder against his arm and stifled a yawn. "Goodness. I don't know where she finds the energy."

Will's cheeks were beginning to ache from smiling politely and his shoulders were stiff from standing with perfect posture but he was perfectly happy by Phoebe's side.

"Well, for one thing I don't suspect Mrs. Richardson was keeping a man up all night," he said dryly.

"Oh, hush." Phoebe playfully batted his arm. "I don't recall hearing any complaints from you."

Will grinned. "And you never shall. Just say the word and we will leave."

He was ready to whisk Phoebe home in his carriage and sneak her into his bedroom once more. Since their engagement, they had managed to spend several nights a week together. But with Phoebe resuming her teaching duties very soon, Will knew their opportunities for that would grow few and far between until they married in December. Until then, he was eager to take what he could get of his future bride.

"All right, but let's stay a little longer," she said.

Just as the crowd was beginning to thin out, a familiar face appeared before them.

Maude Clarke.

Will almost didn't recognize her, as she was dressed in a modest gray gown and straw hat. He knew from Phoebe that she was working in the ladies' section of one of the big department stores, but Will hadn't seen her in person since the night at Fleur.

"Miss Clarke!" Phoebe cried out. "What a lovely surprise." But her face fell as she took in the woman's sober expression. "Is everything all right?"

"I'm looking for your sister. I must speak to her. It's urgent."

"She's over there," Phoebe said and pointed to where Alex had been caught in a conversation with the new drama teacher and not even trying to hide her look of bordom. She then drew closer and lowered her voice. "What is it, Maude?"

"I've just learned about the true owner of Fleur. As we suspected, the earl was used to lure prosperous gentlemen to join."

As Phoebe's eyes sparked with interest, Will crossed his arms. "Well, who is it?"

Would they never be done with this blasted business?

Fairbanks had absconded to the Continent not long after their meeting in Parliament. Rumors had swirled regarding nefarious debt collectors, but Alex claimed to still be receiving payments from his solicitor.

If he's left London, it hasn't been on my account.

Maude cast a glance around the room. "Have either of you heard of the Nun?" Will exchanged a blank look with Phoebe and Maude let out a restless sigh. "Of course not," she muttered. "When I was a girl, he was the most powerful man in the neighborhood. Had his hands in every business imaginable. And if you crossed him, you were lucky to end up dead. Then one day he simply vanished. Some said he left for America, others said he returned to his hometown of Dublin. Most swore he was rotting at the bottom of the Thames."

Phoebe swallowed. "So he's a criminal, then."

Maude gave her a mirthless smile. "That's one way to describe him, yes. And now he's back—that's the rumor at least. I've heard that he was the money behind Fleur, as well as some other ventures the earl was involved in. But they all fell apart when your sister bought up his debts and the earl failed to pass his bill."

Will's sore shoulders tightened. "That's why Fairbanks fled. To get away from him."

"It won't work though," Maude said in an ominous tone that sent shivers down Phoebe's back. "I'm told that if the Nun wants something—or some*one*—he finds a way. Your sister needs to be very careful. Thanks to her actions, she will have gotten his attention now, for better or worse."

Phoebe inhaled sharply and Will placed a steadying palm at the small of her back.

Maude's gaze then caught on someone behind them. "Oh, thank God."

Will glanced back and found Inspector Holland heading for them.

"Detective Inspector!" Phoebe greeted him with a cheery smile that couldn't quite hide the tension around her eyes. "How nice of you to come."

He gave a short bow. "My pleasure. Congratulations on the opening of the new school, and your engagement."

Phoebe's smile grew as she looked up at Will and leaned closer to him. "Thank you so much."

"Miss Clarke," the inspector said with a nod.

"Come with me," Maude replied without preamble. "I need to tell you something." She then hooked her arm through his and steered him toward Alex.

Phoebe watched them with a furrowed brow. "Do you think Alex is really in danger from this man?"

Will shrugged. "I'll look into it. But what I want to know is why a fearsome London criminal is called the Nun."

"It does sound odd. Perhaps he's very religious?"

"Or very chaste."

They exchanged a look and began to laugh. Phoebe then brought a hand to her mouth and the tension returned to her face. "Oh, but there isn't anything funny about this."

"Don't worry, my dear. Alex is quite fearsome herself. And she has good people around her, including a very powerful and important duke," he said with a wink.

Phoebe smiled at that and leaned against him again, but just as he pulled her a little closer someone interrupted: "Goodness, you two *do* realize we're in public."

Will and Phoebe both turned to find Freddie beside them, but her gaze was fixed firmly to Holland's retreating back. "Oh, is that that handsome inspector?" Will didn't much like the look of interest in her eyes. "How nice of him to come. I think I'll just say hello."

"Freddie," Phoebe cautioned, but her sister was already striding toward the unsuspecting chap.

"What does she mean to do with him? Ericson's ring shopping as we speak."

"I'm not sure Freddie even knows," Phoebe said on a sigh. "She's just muddling through, like the rest of us."

"But *you* aren't muddling anymore, are you?"

She looked up at him with that fetching smile that never failed to make his heart soar. "Not in the least. There is nowhere I'd wish to be than right here with you."

"Not even the carriage?" he murmured suggestively.

"Well, perhaps the place could be a *little* more private," she allowed.

He held out his arm. "That is easily arranged."

"All right," Phoebe said as she took it. "Lead the way, Your Grace."

Will let out a harumph. "You'll pay for that, Atkinson."

She then flashed him a cheeky grin. "Promise?"

"Only for you, my love." Will chuckled as he led her toward the exit. "Only for you."

Epilogue

Phoebe let out a dreamy sigh as she leaned against the railing of their hired villa's impressive balcony. Perched on the hillside above Corfu's port, the villa offered breathtaking views of the city and sea below. Phoebe had spent each morning of their stay out here so far and was quite certain she could watch dawn breaking across the Ionian every day for the rest of her life. A pity they would have to return to London eventually. But there were a great many exciting things to look forward to back home. The school was thriving after a busy fall and though she would not be returning to the classroom, Phoebe was developing an enrichment program for woman workers in industry to study subjects like literature and mathematics for eight-week sessions. Marion had already signed on as the head teacher and Will donated the use of a large country house he owned just outside London, which would serve their purposes very nicely. Meanwhile, Phoebe was having an excellent time putting together a roster of guest lecturers. But all that would happen in the spring. For now she lost herself in the hypnotic rhythm of the gentle waves, watching as the deep indigo water slowly turned cerulean in the morning light.

They had arrived in Corfu only a few days before after an exhausting stopover in Rome filled with endless tours, sightseeing, and so *many* statues of badly behaved gods. Though the pasta had been life-changing, Phoebe already preferred this idyllic island to the bustle of the city. They hadn't left their hillside villa as much as she had anticipated given the slower pace of life here—not that she was complaining.

Recalling just *how* they had been occupying themselves brought a smile to her face. She glanced back at the sound of bare feet on the tiled floor. A moment later, Will's arms wrapped around her waist and pulled her against his warm chest.

"Come back to bed, Duchess," he purred by her ear.

Phoebe loved how deep and rough his voice was first thing in the morning. She relaxed against him and reached up to stroke the nape of his neck. "Haven't you had enough of me yet?"

"*Never.*" Will punctuated this with a swift nip at her earlobe and Phoebe let out a delighted laugh.

She turned around and grinned up at him. Her handsome husband. Her whole heart. "Well, I suppose I can. If it is a matter of great urgency."

He leaned down and nuzzled her cheek. "Oh, most definitely. The very greatest." Will then rocked his hips against hers and Phoebe raised an eyebrow.

"Say no more, Your Grace. The matter is in hand."

Will flashed her a wicked grin. "I was hoping you'd say that."

Then he turned and tugged her back inside. But as Phoebe dutifully followed him, something on the floor caught her eye.

"Wait." Phoebe broke away and picked up an envelope that the housekeeper had slid under their bedroom door. "It must have arrived after we retired."

"Then it can wait a little longer," Will said as he began to place distracting kisses along her neck.

Phoebe did her best to ignore him as she tore open the envelope and scanned the heading. "It's from Alex."

Will pulled back. "Why is she contacting us, anyway? She has a whole entire man to occupy her time now."

Phoebe laughed and turned to face him. "You know Alex can always find time for anything. I'm very happy for her."

He caught her hand and planted a kiss on her wrist. "As am I, but I'd rather she didn't interrupt our honeymoon."

"I think you can sacrifice a minute for me to read this."

His mouth curved in answer. "Even when you know all I can do with you in a minute?"

Phoebe rolled her eyes even as her cheeks flushed. "Even then." But as she scanned the short note, she stiffened. "It's Freddie. She's in some kind of trouble. And *Inspector Holland* is involved."

"What kind of trouble?" Will's gaze turned suspicious as he took the paper from her and read it himself. "Oh. *That* kind." He let out a sigh. "Shall I go make the travel arrangements, then?"

Though a great part of her revolted at the idea, there was no way Phoebe could relax here anymore. They needed to be back in London as soon as possible.

"I'm sorry, darling." She wrapped her arms around his waist and rested her head against his chest. "You know how much I've been looking forward to our Grecian winter."

They had even planned to rent a yacht and retrace some of Odysseus's journey. Her heart sank at all that would be lost.

"No need," Will said as he stroked her hair. "We'll come back as soon as we can. Besides, I knew when we married you came with two sisters nearly as given to courting trouble as you."

She looked up and found that unique sense of understanding in his eyes. Never mind the Ionian Sea. She got to wake up to him every day, this man that had been part of her past and now her future. "Have I told you how *very much* I love you?"

He tilted his head in thought. "Not in the last hour."

"Let's remedy that first. Then we'll make the arrangements, as I doubt anyone is awake now anyway."

Will pressed a kiss to her forehead. "Yes, people keep very sensible business hours here." Then he tugged her toward the bedroom. "And thank heavens for that."

Author's Note

Duchess Material is set during the late 1890s, which was a transformative period for women due in part to a growing population of independent, educated women uninterested in traditional ideas of Victorian femininity. Often referred to as "New Women" by their contemporaries, they found meaning outside the domestic sphere and many sought to enter the workforce in order to retain their independence while also engaging in artistic pursuits and social or political activism.

Phoebe was written very much in this vein, and I first considered having her work as an urban investigator similar to Beatrice Webb, a Victorian social reformer who was a volunteer rent collector in London's East End and also assisted her cousin Charles Booth with his landmark survey of the city's slums. While many of Phoebe's ideas were informed by reformist women like Webb, who was also a member of the Fabian Society and a founder of the London School of Economics, in the end I decided to make her a schoolteacher, which was another popular career choice and one I have some personal experience to draw from.

The Sheltering Tree, author Netta Syrett's autobiography chronicling her years as a young schoolteacher working and living in London during the 1890s, was also particularly informative. And while the idea of a gently bred young woman living apart from her family either alone or with friends may sound anachronistic, it was a common enough experience during this time period. One can even find a whole subgenre of fiction written during this time that focused on the lives of such women. Some notable authors include Sarah Grand, Emma Brooke, and Mona Caird.

In addition to *The Sheltering Tree, Odd Women?: Spinsters, Lesbians and Widows in British Women's Fiction, 1850s–1930s* by Emma Liggins and *Walking the Victorian Streets: Women, Representation, and The City* by Deborah Epstein Nord provided a wealth of information about the varied paths women's lives could take during this era, and I highly recommend them if you are interested in further reading.

At the end of the novel, Phoebe has begun to organize a summer enrichment program for working-class women. This was inspired by real-life programs organized by groups like the Women's Co-operative Guild and the London Society for the Extension of University Education, which provided classes to adults on an array of topics and worked to improve equity in education in terms of both gender and class.

Acknowledgments

Many thanks to my family for nurturing my lifelong love of reading and writing. It is a wonderful privilege to grow up in a household surrounded by books. Thank you to my husband for never questioning when or why I needed to shut myself in my office for hours at a time and for always treating me like a professional writer long before I was one. Thank you to my parents and my in-laws for taking care of my busy girl so I could work on this book (and catch up on laundry, but mostly work on the book). Thank you to Elizabeth, Erin, and Suzanne for being so generous with your time and feedback. Thank you to my pocket friends for being a constant source of support and insight. Thank you to the entire team at Forever, but especially Junessa Viloria for her kind words and encouragement and Dana Cuadrado for making sure my books find readers and for championing historical romance. Thank you to the fabulous Lisa Perrin for crafting such a gorgeous cover that captured my characters perfectly. Thank you to my agent, Amanda Jain, for your guidance. And last but never least, thank you to the readers both online and off for your enthusiasm and support.

About the Author

Emily Sullivan is an award-winning author of historical fiction set in the late Victorian period. She lives with her family in New England, where she enjoys taking long drives and short walks, and she always orders dessert.

You can learn more at:
    EmilySullivanBooks.com
    X @PaperbackLady
    Instagram @PaperbackLady
    Pinterest.com/ESullivanBooks